THE
HOLLOWS

ALSO BY MARK EDWARDS

WITH LOUISE VOSS

THE
HOLLOWS

MARK
EDWARDS

Text copyright © 2021 by Mark Edwards
All rights reserved.

Published by Thomas & Mercer, Seattle

www.apub.com

Amazon, the Amazon logo, and Thomas & Mercer are trademarks of Amazon.com, Inc., or its affiliates.

ISBN-13: 9781542026826
ISBN-10: 1542026822

Cover design by Tom Sanderson

Printed in the United States of America

THE HOLLOWS

PART ONE

Chapter 1

Saturday

WELCOME TO HOLLOW FALLS

A few helium-filled balloons had been tied to the wooden sign at the entrance of the resort. They bobbed lazily in the breeze, bumping against each other as if they would like to escape, to sail over the treetops, but couldn't gather the energy to really try.

Beside the reception building another sign announced that this was the *GRAND OPENING WEEK*. I parked next to it and went inside to collect our keys. There were two people behind the desk, a large man and a skinny woman. The man, who was in his mid-thirties, beckoned me forward. He wore a red polo shirt that strained against his bulk, the button at the collar looking like it was going to pop at any moment. His badge told me he was Greg Quinn, the manager.

I handed him my passport and he looked me up on the computer, meaty fingers stabbing at the keys.

'Did you come all the way from England to visit us?' he asked as he handed my passport back.

The answer was more complicated than a simple yes or no, but it was easier to say, 'I did.'

'Hey, Vivian, you hear that? Mr Anderson has come here from the UK.'

Vivian, a grey-haired woman with a no-bullshit air, muttered something like, 'Probably one of them', although that didn't make much sense. One of what? I decided I must have misheard.

Greg gave me the keys along with a welcome pack. 'This your first time in Maine?'

'Actually, it is.'

'I'm even more flattered.' He stuck out a hand for me to shake. His clasp was strong. 'If you need anything, anything at all, please don't hesitate to come see Vivian or me.'

Vivian muttered something else. It sounded like, 'Him, preferably.'

Minutes later, still chuckling at Greg and Vivian's double act, I was steering the rental into the bay outside cabin fourteen, on the far side of the resort. Nestled in the trees, the cabin – like all the cabins here – was brand new. Its windows gleamed in the sunshine. This was our home for the next ten nights.

I looked over my shoulder. Frankie, my fourteen-year-old daughter, was still asleep, and I took the opportunity to stretch my legs before waking her. I got out of the car and inhaled. The air was so fresh it felt like a cold beer at the end of a hard day's work. Like I was breathing properly for the first time in months. Eager to share this moment, I rapped lightly on the car window.

Frankie woke up as I opened the car door. She blinked and plucked at the lock of hair that was stuck to her forehead.

'We're here?'

'We're here.' I jangled the keys. 'Want to see what it's like inside?'

She squinted at the cabin.

'I guess,' she said.

4

It was perfect. Along with the two bedrooms, there was a living area with a tiny TV and DVD player, a small kitchen, plus a main bathroom and an en suite attached to my bedroom. There was a deck with a barbecue and a table for outside dining. The beds were big and comfortable. There was plenty of space but I could already tell that at night, when we were surrounded by the darkness of the Maine woods, it would be cosy. The rear of the cabin backed directly on to those woods, which, according to the map I'd studied before coming here, stretched for miles in every direction. It was a beautiful place.

Even Frankie seemed impressed.

'My room is massive,' she said, coming into the kitchen, where I was trying to figure out how to work the coffee maker. She had her Hydro Flask with her, an expensive drinks bottle that she carried everywhere like a comfort blanket. She went over to the sink and filled the bottle with water from the tap – or faucet, as she had started to call it.

'I'm glad you approve,' I said. 'Would you describe it as "awesome"?'

She cringed. 'Dad. You're so . . .'

'Awesome?'

She groaned and I made a vow to stop teasing her about being American now. The truth was, I was still reeling from when I'd first seen her earlier, picking her up from her new home in Albany. I had parked the car expecting to see a child, my little girl, and a young woman had emerged from the house. A beautiful young woman with her mother's dark-brown hair and lightly freckled skin. She had inherited my hazel eyes and the 'lucky' gap between my front teeth – along with my height. It had been a year since I'd last seen her in the flesh, and all those FaceTime calls and Instagram photos hadn't prepared me for how much she'd grown.

'We can go down to the lake in a bit,' I said. 'Sign up for some activities. I thought we could try archery. Did I tell you Grandad used to be an archery champion? Maybe you'll have inherited—'

'Dad, chill, okay? We've only just got here.'

She had her iPhone in her hand – an older model, which her mum had handed down – and she went around the cabin taking photos, including a few selfies with her fingers held up in that ubiquitous V-for-Victory sign. I watched as she tapped at the screen, presumably choosing which photos were most flattering, applying filters, creating the most perfect version of reality she could.

Then she furrowed her brow.

'I can't find a Wi-Fi network,' she said.

'That's because there isn't any Wi-Fi here.'

She looked at me like I'd just told her we'd have to slaughter ourselves a pig for supper.

'I told you,' I said. 'When I booked it.'

'No you didn't.'

'I'm almost certain I did.'

'But . . . I can't get 4G either. I can't get any signal at all.' She sounded increasingly panicked. 'Have *you* got one?'

I had already checked. 'No. Frankie, that was the whole point of coming here. To get away from everything. No social media. No YouTube. No news. A whole week and a half without staring at a screen. Just you and me.'

I had to admit I had been slightly hesitant about it myself. Ten days without being able to refresh Twitter or check my emails? But then I had thought about it properly and realised how wonderful it would be.

'Come on,' I said. 'I never get to see you . . .' I was about to launch into a speech about how I didn't want her to spend our time together glued to her phone, but managed to stop myself. I knew it wouldn't go down well. 'There's so much to do here,' I said instead, trying to sell the positives.

'Like what?' she said, squeezing her phone like it was a friend who was about to abandon her.

'We can get out into nature.' I mentioned archery again. Boating on the lake. 'It'll be good for us. You can still write in your bullet journal. Read. And I think I saw some jigsaw puzzles over there.'

'*Jigsaw puzzles?*'

It was as if I'd told her that, once she'd slaughtered the pig we were having for supper, she would be expected to knit a blanket using its entrails.

'What if there's an emergency?' she said. 'What if I want to talk to Mum?'

'I'm sure there are payphones.'

She looked blank.

'You know, phones where you have to put a coin in a slot.'

She reacted like this was the weirdest thing she'd ever heard of.

'It will be cool. I promise.'

I remembered my grandparents going on about how in the olden days they would have to make their own entertainment, using such maddening phrases as 'only boring people get bored' and talking about the fun they'd had with an old tin bucket and a stick. I laughed to myself.

'What's so funny?' Frankie demanded.

'Oh, nothing. I was just thinking, maybe we could go scrumping for apples.'

She shot me a look of contempt, the kind that only a fourteen-year-old girl can muster, and stamped back to her room, slamming the door behind her. I tried not to react, to suppress my irritation. This was her vacation as much as mine, and she was almost an adult now, as hard as that was for me to admit.

I went out to the rental car, trying to stay resolute in my belief that a lack of Wi-Fi was a good thing, and got our suitcases out of the trunk.

'Hey.'

I looked up, startled.

There was a man standing maybe five metres away, by the tree line. He was in his late forties, I guessed, same as me, and was wearing shorts, a faded Guns N' Roses T-shirt and a San Francisco Giants baseball cap, with black Converse on his feet.

He strode over, a big grin on his face.

'David Butler,' he said, shaking my hand. He gestured down the path. 'We're staying at the next cabin over. Number twelve. There's no cabin thirteen. I guess they decided that would be a bad idea, with this place's history.'

'Tom Anderson,' I told him. Then: 'What do you mean, "this place's history"?'

He didn't answer my question. 'Oh, you're a Brit. Did you come all this way to stay here?' He sounded impressed. I noticed that he had a tattoo of a circle with a cross through it on his upper arm, kind of crudely drawn. There was something familiar about it.

'It's complicated.'

'Oh yeah?'

He was a stranger. I didn't need to explain anything to him. But I figured I was going to get asked about this a lot so I might as well be open.

'I'm here with my teenage daughter, Frankie. She lives in Albany with her mum, my ex-wife. I come over to the States once a year to see her, and last summer we stayed in New York but it was so insanely hot I couldn't face it again.'

'Very wise.'

'Yeah. I thought so. My daughter seems less impressed.'

8

'Let me guess. There's no internet! It's child cruelty! My son is exactly the same.'

'How old is he?'

'Just turned fifteen.' David removed his baseball cap and scratched his head where a cowlick stuck up. 'I'm trying to remember if I whined as much when I was that age. Pretty sure I did. Least that's what Connie says. That's my wife.' At the mention of her name, he must have remembered something because he said, 'I'd better get back.'

'Okay. Nice to meet you.'

He turned to go, then stopped. 'Hey, we're gonna be neighbours. We should get to know each other. Why don't you come over later? I've got some steaks for the barbecue, plenty of beer and wine.'

'I'm not sure. I'm pretty jet-lagged. I flew over from London overnight and I've been awake for . . .' I had actually lost count. 'Twenty-four hours?'

'You have to stay up as long as you can – acclimate to the time zone.'

'Also, Frankie and I are vegetarian,' I said.

'No problem. We've got plenty of veggie food too.' He strode away before I could protest, calling over his shoulder, 'See you at seven, okay?'

I went back into my cabin. Frankie was still in her room, presumably unpacking. I was going to knock on her door but decided to leave it. Listening to David criticise his son's 'whining' had reminded me I didn't want to be that kind of dad. I couldn't afford to be, not when Frankie and I lived thousands of miles apart.

ʊ

Frankie accompanied me reluctantly, finally giving in because there was 'nothing else to do' and we didn't have any food in the cabin yet.

'I should have consulted you,' I said. 'About the lack of Wi-Fi, I mean. I'm sorry.'

She grunted, but I could see she was pleased.

David was out on the deck, wearing an apron and prodding at the barbecue with a pair of tongs. He greeted us loudly and enthusiastically, then yelled, 'Hey, Connie!'

His wife came outside. She had long, dark hair and striking blue eyes, and walked with the aid of a stick.

'I have arthritis,' she said, seeing us both glance at the stick. 'It's a bitch. But at least it gives me an excuse to carry this deadly-ass weapon with me at all times.'

'In case I'm a bad boy,' said David, giving her an adoring look, which she returned. Some couples you can just tell: they love each other to pieces, no matter how long they've been together. 'Hey, Tom, can you watch this while I grab some drinks?'

I took the tongs and attended to the food while he went inside, coming out a few minutes later dragging a cooler full of beer and wine.

With him was his teenage son. 'This is Ryan,' said David.

I caught the reaction on Frankie's face. She had been standing a few yards from the cabin, scuffing the ground with her shoe, suffering TikTok withdrawal or whatever, but as soon as Ryan appeared she stopped slouching and did a double take.

I wasn't surprised. Ryan was a good-looking boy. He had his mother's dark hair and the kind of cheekbones that have launched pop careers. He looked like something out of one of the teen shows Frankie loved, like *Riverdale*. Or used to love. I wasn't sure. Earlier, in the car, I had said something about Taylor Swift, who used to be Frankie's idol, and she had rolled her eyes.

'Hi,' Frankie said, not quite looking at Ryan.

My instinct as a father was to step between them, to form a barrier, but I recognised immediately that this would be a mistake. Besides, maybe Frankie would stop sulking now.

'You kids want Coke? Sprite? Dew?' David had a great variety of sodas in his cooler.

Frankie and Ryan each took a Diet Coke, and Ryan said, in a confident and friendly tone, 'Hey. I was gonna check out the lake.'

Frankie looked to me for permission and I reminded myself she wasn't a child any more. I nodded.

'A summer fling, huh?' said David after the teens were out of earshot, and I couldn't help but balk at his words. He laughed. 'Hey, it's cool. I don't know what it's like to have a daughter, but Ryan's a good kid.'

'He respects women,' said Connie. 'He's definitely not a serial killer.'

They both laughed.

'And Connie would know,' said David. 'She's an expert.'

'On teenagers?'

That made them laugh again. 'No one is an expert when it comes to teenagers,' David said. 'Connie's an expert on serial killers.'

'Really?'

'Yep. Ask her anything. Ted Bundy. Richard Ramirez. The Zodiac Killer.' He pointed to the tattoo on his arm and I realised where I'd seen it before. It was the symbol the Zodiac Killer had sent to the police. 'It's a tribute to the victims. A reminder he was never caught.' That seemed a little odd to me, but before I had a chance to react, David went on: 'You guys have had some seriously messed-up serial killers across the pond. Like that doctor guy. Harold Shipman. And that dude who kept all those bodies in his apartment. Dennis Nilsen.'

'I read a great book about the Shropshire Viper too,' said Connie. 'Oh, and Lucy Newton. The Dark Angel. She was cool.'

Cool? I thought.

'It's not just serial killers,' Connie continued, settling into a chair and pouring herself a glass of wine. 'I'm just crazy about true crime.'

'We both are,' David said. 'It's why we're here.' He gestured at our surroundings.

'What do you mean?' I asked. I had a feeling I wasn't going to like the answer.

David and Connie both looked confused. 'Wait, you didn't know about this place? Where did you see it advertised?'

'I don't know. I put "cabins Maine" into Google and it was one of the first results.'

Connie almost spat her wine out. 'Really? That's hilarious. Most people here this weekend saw it on The Snuff Guide.'

'The Snuff Guide? What on earth's that?'

'It's a dark tourism website,' David said. 'You really didn't know this? You don't know what happened here?'

'No.'

'This is the coolest,' David said, shoving a veggie burger into a bun and handing it to me. I got a good look at his Zodiac Killer tattoo as he passed it over.

'We get to tell you about the Hollows Horror,' said Connie, and she put down her wine and leaned forward, eager to tell me.

Chapter 2

As Connie and David took it in turns to tell me the story of what had happened here almost exactly twenty years before, the hairs stood up on the back of my neck, as if someone were standing behind me, blowing cool air on to me through pursed lips.

'So, it was July 1999,' Connie said. 'The anniversary is this month, in fact. The twenty-sixth.'

'This used to be a much more basic campground,' said David. 'A place to pitch tents or park your RV. None of these fancy cabins. It wasn't a *resort*.'

'It was popular with schools. Like the one that was staying here the week in question. Wendt Middle School, out of Portland.'

'And it was closed down immediately after what happened.'

'What *did* happen?' I asked. I tried to keep my tone light. 'Don't tell me – it was a dark and stormy night.'

'Ha! Actually, it was a warm, still night, like this. A couple of kids, names of Jake Robineaux and Mary-Ellen Pearce, arranged to meet up after everyone else went to sleep. They were both fourteen, weren't they, honey?'

Connie nodded. 'That's right.' The same age as Frankie. 'Jake wrote a book about it around five years ago. Self-published it.'

'*A Night in the Woods*,' said David. 'That's the title.' He was sitting down, barbecue sauce smeared around his lips. He had already finished one bottle of beer and had moved on to the next. 'Jake said that he found Mary-Ellen in this clearing in the woods, frozen to the spot, pointing her flashlight.'

'What had she seen?' I asked.

Neither David nor Connie replied straight away. They were like a veteran rock band who had played their set so many times they knew exactly how to work their audience.

'Two of their teachers,' said Connie.

'Eric Daniels and Sally Fredericks,' added David.

'Murdered.'

'Slaughtered.'

'Both completely naked.'

Over the next thirty minutes, the Butlers told me, in unnerving detail, what had happened.

Eric Daniels was a thirty-eight-year-old English teacher, married with two children. He was described by those who knew him as 'a great guy': bookish but a big baseball fan; a man who was as comfortable doing home improvement as he was debating the finer points of *To Kill a Mockingbird*. He seemed a little too good to be true to me.

And, of course, he wasn't perfect. Because he had apparently been having an affair with his co-worker, Sally Fredericks.

She was a geography teacher who had organised the camping trip, just as she had every year since starting at Wendt Middle School. She was two years older than Daniels, a fitness fanatic who had, the year before her death, run the New York City Marathon. She was typically skinny for a long-distance runner. In the photos that accompanied the news stories I found later, Sally wasn't classically beautiful or conventionally attractive, but there was something about her. The trace of a wry smile on her lips; an ironic twinkle in her eye. Everyone described her as clever and cool and

14

kind. And the students and colleagues she'd left behind had seemed genuinely devastated by their loss – as had her husband, Neal.

'So what, they snuck off into the woods together to have sex?' I asked, glancing up at the trees that rose behind the Butlers' cabin.

'Yep,' David said. 'I guess it was too good an opportunity to pass up. A warm night. All the kids asleep, or so they thought. It must have seemed exciting. Romantic.'

'It happened a little way from here,' Connie added, pointing up the path with her stick. 'There used to be a nature trail there, with a clearing further along the trail. The perfect place for a midnight hook-up.'

'Nothing like a bit of al fresco fun,' said David, winking at his wife.

She grimaced. 'Don't get any ideas, buster. I don't want any bugs biting me on the butt.'

'But I wouldn't blame them if they did,' he said, kissing her. 'It's so biteable.'

She slapped his chest and rolled her eyes, but she was pleased.

'How were they killed?' I asked, marvelling at how the Butlers had paused halfway through their gruesome tale for some flirtation, as if they were teenagers enjoying a scary movie rather than a married couple recounting a real-life crime.

When I looked it up afterwards, I found that the Butlers had remembered the details as if they themselves were the pathologists who had examined the bodies and written the reports. Actually, it wasn't hard to picture David and Connie at the morgue, in scrubs and surgical masks, scalpels and saws slicing and grinding beneath artificial light.

Eric had been bludgeoned to death with a heavy object, probably a rock. He had died of blunt force trauma. The pathologist noted that he had been struck three times on the back of his head, which had shattered his skull. They speculated that the murderer had first struck Eric while he and Sally were having sex, with him on top. It would have been dark and they were busy; they wouldn't have heard their assailant creeping up on them, weapon raised.

Sally died by strangulation. A makeshift ligature, probably a belt, had been tied around her throat and tightened until she choked to death. Marks on her fingers indicated that she had struggled and attempted to claw at the ligature around her neck.

The traces of semen and saliva on and inside her body belonged to Eric. There was no evidence that she had been raped, although there was bruising on her arms to indicate that she had been pinned down. The pathologist wrote that this bruising could have been caused during consensual sex, but it seemed most likely the murderer had held her down before strangling her. Perhaps he had intended to rape her, before changing his mind or being unable to do it.

As David and Connie told the story, a question formed in my head. It was horrible, yes. But murder was not uncommon, even double murders. Why was this slaying so notorious?

Why had it brought all these dark tourists flocking to this place?

I was about to voice the question when Connie said, 'Here's where it gets weird. At the centre of the clearing is this huge, flat rock. The bodies were left lying across the rock.'

'Head to toe,' said David.

'What?'

'They'd been laid out so his head was by her feet, and vice versa. But that's not the weird part.'

'There were symbols painted on the rock beside their bodies,' Connie said.

'In their own blood. Or Eric's blood, I should say. Sally wasn't bleeding.'

Now I was beginning to understand the murders' gruesome appeal. 'What kind of symbols?'

David's eyes widened with excitement. 'The horned god.'

'And the triple goddess,' said Connie. Unlike her husband, she said it in an almost reverential tone. Serious and unsmiling.

I blinked at them. 'What are they? Satanic symbols?'

'It's more pagan,' Connie said. 'They're two of the primary Wiccan deities.'

'The horned god represents male power,' said David. He had dropped his voice as if there might be ears in the forest, listening in. Perhaps the trees themselves. 'He's the lord of life.'

'And death,' said Connie. 'The triple goddess represents the divine feminine. They were kind of crudely etched, but all the experts agreed that's what they were meant to be.'

'Here, hold on,' said David. 'I'll show you.'

Show me what, *for God's sake*, I wanted to ask, but he'd already disappeared into their cabin. A moment later, he came out with a blank sheet of paper and a Sharpie. He drew a large circle, then a crescent on top. It looked like a crudely drawn head with thick horns. 'That's the horned god. And this is the triple goddess.' He drew another circle, then a crescent on either side, facing outwards.

'Do these represent the moon?' I asked.

'You got it,' he replied. 'The goddess symbol represents the waxing and waning of the moon. The male one is more a literal representation of a dude with horns.' He chuckled. 'But yeah, the moon is important to pagans.'

'And it was a new moon that night,' said Connie.

'So this was . . .' I was loath to say it. 'Some kind of offering? A sacrifice?'

'That's the theory,' she replied.

Light was beginning to drain from the sky, the spaces between the trees darkening. I looked up, wondering where the moon was in its cycle, but it hadn't yet appeared. I had an image of the bodies, pale and bloody in the moonlight, flies already gathering, drawn by the sweet, sticky blood . . . and just like that, I'd been transformed into a dark tourist. I couldn't help but see, peeking through a gap in the trees, the yellow eyes of some creature, some god – and a shiver of nausea and horror went through me.

'It only took the cops a few hours to figure out who did it,' Connie said, bringing me back to the real world.

'His name was Everett Miller,' David said.

'A local?'

'Yep. He lived in Penance.'

Penance was the nearest town, several miles from Hollow Falls. I had looked it up before coming to the US, wanting to know what was nearby and if there were any places worth taking day trips to. Penance, which had a population of 2,068 at the last census, didn't appear to have anything worth seeing. There wasn't even a cinema; just a couple of bars, a Baptist church and a handful of shops.

'Everett Miller was the local weirdo,' David said. 'The guy that everyone whispered about or laughed at when he went by.'

'He had long hair and dressed all in black,' Connie said. 'He wore make-up and had piercings all over his face.'

'And he was into black metal,' said David. 'All these crazy-ass bands out of Norway and Finland or wherever. Screaming about Satan and death and all this bizarre pagan shit. There was this one band he was into, Wolfspear – all their songs were about blood sacrifices and murder and burning churches. Their newest one at the time had a video where the lead guy dressed as the horned god and rampaged through the woods with all these naked women, and then murdered them and had sex with their bodies. Real X-rated horror-film stuff. It was banned but Everett had a videotape that he'd imported from Norway. He had the band's symbol painted on the back of his leather jacket too.'

18

'The police thought it probably wasn't planned,' Connie said. 'Or not properly thought through, anyway. The theory was that he'd seen them having sex and been sent into some kind of frenzy. There was speculation he was on drugs. Out of his mind.'

'Hold on,' I said. 'They blamed him because he watched a music video and had a pagan symbol on the back of his jacket? Isn't that, like, circumstantial evidence?'

'It is. But there was forensic evidence too. That's the important part.' Connie looked over my shoulder as she spoke, and I turned to see Frankie and Ryan coming back up the path towards us. They were laughing; clearly, they had hit it off.

'Everett always used to wear this scarf,' David said quickly. 'A bandana? And guess what was used to daub the symbols on the rock? The cops found it on a path near the clearing, covered in Eric's blood.'

I'd heard of criminals being caught because of their own stupidity before, but this was something else.

'Did Everett confess?'

Frankie and Ryan reached us just then, a big smile on Frankie's face, the sulkiness of earlier forgotten. 'What are you talking about?' she asked.

Ryan rolled his eyes. 'I bet I can guess. The Hollows Horror. My mom and dad are obsessed.'

'We're not obsessed, Ryan,' said David.

'You could have fooled me.'

'Yeah, well, our podcast paid for this vacation. Don't forget that.'

'How could I?' said Ryan. 'You only mentioned it twenty times on the way here.'

He went inside, muttering something about needing the bathroom, before his dad could respond.

'So what happened to Everett Miller?' I asked, giving Frankie a wary glance. I didn't feel comfortable talking about this stuff in front of her. 'Does Maine have the death penalty?'

'No, it doesn't,' David said. 'But it wouldn't have mattered in this case anyway. Because they never caught him. The night of the murders, he disappeared.'

Connie leaned forward. 'And no one ever saw him again.'

Chapter 3

Sunday

Sunlight splashed through the trees, the sounds of the resort fading behind them, as Frankie and Ryan took the path towards town.

It had been his idea. Last night, down by the lake, she'd complained about not being able to get online and he'd suggested this: a walk through the woods to Penance the next day.

'They've got to have 4G there,' he'd said. 'Or we'll be able to find a Subway or a Dunkin' or something. Somewhere with Wi-Fi.'

'It's just cruel,' Frankie had said, hoping Ryan could tell she was being ironic. 'Expecting us to exist without internet.'

Despite what she'd said to her dad, she wasn't *that* bothered about the lack of a connection. It was nice to have a break from all the drama in the WhatsApp group she was in with Sienna and Abby, and they'd be able to catch her up when she got home.

The real reason she'd wanted to go on this little expedition was walking beside her. Fifteen years old, six foot tall, fit as hell. He looked just like Harry Styles. Actually, that would be one good reason to get back online. To share a picture of Ryan. Her friends would *freak*.

She glanced at him now, daring to wonder if he liked her too. He'd certainly seemed keen to spend time with her, but she wasn't getting any 'I fancy you' vibes from him. He hadn't made any lame sexual jokes. He was, so far, being a perfect gentleman. And that made her like him even more.

They continued along the path and she tried not to worry about how much she was sweating. Mosquitoes buzzed around them and she swatted at them as casually as she could, not wanting Ryan to know how much bugs freaked her out. He barely even seemed to be sweating. He gave off more of a glow, like from an Instagram filter.

'So you're from California?' she asked.

'Uh-huh.'

'Whereabouts?'

He flicked his hair out of his eyes. 'San Jose. I wouldn't recommend it. It's all big tech companies and homeless people.'

'Is that what your parents do? Work for a tech company?'

He pushed a low-hanging branch out of the way and held it so Frankie could step past. 'No. My dad sells insurance. The most boring job in the world. My mom stays home and does her podcast.'

'The famous podcast.'

'Yeah. It actually is famous. It was like, number three on the Apple Podcasts chart at one point.'

'That's amazing.'

'I guess.' She could tell from his expression that he really didn't think it was amazing. 'So . . . do you mind me asking? What's the deal with your parents? Is your mom British too?'

'No. She's from Albany but moved to the UK for college, which is where she met my dad. And after they got divorced she came home, bringing me with her.'

'And how did you feel about that?'

The answer to this always left a sour taste in her mouth. 'I didn't get a say. I hated it at first. Schools in America are so different. It's kinda . . . it's actually like *Mean Girls* at my school.'

22

He laughed.

'But I'm used to it now. I like it. I've made friends.'

Geeks and nerds. But that was okay. She fitted right in.

'And I don't want to flex but I'm getting good grades. It's all right.'

'And what do your parents do for work?' Ryan asked, saying it like he wasn't interested but was trying to keep the conversation going.

'Mum works in HR and dad's a music journalist. He's met everyone,' she found herself saying. 'Eminem, Pink, Jay-Z. He interviewed Kurt Cobain a month before he killed himself.'

Now Ryan's interest was piqued. 'For real?'

'Yeah. Dad worked for this really popular magazine, back when magazines were still a thing.'

'Meeting Cobain and Eminem. I guess your dad's pretty cool.'

'Hmm.'

'What is it?'

'Well. It's like . . . I left England when I was eleven. A kid, you know? And he still thinks I'm a baby, like he can order me around, not ask for my opinion about stuff. I'm almost fifteen.'

'Parents,' Ryan said. 'Mine are the same. I didn't even want to come here. Why would I want to go somewhere just because a couple of teachers got murdered there? It's creepy AF. I mean, it's all right during the day, I guess, but I looked out of the cabin window last night and it was *Friday the 13th* out there.'

Frankie laughed. 'Camp Crystal Lake.'

'Does being a virgin mean I'm safe?' Ryan asked, and Frankie felt herself blush.

'I think we're almost there,' Ryan said, rescuing her from the super-cringe moment. The light streaming through the trees ahead of them was brighter, indicating they had reached the edge of the woods.

Frankie checked her phone. 'I don't have a signal yet. Do you?'
'No.'

They found themselves stepping out on to a road on the outskirts of the town. To their left, there was what appeared to be a junkyard, with a tall chain-link fence and a sign that read *Honest Salvage and Recycling*. A crumbling house with broken windows sat beyond the empty yard.

'Yep. Horror-movie central.' Ryan took a photo then gestured for Frankie to stand beside him so he could take a selfie of the two of them with the junkyard in the background.

There was no one in sight, not even any cars on the road. All Frankie could hear was a faint tinkling in the distance. Wind chimes? For some reason, the sound – one she usually found pleasant – made goosebumps spring up on the flesh of her arms, and she hugged herself.

'Welcome to Penance, Maine,' said Ryan, checking his phone again. There was still no signal. 'Seems like just the kind of place a murderer would grow up in, huh?'

They walked along the road. The sun beat down on them as the wind chimes continued to ring out softly, somewhere far away. They chatted as they walked: about school, their friends, the differences between Britain and America, and, to Frankie's surprised delight, books they'd both enjoyed. She didn't know any boys who read. At her school, any boy caught reading for pleasure was setting himself up for months of bullying. Ryan was a fan of lots of books she'd enjoyed, like *The Hate U Give* and *The Fault in Our Stars*. He also loved Stephen King and was astonished she'd never read any. 'I've got one with me. *Pet Sematary*. I'll lend it to you. Get you in the Maine mood.'

They passed a street called Paradise Loop. There was a group of four teenagers, three boys and a girl, all white, hanging out on the sidewalk. A couple of the boys bounced a basketball between them while the other two, who might have been girlfriend and boyfriend, stood nearby, not doing anything but watching. They were all around Frankie's age and she didn't like the look of them. There was something intimidating about them.

But Ryan didn't seem to share her concern.

'Hey,' he said, approaching them. The two boys who were bouncing the basketball stopped. The girl and the boy who'd been watching stopped their conversation and turned to face Ryan. The girl was very pale, with strawberry-blonde hair and eyebrows that were almost non-existent. The boy had very short hair, with huge eyes and pale skin stretched over hollow cheeks.

The boy looked Ryan up and down like he was trash.

'Hey,' Ryan said again. 'Is there someplace around here we can get Wi-Fi? Like a McDonald's?'

'A McDonald's?' said the girl, with a mean laugh.

'Subway?' Ryan said.

All the kids laughed except the boy with the cropped hair. He just continued to stare at Ryan. Looking at him, and the girl, Frankie realised they were probably brother and sister. Twins? They had the same hair colour. The same pallid skin, like teenage vampires. Frankie noticed the boys with the basketball edging away from the siblings, and realised they weren't all together. The probably-twins had just been watching them.

'All right, whatever,' Ryan said. 'You all have a good one.'

He'd started to walk away, with a relieved Frankie at his side, when they heard a high-pitched male voice from behind. 'You staying at Hollow Falls?'

Ryan turned back and Frankie reluctantly turned too. 'Yeah, we are.'

'Seen any ghosts yet?'

'What?' Frankie said.

The boy looked at her like she was a moron. 'I asked if you'd seen any ghosts.'

His voice was odd. Like it hadn't broken properly yet. His eyes, though huge like an anime character's, were sleepy. Was he stoned? Frankie was holding her Hydro Flask and she noticed the girl looking at it. Instinctively, she moved it behind her back.

'You're trespassing,' said the boy, staring right into Frankie's eyes.

'It was so great to meet you guys,' said Ryan, after a stunned pause. 'Come on, Frankie.' And he walked away quickly. Frankie followed.

ω

When they were out of the teenagers' earshot, Frankie said, 'Oh my God.' She tried to laugh but it wouldn't quite come.

'You okay? You seem rattled.'

'I'm fine. Jesus.'

Ryan laughed. '*You're trespassing.* Wow. What a pair of freaks.' His words struck the note he was after, but somehow he didn't quite sell them. It seemed possible to Frankie that he might be as rattled as she was.

They turned a corner and found themselves on what was presumably Main Street. A wide road, with a few stores and other establishments on either side: a post office, a bar, a minimart and, Frankie was pleased and surprised to see, a bookstore.

There was hardly anyone around. An old man sat on a bench beneath a tree, fanning himself with a hat. A woman strode along the sidewalk with a couple of kids struggling to keep up with her. A few cars went by.

There was a war memorial nearby, a statue of a soldier with a plaque commemorating the *brave men of Penance* who had died in World War Two. A crow sat on the soldier's head, gazing down at them with a beady eye. Frankie took a photo. Then she looked down and saw that someone was sleeping in the shadow cast by the memorial. A homeless man, with an empty bottle beside him. Ryan took a picture of him.

'You probably shouldn't have done that,' Frankie said.

Ryan shrugged. 'It's fine. He'll never know. Hey, look, a bookstore.'

They crossed the road, Frankie thinking she might be able to impress Ryan by popping in and buying a Stephen King novel – she'd let him choose which one – but as she got closer to the shop her heart sank. It was shut.

They walked away from the bookstore towards a diner. 'I'm dying of thirst,' Ryan said. 'And I haven't eaten since breakfast.'

The diner was shut too.

'Oh, you're kidding me. What is this place? Did all the adults die or something?'

But Frankie had taken out her phone and noticed something wonderful. A Wi-Fi signal, apparently coming from one of the nearby buildings. And it wasn't password-protected.

'I'm online,' she said, and seconds later her phone went *ping ping ping* as a flood of WhatsApp messages came pouring across state lines from her friends back home. Distracted, she sat on a low wall and scrolled through the most recent ones. As she'd suspected, loads of drama.

'Hey,' she said, trying to sound casual. 'Can you send me that selfie?'

'Yeah, course. Give me your number.' He handed her his phone and she tapped her number in.

The selfie arrived and she forwarded it to her friends. The replies came back instantly.

OMG!!

Who dat?

Frankie got a new boo LOL!

As she smiled at her phone, she noticed Ryan tapping away at his. She could see he had opened Instagram. 'What's your Insta name?' he said.

She told him. 'What are you doing?'

'Just posting. Hey, I've followed you, if you want to follow me back.'

She clicked on to his profile and scrolled through. There were a lot of pictures of buildings, rooftops, graffiti. A video clip of Ryan leaping across a gap between two buildings.

'You do parkour?' she asked.

'Oh yeah. Mom hates it. Says I'm gonna end up walking with a stick, like her.'

Frankie scrolled down. There was a photo of Ryan with his arm around another boy.

'Is this your best friend?'

He glanced up from the post he was still composing and pulled a face. 'That's my ex. I should delete that.'

She scrolled down further. There were photos of Ryan and the other boy at what appeared to be a Pride parade, rainbow flags aloft. Of course, the best-looking, coolest guy she'd met, like, *ever* was gay.

'Do you have a *new* boyfriend?' she asked.

He was still tapping at his phone. 'Hmm? Not yet. But there's this boy in my class. Glen Troiano. There, done.'

He showed her his screen. He had put up the photos he'd taken of the junkyard, Penance's Main Street and the homeless man, with his face blurred. The pictures were accompanied by a caption:

Come to the asshole of the world! Penance, ME. Where the dogs in the junkyard have higher IQs than the people. #Penance #shithole #vacationfromhell

She tried to hide her shock. She didn't want Ryan to think she was a killjoy. This place *was* a shithole. A weird, creepy shithole. But that post was mean. She guessed Ryan really had been rattled by the encounter with the other teenagers.

And the homeless guy across the street was staring at them.

Frankie nudged Ryan and he followed her gaze.

'Let's get out of here before someone else accuses us of trespassing,' he said.

Chapter 4

On the way back from the on-site shop, carrying a bag containing coffee, bread, milk and some snacks for Frankie, I paused briefly to peruse a map of Hollow Falls. It was a big place, with the lake forming a border at its southern edge and the general store and the restaurant at its centre. There were tennis courts, an archery field, a stables and a children's playground. The cabins were grouped in clusters around the edges of the resort, with mine and Frankie's in the north-west corner, before the resort gave way to the woods that separated Hollow Falls from Penance.

I wondered how many of the people staying here were dark tourists. The mindset was alien to me. Of course, I understood the human urge that makes people slow down at the scene of an accident, or that draws us to read news stories about murders and child abductions. But to choose your holiday destination based on such terrible things? *Where do you fancy going this year? Disneyland? A Spanish beach? I know – how about that place where two teachers were ritually murdered?* If I'd known, I wouldn't have brought Frankie here. I would have chosen one of the many other resorts in New England.

As I neared our cabin, I spotted our other nearest neighbours on the deck of cabin fifteen, sitting at their outdoor table with coffee mugs in front of them. Two women in late middle age. One of them caught my eye as I passed so I went over to say hello and introduce myself.

They were both dressed as if they were going on a hike. The woman closest to me had curly brown hair with grey streaks and introduced herself as Tamara.

'Donna,' said the other one, a thickset woman with a slightly startled expression. She had auburn hair and looked a little older than Tamara. There was a walking pole leaning against her chair. Yes, definitely going on a hike.

We exchanged small talk for a minute, before I decided to bring up the topic that was lurking like an elephant in the woods.

'So . . . are you guys here because of Everett Miller?'

'Who?'

'You haven't heard of him? Jesus, I'm glad I'm not the only one.'

I'd noticed Donna wince while I spoke. It took me a beat to figure out why: the gold cross dangling from a chain around her neck. Her fingers kept straying to it, in the same way a tongue constantly returns to a sharp tooth.

'Sorry,' I said, feeling myself flush. 'My language.' This earned me a tight smile. Eager to leave the awkwardness behind, I pushed on, giving them a short version of what David and Connie had recounted the night before.

'Oh, isn't that just great,' said Donna. 'I came here to get away from all that.'

All that? Had there just been a spate of ritual murders where they came from? I was afraid to ask for clarification.

'She's been under a lot of stress lately,' said Tamara, patting Donna's shoulder. 'We both have.' She gave Donna an affectionate look. It made me wonder all the more what had happened to them. Had one of them been ill? I was also unsure if they were a couple or if they were just friends.

31

'Perhaps we should find somewhere else to stay,' Tamara offered. 'I don't want you fretting.'

Donna frowned and addressed me as if I were the expert. 'It happened twenty years ago, you say?'

'Almost exactly. It was a one-off.' I wished I hadn't mentioned any of it to them. 'As far as I know, nothing has happened since. If I didn't think this was a safe place, I wouldn't stay here with my daughter.'

'Twenty years,' Donna said, touching her gold cross again. 'I'm sure we have nothing to worry about.'

Tamara seemed relieved.

As I headed back to my cabin, glad my need to gossip hadn't caused them to overreact, I found someone on the front steps, knocking on the door. A large man wearing a red polo shirt and holding a clipboard. It was the guy who'd checked us in. The manager. What was his name? As he turned to greet me I saw it pinned to his chest. Greg.

'Hey, Mr Anderson. Just doing my rounds, making sure everything's okay.'

Was I imagining it, or did he seem a little nervous? Like he'd had lots of complaints and was bracing himself for another.

'Everything's great,' I said.

'I'm so glad.' He definitely looked relieved. He was sweating in the heat and he produced a handkerchief from his pocket and mopped his brow. He plucked a sheet of paper from his clipboard and handed it to me, his thumb leaving a damp imprint behind. 'I'd encourage you and your daughter to sign up for as many activities as you can before all the slots fill up.'

He carried on, telling me about all the wonderful things they had on offer. To be fair, it did all sound appealing. Rafting, kayaking, tennis, a 'teddy-bear hunt' for small children, even a moose safari. Horse riding leapt out at me – Frankie would love that – and I still fancied trying archery again.

'Can I put your names down for our big campfire event? It's on Wednesday night and there's going to be a barbecue and live music. We have an awesome band booked. It's a great chance for all our guests to meet.'

'And talk about their favourite murderer?'

He froze. 'Excuse me?'

'I'm just kidding.'

But Greg's smile had vanished and the sweat was pouring off him even more profusely. 'That's really not something we like to talk about. It was a long time ago and it was a completely different place then.'

'I'm sorry,' I said. 'It's just that David and Connie in cabin twelve told me there are lots of dark tourists here.'

His expression of shock seemed genuine. '*Dark* tourists?'

'I assumed you would have known that. They're all talking about it on some website for people who are into serial killers and grisly crimes.'

The remains of his smile slipped away. 'I'll have to look into that. Shall I put you down for two tickets?'

I had forgotten what he was talking about.

'The campfire?' he prompted.

'Oh, yes. That would be great. Thanks.'

Inside, I found a note on the table.

Have gone for a walk with Ryan. See you later. Frankie.

I held the sheet of paper, trying to work out how I felt. I had been looking forward to spending time with her. That was the whole point of this trip, after all. I didn't see her for fifty weeks of the year. It didn't seem so long ago that she had wanted to spend every possible minute in my company. I had pictured us exploring the resort together, going out on to the lake, signing up for the activities on the sheet Greg had given me. Filling the tank before I had to go back to England and my solo existence there. Instead, she had chosen to go off with some boy . . .

I stopped myself. She was a teenager now. All that mattered was that she was happy. I would still see her plenty, and this was my holiday too. It would be good for me to spend some time alone, and the last thing I wanted to be was clingy.

I put the shopping away and walked around the cabin for a little while. It was too beautiful to stay indoors. I grabbed a bottle of water and headed down to the lake.

ω

I sat at a picnic table by the water's edge. Close by, families and couples were lining up to hire boats: kayaks and paddleboards and even sailboats. I wasn't sure how big the lake was but its far shore was hazy, its surface still and blue. In the distance I could see a few people fishing and I remembered the website detailing how the lake contained trout and bass and landlocked salmon. There was the buzz of a motorboat, a water-skier gliding across the water behind it. On the edge of the lake, beneath the shade of pine trees, I could see a yoga class taking place.

'Man, it's beautiful, huh?'

It was David. He sat opposite me without asking. Connie was standing over by the little ice cream hut, talking to a couple in their sixties.

'So, I learned something interesting,' he said, leaning forward conspiratorially.

'Oh?'

34

'You know I told you how Everett Miller disappeared? And that he never showed up?'

'Uh-huh.'

'Well, there have been sightings of him, supposedly. One of the women who works in the kitchen was telling me about it. A few times, people walking in the woods have reported seeing a bearded guy with long hair lurking in the trees, and apparently some of the guys building this place reported all sorts of weird shit going on. Like equipment being moved. Car tyres going flat. Some of them said they were sure they were being watched. And they found food wrappers on the edge of the woods – like, candy bars and shit.'

'Wait. You think this Miller guy has been living out here in the woods for twenty years?'

He shrugged. 'Weirder things have happened.'

'If Everett Miller was guilty, would he really hide out here? Surely he'd have hot-footed it to Canada or somewhere.' We were only a thirty-minute drive from the border.

David grunted and turned his attention to Connie, who had arrived at his side while we were talking. He nodded towards the couple she'd been speaking to. 'Who was that?'

'They're fans,' she said. 'They even asked for my autograph. Said they'd come here after hearing about it on my podcast. Hey, Tom.'

'Hi.' I was impressed. She had fans?

'So, are you ready?' she asked David.

'As I'll ever be.' He stood. 'You want to come, Tom?'

'Where are you going?'

He grinned. 'We're going to take a look at where it happened.'

Chapter 5

We pushed our way through the trees, stepping over rocks and treading through tall grass. I wasn't sure exactly how David knew which way to go – as far as I could see all the trees on the path that led north looked the same – but he was like a sniffer dog who'd picked up a scent. We paused frequently so Connie could keep up, before ducking beneath some low-hanging branches.

'This is it,' David said, a little breathlessly, like an explorer who'd just found some long-lost burial chamber. He took a few steps forward and looked around, not speaking. He seemed in awe. Reverential.

There, at the centre of the clearing, just as he'd described, was a large, flat rock, about two and a half metres across. We approached it and David reached out a hand to touch its smooth surface.

'I can feel them,' he said after a short while.

'What do you mean?'

'Them. The victims. Can't you feel it? The energy.'

I couldn't. It was a beautiful day, the sun flickering through the trees. The bloody symbols on the rock had been washed away long ago and it was hard to imagine anything horrific happening here. David and Connie had obviously spent a lot of time immersed in the minutiae of this case, and Connie had, I guessed, described the crime scene in great detail to her podcast listeners. But for me, it was just a rock in a clearing.

'Eric and Sally weren't the only victims,' Connie said.

'What do you mean?'

'Jake Robineaux.'

'The boy who found them?'

'Yeah. He killed himself a couple of years after his book came out.' Connie leaned on her stick and looked down at the rock. 'You can tell by reading his book that he was deeply wounded by what he saw. He loved Sally Fredericks. She was his favourite teacher. Imagine finding her like that. Naked, her face turned blue from where she'd been strangled, her lover beside her with his brains leaking out of his skull.'

I was beginning to see why her podcast was so popular. She had a way with the ghoulish details.

'It must have really messed him up,' said David.

'You're not kidding.' I paused. Despite my insistence that I wasn't interested in true crime, I could feel myself being drawn in. The picture the Butlers had painted, last night and now. I was starting to see it. 'What do you know about Everett Miller? What was he like, apart from being a death-metal fan?'

Connie answered. 'Everyone said he was a pussycat. A pacifist. He had no record of violence. Kids he went to school with said how shocked they were, because Everett had always been bullied but never fought back.'

'Exactly the kind of person who's most likely to snap,' said David.

I could see that, even if it seemed like pop psychology. I wondered how many murderers had no record of violence in their past, though. I could understand it of domestic abuse victims who killed to escape. Or someone who committed a so-called crime of passion. But a murder like this? Surely there would have to have been some propensity towards violence. Wouldn't they need to build up to it? Could he really have been influenced by the music he listened to and videos he watched?

Maybe, as David suggested, he'd got sick of being ostracised and bullied and had snapped.

'Did he have a history of being into the occult?' I asked.

'Kinda,' said David. 'There was the music he was into, of course. They found tarot cards and a Ouija board in his room too. A big collection of horror videos.'

'That doesn't mean he believed in pagan gods, though, does it?'

Connie was looking around her. 'I don't know. These small towns, on the edge of the wilderness. People believe in all sorts of weird shit. And if he was being influenced by the music he listened to and the movies he watched . . .'

'Or maybe he just stumbled across this real-life porn show in the woods, wanted to join in and things got messy.' David shrugged. 'I guess we'll never know.'

'Unless he really is out here still,' I said, not believing it for a second. 'And someone catches him.'

'Huh. Yeah. Wouldn't that be something? I bet you'd love the chance to sit down with him for ten minutes, huh, Connie? Interview him for the podcast?'

'Imagine the ratings,' she replied.

David took a few photographs and was about to say something when we heard voices. A man and a woman, chatting and laughing.

David gestured for us to follow him into the trees. We crouched in the shadows behind a fallen log.

'What are we doing?' I asked.

He held up a finger. 'Wait.'

A man stepped into the clearing on the far side, almost at the same spot where we had entered it a few minutes before, followed by a woman. The man was balding and bearded, wearing knee-length shorts and a T-shirt bearing Charles Manson's face, and the woman was tall and broad, dressed all in black with purple streaks in her bleached hair.

'Oh my God, this is it, this is the place,' I heard him say, and the woman let out an excited squeal. They stood before the flat rock.

'Do you know them?' I hissed.

David shook his head. 'Oh, sweet Jesus,' he said. 'They're not going to . . .'

But they were. The two of them stepped into an embrace, their lips mashing together, and then they were lying on the rock and she was tugging at his shorts.

We three looked at each other, eyes wide. I didn't know whether to laugh or throw up. Connie, who had her hand over her mouth, was clearly going through the same struggle.

'We need to get out of here,' I whispered.

A high-pitched giggle rang out. The woman had hitched up her skirt and the man was unbuttoning his shorts. I tore my eyes away.

We crept further into the trees, trying to be quiet. We looped our way back to the main path until we were out of earshot of the sick pair.

'I hope you don't think we're like that,' David said. 'Turned on by death and murder.'

'It hadn't occurred to me.'

'Good. Fucking ghouls. They disgust me.' He was quiet for a moment. 'People often accuse us of, what's the word?'

'Prurience,' said Connie.

'That's it. Well, we're not prurient. We care about the victims. We're interested in justice. That's our motivation.'

He looked so pissed off, like I'd accused him of being a pervert, that I had no choice but to say, 'Okay, I believe you.' And I did, to an extent, though I was sure it wasn't only about justice. It was an interest in the dark side of human nature, mixed up with the thrill of trying to solve puzzles. I understood it, and recognised it in myself too. And, inside my head, an idea was beginning to take shape.

But my train of thought was interrupted. There was someone coming along the path, young voices ringing out through the trees, and I recognised one of the voices before their owners came into view.

It was Frankie and Ryan.

They both looked shocked to see us.

'Dad?' said Frankie.

David smiled. 'Hey, guys. Where have you been?'

'We went into Penance,' Frankie said. She seemed flustered.

'Are you all right?' I asked.

'Yeah. Why?'

'You seem a little . . . Oh, forget it. How was Penance?'

The two of them exchanged a look that told me something had gone down there, but they both shrugged as if the topic was too boring for words. I studied them, looking for hints of romance, unsure how I would handle it.

We all started down the path. There was a rustling in the trees and the couple emerged, looking flushed and pleased with themselves. Seeing us, they laughed and hurried off towards the resort, heads close together.

'Perverts,' David said, drawing a confused look from his son.

'What?' he said.

'Oh, nothing. Just . . . there are a lot of weirdos staying here this week.'

'Like you and Mom?'

David laughed and reached up to ruffle his squirming son's hair. I paused. *A lot of weirdos staying here.* The idea that had begun to form quietly a few minutes ago was now shouting for my attention.

'Hey, Frankie,' I said. 'Why don't you show me the town? I want to check it out.'

She shot a glance at Ryan. 'I've just come from there.'

'I know but—'

'You want to hang out with us, sweetheart?' Connie asked. 'While your dad does whatever it is he wants to do?'

'Sure. That would be nice. Thank you.'

Now I was torn. I wanted to spend time with Frankie. But it was pretty obvious she wanted to stay with Ryan.

'Maybe I'll come with you,' I said. 'I can go into town another time.'

'Dad. It's cool. You don't need to babysit me.'

'That told you,' said David with an annoying smirk. 'You go and do whatever it is you want to do and Frankie can hang with us.'

Now I felt like I had no choice.

'All right,' I said. 'I'll see you back at the cabin at one.'

I watched them walk away in the direction of the resort, then headed along the path around the clearing. As my daughter and the Butlers vanished from sight, a gloom came over me, as if the sun was no longer able to penetrate the trees and the path on which I walked was dark. Now that I was alone, what David had said about being able to feel the energy of what had happened here came back to me. I could sense it. An imprint in the air, the memory of an evil act stamped upon this place.

I hurried away from the clearing as quickly as I could.

Chapter 6

Later, I found out that Frankie and Ryan had gone into Penance to look for an internet connection. Now I was doing the same – because the idea I'd had in the clearing was starting to excite me. There was, I was sure, a story here worth writing about. Firstly, there were the murders. A pair of unfaithful schoolteachers bludgeoned and strangled on a school trip. The ritualistic nature of it. A shocking crime, but not one that had ever, as far as I knew, been reported in the UK – and I didn't think the popularity of Connie's podcast had reached our shores either.

Then there was the ongoing mystery. Everett Miller was apparently guilty but had never been found. Where had he gone? Was he still alive, living under a new identity? Had someone helped him get away? Had he gone on to commit more murders? There were enough questions there to pique the curiosity of anyone with the slightest interest in true crime.

Finally, there was the element that, I believed, really gave this story an edge: the opening of the resort and the influx of dark tourists, many of them obsessed with this case they'd learned about on a true-crime podcast.

I had never written a crime article before, nor any investigative journalism. But the idea excited me. This could be the new start I had been desperate for. Because, after clinging on for a long time, even through the horrific period of my divorce from Sarah, I was finally facing up to the truth. My career was dead.

Music journalism was all I'd ever wanted to do. I started in the early nineties, when the UK music scene was in rude health and there were numerous publications who were willing to pay decent money. For a few years, I lived the dream: being flown to LA and New York to follow British bands on tour; hanging out with rappers, and joining in the hedonistic rituals of rock stars who wanted to be seen to be living it large. Parties, awards ceremonies, private jets with record company execs, an endless supply of CDs and concert tickets.

But every boom is followed by a bust. At the same time that illegal file sharing started taking huge bites out of the record industry, the internet did the same to the music-magazine business. No one needed to wait to find news or reviews any more. And everyone was now a writer, willing to fill the Web with their opinions for free. Suddenly, publications that had been household names for decades were closing down. Others merged, or moved online. I watched as half my friends lost their jobs. It was like a virus ripping through a community, taking out the weak and strong alike. The business I had loved, lived and breathed was ravaged.

Suddenly, I too was part of a great army of freelancers, battling for a dwindling number of paying jobs. And as supply outstripped demand, prices went down and continued to drop. For years, I scraped by, living from commission to commission. A few stars who I'd befriended in the nineties gave me work writing sleeve notes for retrospective box sets. A book I'd written about David Bowie was republished after his death. I had an incredible collection of memorabilia – a platinum disc signed by Depeche Mode; a leather jacket worn by Courtney Love – which I reluctantly auctioned off. The stress made me drink and, I confess, act like a morose arsehole. I resisted Sarah's pleas that I retrain and get a proper job. I refused to move on and, eventually – nearly three years ago – Sarah moved out, taking Frankie with her.

Professionally, I managed to limp on. A friend who edited the culture section of a national newspaper promised me regular work writing reviews, which paid the bills – barely. I lived frugally and saved all year for these holidays with Frankie.

But I was wounded. The slow death of my career. The breakdown of my marriage. The loss of my daughter.

Some days – most days, in fact – it felt like I had nothing to be proud of. Nothing to get out of bed for.

And I was sick of feeling that way.

I didn't want to get ahead of myself, but if a great story had just landed in my lap – or rather, I'd landed in *its* lap – maybe this was my chance to start again. I had often thought about relaunching myself as a different kind of journalist. Could this be my chance to do just that?

The first step would be to do some research beyond talking to David and Connie. Read more about the case. Chat to a few locals. Then, if it seemed like there really was an intriguing story here, pitch it to some editors.

I tried to keep my excitement in check, but it was hard. Because when you've been starved of hope for so long, it's hard not to snatch at it when you see it dangled before you.

ω

Penance felt like it had been evacuated because of an emergency, with one or two refuseniks hanging on, including a homeless man who sat at the foot of a statue on the west side of the street. He had a thick beard and a sun-scorched face, and was wearing combat trousers and a black T-shirt that hung off his skinny frame. I had a few dollars in my pocket, which I handed to him as I passed by. He looked shocked, like he wasn't used to charity.

'You from the camp?' he said. 'The Hollows?'

I guessed he meant Hollow Falls. 'I'm staying there, yes.'

He nodded. 'It won't last long.'

I took a step towards him, shielding my eyes from the fierce sun. 'Why do you say that?'

'Nothing around here lasts. Nothing good, anyway. This place has been cursed for a long time.' He mumbled something else, the words getting lost in his beard. 'Hey, you got any more money?'

'Sorry.'

He mumbled something else.

'What's your name?' I asked.

He regarded me suspiciously before telling me. 'Wyatt,' he said.

'I'm Tom. Can you tell me where the police station is?'

He laughed. 'Ain't no police here no more. It's all looked after by the county sheriff in Houlton.'

'Where's that?'

He smiled. 'About ninety miles away. State police are based there too.' He started to cough and said, 'You sure you ain't got any more of them dollars?'

I genuinely didn't. He waved a hand like he wanted me to leave him be, so I crossed the street and found myself looking into the window of a bookstore. I was surprised that a town this small had one. The sign on the door said *CLOSED* but the lights were on, and according to the list of opening times in the window it was supposed to be open. Thinking the staff must have forgotten to flip the sign, I tried the handle anyway. The door opened. After the briefest hesitation, I went inside.

It was mercifully cool inside the shop. There was a decent selection of novels and children's books, a mix of new and second-hand.

There was no one behind the counter. I called out, 'Hello?' and, getting no response, wondered if I should leave.

But then something caught my eye: a section of shelving labelled *LOCAL INTEREST*. I decided to take a quick look. There was a book entitled *Penance in Old Photographs*, the cover of which showed the same Main Street I'd just walked down. It was far more bustling in this old sepia photo than it was now. There were books called *Wood You Believe It: My Life as a Logger* and *That Crazy Johnston Family*, the kind of vanity projects one often finds in local bookshops.

I was looking for a particular title: Jake Robineaux's memoir. But there was no sign of it.

I was so busy browsing the shelves that, when a voice in my ear said, 'Can I help you with anything?', I jumped and fumbled the book I was holding.

For some reason, I had expected the proprietor to be a grey-haired man, the kind of person who'd run a curiosity shop full of monkeys' paws and cute creatures that can't be fed after midnight, but the person smiling at me was a woman in, I guessed, her mid-thirties. She wore fashionable glasses and equally fashionable clothes.

'I don't suppose you have *A Night in the Woods* by Jake Robineaux, do you?'

Her pleasant smile slipped away. 'We don't stock that.'

Hiding my disappointment, I went back over to the table near the front of the store and picked up a dusty novel, thinking that if I looked like I was going to spend money, the shopkeeper would be easier to engage in conversation. But as I picked the book up, the dust made me sneeze.

'Bless you,' she said.

She held out a hand and I realised she wanted me to give her the book. I obliged and she produced a tissue, wiping the cover of the novel then giving it back to me. 'That's a good book. A lot better than that Robineaux trash.'

'You've read it?'

She didn't reply.

'I'm Tom,' I said. 'I'm staying at Hollow Falls.'

'Nikki. And I thought you might be. That's why you want to read *A Night in the Woods*.'

'People there are talking about what happened twenty years ago.'

'I bet.' She stared at me for another moment – it was the kind of stare that made me want to confess to crimes I hadn't committed – then she sighed. 'So what's it like, the resort?'

'You haven't been to check it out?'

'I don't go into the woods much these days. Not if I can help it.'

It was as if she were talking about some awful city slum or a nightmarish shopping mall, not the beautiful area that was right on her doorstep.

'Maybe you should,' I said. 'The place is impressive and there are a lot of people staying there. There's no internet or TV, so it seems like the kind of place you'd find a lot of customers.'

'You think? When they reopened the campground, turned it into a fancy resort, they told us it was going to save Penance. Provide jobs. Bring people to the area. They'd all come to town, spend money, make this place thrive again.' She gestured at the empty shop.

'It's only been open a few days,' I said. 'Maybe if you hand out flyers at the resort . . . Let people know you exist. And get a true-crime shelf for the dark tourists.'

Her frown returned.

'I guess you were here when it happened? The murders?'

'I was a kid,' she said. 'But yeah, I remember that summer. We all remember it.'

Without saying anything else, she went behind the cash register, disappearing into a back room. She came back out a minute later carrying a book.

'There you go,' she said, handing it to me. It was a copy of *A Night in the Woods*. 'I don't sell it. But I've read it.'

From the book's tatty condition, it looked like it had been read, or at least flicked through, many times. The cover showed the clearing where the murders had happened. Inset was a photo of Everett Miller.

'You can borrow it,' she said.

'I'm . . . Thank you.' I touched the picture of Miller. 'Did you know him?'

'It's a small town. Everyone knew him.'

'And you were a teenager when it happened?'

'Fifteen.'

'What was he like?' I asked.

'He was all right. People around here treated him like he was trash because he dressed different, listened to "freaky" music. But he wasn't a freak. At least, he didn't seem like one.'

'Some people are saying he's still around,' I said, wanting to gauge her reaction. 'Living in the woods.'

She smiled thinly. 'Or Canada.'

'That's what I said.'

'Great minds, huh?' She gave me a look that momentarily made me speechless. Was she flirting with me? It had been such a long time that I wasn't sure I was reading the signs correctly.

'So you really think he went to Canada?' I asked, stumbling a little over my words. Her eyes were a striking shade of green and she had a tiny scar above her lips. I had to force myself to break eye contact.

She shrugged with one shoulder. 'That's where I would have gone.'

'And do you think he did it? Murdered those teachers.'

'Well, he never liked school much.'

It was my turn to laugh.

'I'm sorry,' she said. She wasn't smiling. 'I'm just tired of hearing about it. It's been twenty years. Am I going to get someone coming in here every day asking about it, now the resort's open?'

I was trying to think of a good response when there was a high-pitched chirruping sound and a huge cat came strolling out of the back room and leapt up on to the counter. A tabby with a tail as thick as my arm.

'That's the biggest cat I've ever seen,' I said, stroking it.

'This is Cujo. He's a Maine Coon,' said Nikki, smiling at the cat like a proud mother.

'Cujo?'

'Well, I thought it was funny.'

The cat rubbed his head against my hand and chirruped again.

'He's beautiful,' I said.

'And he knows it.'

I petted the cat for a minute. Finally I said, 'Does Everett Miller have any relatives left in Penance? Any friends?'

'No, he doesn't.' Her frown had returned. 'Why are you asking all these questions? Are you a reporter or something?'

'I am a journalist, yeah.'

Her smile vanished. 'In which case, I'm going to have to ask you to leave.'

She escorted me to the door before I had a chance to protest. I thought she was going to snatch back the copy of *A Night in the Woods* she'd lent me, but instead she just held the door open. A little sheepishly, I went out.

'If you know what's good for you, you'll leave it. Stop asking questions.'

I must have looked confused.

'Sooner or later, you'll bump into somebody less friendly than me.'

She shut the door and locked it behind her.

Meet someone less friendly than her if I kept asking questions? Okay, now I really was intrigued.

Chapter 7

Monday

There was something on the ground in front of the Butlers' cabin. I stood by the kitchen window, peering out and wishing my eyesight was as good as it used to be. I was tired. Jet lag had prevented me from getting to sleep, so I'd stayed up late making notes for the article I was now sure I wanted to write.

Before leaving Penance, a little shaken from how my encounter with Nikki had ended, I had managed to get online. I immediately searched for 'murders Penance 1999' and found a few news stories that had originally been published in a Portland newspaper and a now-defunct paper that covered Aroostook County. There were photos of the two victims, Eric and Sally, including a photo of her on her wedding day, smiling beside her husband, Neal. It seemed as if the editor of the *Aroostook Eagle* was trying to make a point, and I detected a whiff of judgement in the way the story was written, as if the teachers had paid the price for their adultery. *Cheat and die* was the subtext.

Most interesting to me was the reproduction of Everett Miller's school yearbook photo. I was shocked to learn how young he was: he would have been just seventeen at the time of the murders.

In the yearbook photo he had long black hair and a wispy beard. There was a hint of eyeliner, like he'd been wearing make-up and hadn't scrubbed it off properly before the picture was taken. He was scowling, his gaze refusing to meet the camera lens. The Portland paper had interviewed several people in Penance who described him as 'odd' and 'a freak'. Of course, more than one person had blamed 'that Devil's music he listens to'. Somebody said they'd heard he was a Marilyn Manson fan.

I thought back. The Hollow Falls murders had happened just a couple of months after the Columbine shootings. The perpetrators of that terrible massacre had apparently been part of a group called the 'Trenchcoat Mafia', and the media had latched on to the idea that they were fans of Marilyn Manson. I'd written a piece about it at the time. In the summer of 1999, shock rockers like Manson and his fans were taking their turn as scapegoats for everything that was wrong with the world. From what I'd learned, Everett's tastes were more hardcore than Manson, stuff that was too noisy to ever make it on to MTV, and I could see how the people of Penance would find it easy to believe that the local 'weirdo' was guilty – especially when they learned about the Wolfspear music video David had mentioned to me. Later, I found a link to the video on Reddit and it was indeed disturbing, with its scenes of sex and bloody murder in the woods. I could imagine it being shown to a jury to convince them of Everett's warped tastes and love of violent imagery. It was the kind of thing that could send someone to prison.

Not that there was anything to say he wasn't guilty. There was forensic evidence, namely Everett's bandana. On top of that, the moment suspicion had fallen on him, he had run. In fact, as far as I could tell from the reports, no one had seen Miller since a few hours before the murders, at dinner. His mother couldn't tell if his bed had been slept in because his room was such a mess she rarely went in there. 'Everett pretty much kept to himself,' she'd said.

Was he guilty? He certainly seemed to be. I had no hope of finding out where he was now, so that wasn't going to be the thrust of my article, but I wanted to be able to paint a portrait of him. Nikki had said that everyone around here had known him. Hopefully I would be able to find someone who wasn't as averse to talking to a journalist as she was.

My focus returned to the object on the grass in front of David and Connie's cabin. Was it an animal?

Taking my freshly brewed coffee with me, I went out to take a look, still wearing the white towelling robe that had been provided by the resort. I walked barefoot across the lawn and down the path towards the Butlers' cabin.

It *was* an animal. From a distance I thought it was a cat, but as I got closer I realised it was a rabbit, a huge one, with white fur that was stained with blood across its belly. Flies were crawling over its face and had settled upon its staring eyes. Its throat was torn or cut open, and more flies had gathered there.

I was glad Frankie was still asleep. If she saw this, she would freak out, particularly since the rabbit looked just like Swifty, Frankie's pet rabbit, who was back at home, being looked after by her mum. Frankie was besotted with her pet, and her Instagram feed was full of pictures of him. Swifty even had his own Instagram account, which was considerably more popular than mine.

I glanced at our cabin, worried that Frankie might emerge and see this grisly sight. At that moment, David emerged from his cabin. It was still only seven and he was dressed in a T-shirt and boxer shorts, his hair sticking up almost vertically.

'Tom? What's going on?'

I pointed to the dead rabbit.

'Whoa. That's a big bunny.'

He slowly came down the steps and across the grass, staring at the animal. Then Connie appeared in the doorway, in a robe that matched mine, propping herself up with her stick. Behind her, peering out with eyes like dinner plates, was Ryan.

'I'll run up to reception,' I said. 'Get someone to come and . . . deal with it.'

David wasn't listening. 'What do you think did it? A cat? A fox?' He stooped and bent closer to the rabbit, examining its throat. 'That cut looks pretty clean to me.'

I stared at him. 'What, you think a person did this? With a knife?'

He chuckled and got to his feet. 'Nah, I'm messing with you. Must have been a fox. Or one of those massive cats they have around here. A Maine Coon.'

I thought about Nikki's cat, Cujo.

'We don't need to bother reception,' David went on. 'We can deal with it ourselves.'

He went back into his cabin and came out with a black rubbish sack and a pair of gloves, which he slipped on. He picked the rabbit up by its hind legs – 'Jeez, he's a heavy bastard' – and dropped it into the bag. Then he put it in the trash can.

'There. Done.'

'Listen,' I said, addressing Ryan as much as his parents. 'It's important not to say anything to Frankie about this. She has a pet rabbit and she'll be upset.'

'Of course,' said Connie.

'Swifty,' said Ryan. 'She told me about him.'

Connie sat down at the table on their deck. 'You know, I think I heard it happen. I woke up around three, needing the bathroom, and when I got back into bed I heard something out here. I figured it was raccoons or something and went straight back to sleep.'

'I bet it was a fox,' David said. 'I can't freaking stand foxes. We had chickens when I was growing up. Hey, Tom, do you want a refill?' He nodded at my coffee cup.

'I'm good. Thanks.'

As I walked away I clocked the expression on Ryan's face. He was staring at the place where the rabbit had been, deep in thought. Perhaps thinking about what his dad had said about a clean cut. Then he noticed me looking, shrugged and turned away.

Heading back, I spotted Tamara on the deck of the cabin on the opposite side of ours, straining to see what was going on.

I went over.

'What's happening?' she asked.

I explained about the rabbit.

'Nature, red in tooth and claw,' she said. 'Though it's kinda weird.'

'What is?'

'Oh, I'm sure it's nothing. It's just I'm a pretty light sleeper, especially since . . .' She left the sentence dangling tantalisingly. 'I thought I heard someone out here in the middle of the night. Two people, maybe. Whispering.'

I must have looked alarmed because she said, 'I'm sure it's nothing. Probably my imagination. In fact, I bet I know what sparked it. Yesterday I got chatting to this elderly couple down by the front desk. They were planning to ask if they could change their cabin. Want to guess why?'

I waited.

'It's because they think their cabin is haunted.'

'You're kidding me.'

'Nope. They swear they heard voices in the night. They said they felt a presence too. Like, a feeling there was someone outside their cabin. They're convinced it's those teachers you were telling us about, haunting this place.'

'Eric and Sally.'

'Yeah, if that's their names. A load of hokum. But I guess that's what triggered my imagination.'

'Or it could just be other vacationers going for a wander in the moonlight.'

'Could be.' She looked over to the spot where I'd indicated the rabbit was found. 'Nothing to worry about. Unless you're a rabbit. But listen. Please don't mention this to Donna if you see her. She can be . . . kinda superstitious.'

Again, I got the impression she wasn't telling me everything. That she was protecting Donna's privacy. But I nodded and said, 'Of course. My lips are sealed.'

ϖ

Two hours later, Frankie and I stood in a field on the edge of the resort, being kitted out for our archery lesson. I had put our names down yesterday, and sprung it on her as a surprise over breakfast. She had moaned at first, but on the walk here her mood had lightened. I hadn't said anything about the dead rabbit.

'So, what do you think of the holiday so far?' I asked. This was our first activity together, if you didn't count eating dinner last night.

'It's pretty good.' She smiled, knowing I would be disappointed by this faint praise. 'No, it's okay here. I'm not even that bothered about not being able to go online.'

'Really? Because I am.'

'Missing Netflix, are you? Or *Facebook*?'

She said this in the same way I might have gently ribbed my gran about still having a black-and-white TV in the 1980s.

'All right. Just because I don't spend my days learning the latest TikTok dance moves.'

'Okay, boomer.'

I laughed. 'Hey, I'm Generation X, I'll have you know. The best generation.'

'You keep telling yourself that, Dad.'

This was more like it.

Our archery instructor was a thirty-something guy called Carl. He had a shaved head and a reddish beard and moustache. He reminded me a little of Walter White from *Breaking Bad*, but fifteen years younger. He asked us if we'd ever tried archery before.

'Not since I was a little kid,' I said, deciding not to tell Carl that my dad had been an amateur archery champion, in case it raised his expectations.

'You guys are Brits? You should be good. Robin Hood and all.'

'I think we might let our country down,' I said.

Carl winked at Frankie. 'I've got a feeling you're going to be good, even if your dad isn't.'

That made her smile.

He showed us the parts of the bow and measured our draw length to decide which size we needed.

'Okay, who wants to go first?' Carl asked. 'You want to show your dad how it's done?'

'You go first,' said Frankie, looking at me.

'Sure.'

My first attempt sailed past the target.

'Maybe I shouldn't have mentioned Robin Hood.' Carl laughed like this was the most hilarious joke he'd ever cracked.

But I improved. I was soon able to hit the target, and though most of my arrows landed in the white, scoring one or two, I got a few in the black and blue. It was frustrating but fun. It took me back to when I was a kid and my dad used to take my sister and me to watch him and occasionally let us have a go.

'Not bad,' said Carl. 'Now, Frankie, it's your turn.'

He handed Frankie a bow. 'Your feet need to be shoulder distance apart. Stand perpendicular to the target. That's it. You need to hold the bow gently, not in a death grip. That's it. Good. Now, when you pull back, use your whole body, not just your arm. Pull it back to the corner of your mouth and aim the sight pin at the centre of the target. There you go.'

Frankie released. The arrow flew past the target.

'Great effort,' said Carl. 'Nobody hits it their first go. Your dad didn't.'

Frankie wore the determined expression I recognised, the one that had accompanied many challenges throughout her life, from learning to tie her shoelaces to kicking Bowser's ass in *Super Mario*. This time, on just her second attempt, she hit the target, the arrow thudding into the blue.

'Awesome!' Carl exclaimed.

She let another arrow fly. It landed on the outer edge of the first gold ring. She grinned.

'Whoa,' Carl said. 'I'm going to start calling you Katniss.'

He grinned at her and held his palm out for a high five. I could see Frankie squirming with embarrassment, but she high-fived him back.

'Keep going, Katniss,' he said. Again I saw Frankie cringe at the reference to the character. She'd loved *The Hunger Games* books and movies, but I guessed it was one of those things she'd outgrown, that wasn't cool any more. It was impossible to keep up.

Frankie released arrow after arrow. I watched her. The concentration. The way the bow quickly came to seem like an extension of her arm; her eye unwavering as she fixed it on the target.

Within minutes, she was hitting the gold, again and again.

'Wow,' said Carl, genuinely impressed. 'You're a natural.'

'Thanks.'

Frankie kept going, and Carl was about to move to the next pair of novices, but I stopped him. Casually, I said, 'Did you grow up around here?'

'Yep. Beautiful part of the world, isn't it?'

'It is.'

I figured he was about the same age as Nikki from the bookstore.

'I heard about—'

'You're going to ask me if I remember what happened in '99, aren't you?' I clearly wasn't the first person to bring it up. 'I'm sorry, but I really don't want to talk about it. And I don't want to talk about the rumours either.'

'Which rumours?'

Frankie was oblivious, firing arrows at the target.

'If you haven't heard them, I'm not going to help spread them,' he said, clearly annoyed.

'Are you talking about Everett Miller still living somewhere in these woods?'

He turned to face me. 'You came all the way from England because of what happened here?'

'No. I—'

He didn't let me finish. 'Look around you. These beautiful woods. The lake. Smell that clean air. This place is special enough as it is. It's not a freaking theme park for ghouls.'

'But I'm not a dark tourist.'

'Whatever.' He took a last glance at Frankie, said, 'Keep it up, Katniss', then walked away.

Chapter 8

Frankie couldn't find her Hydro Flask anywhere and her dad was going to kill her.

She remembered the conversation they'd had when she'd first asked for it. Her mum had already said no, so she'd FaceTimed him and casually mentioned that there was this bottle she really wanted.

'A water flask?' he had said. 'Sure. Send me the link.'

Frankie had done just that and braced herself for his reaction.

'Wait. *Fifty dollars* for a water bottle?'

'It's not just a bottle. It's better than a bottle. And this one's limited edition.' It was aquamarine, wide mouth, with a straw lid. All the girls at school had them, but none as awesome as this. Frankie was certain that owning this bottle would improve her social status by about 200 per cent.

A week-long back and forth of messages had ensued, about how much Frankie needed one, how *essential* it was, with her dad offering terrible off-brand alternatives. Finally, *finally*, when Frankie had achieved top grades in her exams, he'd surrendered and since then Frankie had taken it with her almost everywhere. Of course, it hadn't made her popular at school – though she'd seen a few girls eyeing it enviously – but she loved it as an object in its own right.

And now she couldn't find it.

It didn't make sense. She honestly just about never let it out of her sight. The last time she remembered having it was when she and Ryan had walked into Penance yesterday. Then this morning, before the archery class – which had been surprisingly fun – she'd looked for it but couldn't find it. Now, back at the cabin, she racked her brain, trying to recall when she last saw it. She was certain she'd brought it back to the cabin with her yesterday, after having lunch with Ryan and his parents. Hadn't she?

Her belly had a hard, cold lump inside it.

She loved that flask and she had promised her dad she would always look after it. She wasn't like some of her friends, who didn't care about breaking their phones or losing stuff because they knew their parents would replace it with barely a moan. She prided herself on looking after her things. But where the hell was it?

'Hey,' she called. 'I'm going out.'

Her dad called back, 'Where are you going?' He seemed in a better mood. Excited about something, scribbling away in a notepad. She knew he'd enjoyed the archery too, though he kept going on about how she was a natural talent, that maybe she ought to take it up when she got home, that he could see her competing for prizes. Why couldn't it just be something fun she'd tried? Why did parents always seize things they thought you were good at and try to squeeze all the joy out of them?

'Just to get an ice cream,' she replied.

But she didn't go to the ice cream stand. Instead, she went into the general store, trying to remain calm. It was pretty small, with basic groceries plus some books, magazines and DVD rentals. DVDs. That was how quaint this place was. The shelves were full of all the stuff her mum wouldn't let her have at home: Twinkies, Reese's Peanut Butter Cups, that spread made out of marshmallow. She hovered by the shelf, distracted from her mission, wondering if her dad would buy some for her, until she remembered she was trying to convince him she wasn't a kid any more. Marshmallow spread was hardly the best way to achieve that.

She approached the counter, where a woman who reminded Frankie of her grandma in Albany was standing.

'Hey, sweetie.'

'Um, can you help me? I can't find my flask. It's like, a metal water bottle, a kind of bright greeny-blue colour. Has anything been handed in?'

The woman shook her head, but went into a back room to check and ask her colleagues.

'Maybe try at reception? They have a lost and found there.'

Reception was located in a large cabin near the entrance to the resort. Close to tears, Frankie hovered near the desk, waiting for the grumpy-looking woman seated there to finish her phone call, when a man appeared through another door. He was huge, his red polo shirt threatening to ride up and expose his belly. There was a badge pinned on his chest. *Greg Quinn. Manager.*

'Hey,' he said brightly, doing that twinkly thing that a lot of men did in her presence these days. 'Can I help, sweetheart?'

She hated being called 'sweetheart', but she kept her face neutral.

'Do you have a lost and found?' she asked, wishing she didn't always feel so nervous about talking to adults, especially men.

His shoulders slumped, like he was thinking, *Not another one.*

She told him about her flask.

'Hmm. It doesn't sound familiar.'

'Are you sure? I really need to find it or my dad will kill me.'

Greg seemed taken aback. 'Hey, I'm sure your dad won't . . .' But he must have seen the panic on her face because he said, 'Why don't you come through and we can take a look.'

He opened the door and beckoned for her to follow him. Normally, she would have hesitated, all the years of warnings about stranger danger causing her to be wary, but there was that grumpy woman behind the desk, which made her feel safer. Frankie could scream if anything happened, which it probably wouldn't – she could hear her friends in her head, telling her she was *so* dramatic – and, anyway, she was desperate.

She went through into a large office. A desk with a computer, some filing cabinets, and framed photographs on the walls.

'Okay,' he said, rooting around. 'Where's that lost-items box?'

While he rummaged through the cupboard, Frankie inspected the pictures on the walls. They showed a campground. Rows of tents. Scouts and Guides and groups of schoolkids with funny hair-cuts and retro clothes, from the eighties or nineties, she guessed. One photo showed a small group of teenagers, two boys and a girl, in jeans and T-shirts, gathered by the edge of a lake.

Greg emerged from the cupboard with a large cardboard box and saw her looking at the pictures. 'Cool, huh?' he said, putting the box down.

'I love their clothes,' she said, for want of anything more profound to say.

'Ha, yeah. We all dressed like that in the nineties.' He pointed at one of the boys. 'That's me.'

'No way.' The boy was considerably bigger than his two friends and – Frankie was appalled with herself for thinking this – kind of cute.

He grinned. 'Yes way. That was taken quite close to here, by the lake.'

Yes way? She cringed. But Greg was looking at her expectantly, waiting for a reaction, so she said, 'So did you, like, stay here when you were young?'

He chuckled. 'Me? No. I'm local. From Penance. But me and my friends used to hang around the Hollows a lot.'

He hunted through the cardboard box while he spoke. She held her breath.

'Sorry, sweetheart. There's no flask in here. Do you know where you lost it?'

'No.' She felt tears pricking the backs of her eyes and, apparently seeing how upset she was, Greg said, 'Let me just go and ask Vivian.'

He left the office and Frankie noticed something. A Wi-Fi router sitting on the desk beside the computer.

She checked her phone. There was a Wi-Fi network here! But it was password-protected.

Greg came back in, dabbing his forehead with a handkerchief. 'Sorry, there's no . . .' He saw the phone in her hand. 'Trying to connect to the broadband, are you?'

She scrambled to make an excuse but he smiled, showing a set of dimples. 'Getting internet withdrawal, are you? Want a quick hit?'

He picked up a sheet of paper from the desk and handed it to her. There, in black and white, was the password. *Hollow321*. It could hardly have been easier to guess.

'I don't mind if you want to hang out here and check your emails, or look on TikTok or whatever. Just don't tell anyone, okay? It's our little secret.' He winked.

Okay, that was creepy.

The Wi-Fi symbol appeared on her phone, telling her she had a connection.

He went on. 'I bet your dad doesn't realise how lucky he is, does he? I bet you get good grades, don't cause any trouble for your folks. If your dad gives you any grief over losing your water bottle, send him to me and I'll tell him he should be grateful to have a kid like you.'

Greg, Frankie had decided, was super weird. She stood up. But as she did, her phone let out a series of pinging noises, just as it had when she'd connected in Penance. WhatsApp messages appeared from her friends. Then a flurry of notifications from Instagram. That was unusual. She didn't usually get that many likes or messages on there, unless she posted a photo of Swifty looking extra cute.

'If you ever want to come here and check your messages or whatever, I'm totally cool with that. It would be nice to—'

She tuned him out. She was reading through her Instagram notifications, her Hydro Flask forgotten, the blood in her veins gone cold.

She hurried from the office, leaving Greg mid-sentence.

She needed to find Ryan. Like, right now.

ω

Ryan's mum was seated out front of their cabin, reading a book called *I'll Be Gone in the Dark*.

'Hey, Frankie. Ryan and David are playing tennis,' she said.

The tennis courts were on the other side of the resort, down a path behind the reception building she'd just left, in a large clearing that also contained a children's playground. As she passed the playground, which was quiet – there weren't many little kids at the resort, which was odd – she stopped. Ryan was sitting on one of the swings. A tennis racket lay on the ground at his feet.

She went over.

'Have you finished your tennis game?'

'Huh.' He scowled. 'I was supposed to meet my dad here, like, twenty minutes ago.'

'And he didn't show up?'

'No. Asshole.'

The venom in his voice was shocking.

'He probably ran into some *fans*,' he said.

'Fans?'

'Yeah. Turns out quite a lot of the losers staying here are fans of Mom's podcast, and Dad's been on it a few times.' He frowned. 'This was supposed to be a vacation . . .'

With a grunt, Ryan got off the swing, picked up his racket and strode away. Frankie followed.

'Listen,' she said. 'I need to show you something.'

He kept walking and she had to hurry to keep up. Finally, she caught him by the elbow and yelled, 'Look!'

He stopped, staring at her. She had her phone out, Instagram open. It was disconnected from the internet now, but the photos that had loaded in the office were still on the screen. Ryan started to ask how she'd managed to get online, but she shushed him. 'Just read the comments.'

There was the photo he had posted when they'd been in Penance. She hadn't noticed at the time but he'd tagged her in the post.

> *Come to the asshole of the world! Penance, ME. Where the dogs in the junkyard have higher IQs than the people. #Penance #shithole #vacationfromhell*

Beneath were a couple of comments:

> *Fuck you, tourist.*

> *My dog has a higher IQ than YOU!!*

Ryan laughed. 'Whoops. I've pissed off the locals.'

'Those comments are nothing. Look.'

She had taken screenshots of her direct messages:

Watch yr back we're coming for you.

Run rabbit run rabbit run run run . . .

*First I'm gonna rape you and make your dumb bf watch
and then I'm gonna murder you BOTH.*

There were dozens. All the messages had been sent from different accounts with anonymous names and avatars. Frankie felt shaky and sick. Of course, she'd encountered trolls on social media before, but nothing like this.

'Look at this one,' she said. '*We know where u r staying.* And this one. *Sleep tight. DON'T LET THE BED BUGS BITE!!* What does that mean?'

She had expected Ryan to be as shocked as her. As frightened. But he laughed again. 'Come on, this is typical troll behaviour, that's all. It doesn't mean anything. It could be anyone.' He stopped, finally noticing how upset she was. 'It's not a serious threat. Just ignore it.'

'I think you should delete the post,' she said. 'Or apologise. Actually, you should do both.'

'What? I'm not apologising. It's probably some ten-year-old keyboard warrior anyway, with multiple accounts. Don't worry about it.'

'But—'

'Stop,' Ryan said, giving the phone back. 'Frankie, relax, okay? I promise you, they're empty threats made by a bunch of backwoods losers. Let's go get an ice cream. My treat.'

He strolled off ahead of her, like he didn't have a care in the world. She tried to follow his example, to persuade herself it was just trolls; nothing to worry about. But she was sure she had seen something on Ryan's face when he'd been reading the messages. Surprise. A flicker of fear before his smile returned.

Chapter 9

Frankie and I had dinner at the site restaurant, then went to the store to hire a DVD: *School of Rock*, starring Jack Black.

When we got back to the cabin, Frankie paused just inside the doorway.

'It seems different in here.'

'What do you mean?'

She looked around, sniffing the air. 'I don't know. I guess I'm imagining it.'

The movie was one of her favourites but she didn't laugh as much as usual. She seemed jittery, but insisted there was nothing on her mind. I wondered if she'd fallen out with Ryan already. Perhaps she was missing her mum or friends, and feeling cut off from the 'tea'. Not that I was allowed to attempt to use teenage slang; it apparently made me sound like a sad old man.

'I'm going to bed,' Frankie said when the film finished. She had a Stephen King book she'd borrowed from Ryan, one I'd read years before, and even though I worried it might be a little scary for this setting, I was of the firm belief that any reading should be encouraged – not that Frankie needed any encouragement to bury her head in a book. Despite her attachment to her phone, she was always reading, which pleased me enormously. Another book lover on the planet.

'Are you sure you're okay?' I asked. 'You know if there's something on your mind you can always talk to me about it.'

She hesitated.

'Come on, you can tell your old dad.'

That was obviously the wrong thing to say because she pulled a face and said, 'I'm going to bed.'

I poured a glass of wine and went outside. It was balmy on the deck, and stars were dotted in the spaces between the trees. Out of nowhere, a wave of melancholy hit me. My failed marriage. The thousands of miles between my daughter and me. My failed career and my empty bank account.

That prompted me to go inside to fetch my notebook. I'd already scribbled down a bunch of stream-of-consciousness ideas, but they needed organising. I turned to a fresh page and started to write.

The murders. Was it Everett Miller? Why did he do it? Where did he go? Rumours he's still here now – crazy but could add extra element of mystery.

Dark tourism. Growth of true-crime podcasts. What makes people so obsessed with this stuff? Talk to some of Connie's fans. How do management of Hollow Falls really feel about it? Good for business?

Greg had seemed shocked when I'd mentioned it to him, but would he really care, if it brought in visitors?

Rituals/paganism. Local history of dark beliefs? Influence of music/media?

Victims. Who were they? Reach out to their relatives?
How do they feel about fact justice was never done?

That, I realised, was an important angle. Eric and Sally had been cheating on their spouses. What must it feel like to discover your husband or wife had been murdered while being unfaithful? That alone, I was sure, would make this an interesting article. Perhaps I could talk to Eric's wife and Sally's husband, if I could track them down.

Finally exhausted, I took a shower. When I wasn't thinking about my article, Nikki from the bookstore kept popping into my head. Of course, I encountered women I found attractive all the time, but few of them lingered in my mind the way she did. I was sure there was some chemistry there. I had only spoiled it by revealing I was a journalist. Maybe I should go back and see her . . .

I was lost in reverie for so long that the water began to run cold. When I got out of the shower I found that steam had drifted from my en suite into the bedroom, filling the room and fogging the windows. I dried myself and put my robe on. The windows were still steamed up and I absent-mindedly went over to wipe at them with the palm of my hand, revealing the glass beneath.

A face stared in at me.

I jumped back, then quickly went to the window again, peering out.

There was no one there. Had I imagined it? Seen my own reflection? It had definitely seemed real: a face a few feet from the window, looking right at me. Except – and I shuddered to think of it – there had been something wrong with it. Like it wasn't human. It was as white as milk with large, black eyes, and there had been something protruding from its head.

The horned god.

I tried to laugh, to tell myself it was ridiculous. I remembered Tamara in the cabin opposite telling me about the couple who were convinced their cabin was haunted. I was as bad as them. I guess I must have been unsettled by what Frankie had said too, about our cabin seeming different.

I looked out again and convinced myself it must have been my own mirror image, distorted by condensation. Or maybe light reflecting off the rental car parked outside.

I closed the blinds.

And heard a scream.

Frankie.

I sprinted through the door and ran straight to her room.

She was standing in front of her bed, in her pyjamas, frantically brushing at them. She was making distressed sounds, almost as if she were still sleeping, trapped in a nightmare. I immediately looked over at the window, expecting to see it open, signs that an intruder had been in the room.

'Frankie?'

She stared at me, wide-eyed. I took hold of her shoulders.

'Sweetheart.'

She blinked and came back to life. Pulled away from me.

'What happened?'

Frankie pointed at the bed. The duvet was pulled back, the pillows on the floor.

'Just look,' she said.

I turned the light on and saw what had freaked her out.

There were ants in her bed, crawling across the sheets, caught in the folds at the end of the duvet. These weren't the tiny black ants you get in England. They were a brownish-red colour and about half an inch long. And there were dozens of them, darting in all directions on the bed.

I turned back to Frankie. She was scratching herself and trembling. 'It itches. I think they bit me. Oh God, they could be in my pyjamas.' She was on the verge of sobbing, plucking at the fabric of her pyjama trousers and jogging on the spot, her knees pistoning up and down.

'I think they're carpenter ants,' I said. I've always been a fan of nature documentaries. 'It's okay, they're not poisonous.'

'But it *itches*. I need a shower.' She let out a shuddering breath. 'I can feel them on me.'

'Okay. Go and get in the shower. I'll call maintenance.'

She ran from the room. Was I really going to call maintenance now? It was almost midnight. I decided the call could wait until morning.

I heard the shower come on, followed by a cry of dismay. 'There's no hot water.'

'I'm sorry,' I called through the bathroom door. 'You'll have to wait.'

But the water came back on and I guessed she'd decided to go ahead anyway, so desperate was she to wash away the sensation of the ants.

I went back to Frankie's bedroom, bundled up the sheets and duvet and took them outside, dumping them on the deck. I went back inside. There were still a few ants on the floor of her room, scuttling towards the corners. I watched them vanish into the shadows.

Frankie came out in her robe, a towel wrapped around her hair. She was shivering, her teeth chattering.

I wished she was still little so I could help her, but I felt useless.

'I hate it here,' she said. 'I wish we'd gone to New York.'

'You don't mean that.'

'I do,' she said between teeth chatters.

'I thought you were . . .' I stopped. This wasn't the best time. She'd just been bitten by a load of ants in her bed. Of course she hated Hollow Falls right now. 'Go on, go and get dry. Do you want me to make you a hot chocolate? I bought some earlier.'

'Thank you,' she said, sniffling.

She didn't want to go back into her room in case there were still ants lurking in there, so I fetched a clean pair of PJs for her and she went into my bedroom to get dressed while I made her hot chocolate. I didn't, of course, mention the face I thought I'd seen at the window. I had to tell myself that there was no connection between the two incidents. One of them hadn't even been real.

I heated milk to make her drink. But a few minutes later she poked her head out of the bedroom. 'I'm exhausted, Dad. I'm just going to go to sleep.'

'Of course. You can have my bed.'

But she had already decided that.

I drank the hot chocolate myself then lay down on the couch. It was lumpy and too short. It took me a long time to get to sleep, and when I did I dreamt of a face at the window. A giant insect, tapping at the glass with its mandibles, trying to eat its way through like the window was made of sugar and I was the second course.

Chapter 10

After her dad called the office in the morning to complain about the ants, the grumpy woman from reception turned up. This was apparently the Vivian that weird Greg had gone to check in with about the flask. She went into Frankie's room, got down on her hands and knees and said, 'Yup, looks like you got yourselves some carpenter ants.'

Frankie's dad said, 'What are you going to do about it?'

Vivian got to her feet and dusted herself off. 'We'll put some powder down. Not much else we can do.'

'You can't move us to another cabin?'

Vivian seemed surprised, like this was a massive overreaction. 'I'm sorry, but we're completely full. They're just ants, Mr Anderson. They won't do you any harm.'

Frankie cringed. Her dad had folded his arms. He was this far away from asking to talk to her manager. 'They bit my daughter.'

'Oh shoot. That's not nice.' Vivian addressed Frankie directly. 'I guess you must have scared them off.'

'Can she get a new mattress?'

'What? There's no sense in that. They're not living in there. They've all skedaddled.'

'Has anyone else had an invasion of ants?'

This made Vivian chuckle. 'Invasion? Not that I've heard of. But that's one of the risks we all take when we vacation in nature. It's like these folk that go camping, then get upset when a bear goes rifling through their stuff.'

Frankie's dad had gone bright pink and she was gripped by the urge to laugh. Maybe Vivian was right. Now it was morning, Frankie could see they had overreacted. It was quickly turning into a funny story she could tell her friends when she got home. *And then my bed was invaded by a swarm of killer ants . . .*

She left the room, leaving her dad repeating his demands that Vivian do something about the ants and replace the mattress.

Through the front window she could see Ryan sitting outside his cabin, drinking coffee and reading a book. He was so grown-up and sophisticated. Why weren't there any boys like him in her class? They were a bunch of pimply perverts who talked about nothing except baseball and *Fortnite*.

She went outside.

'Hey,' she said, approaching the deck where Ryan sat.

'Hey.' He put the book down. It was a horror novel called *Sweetmeat* with a big sticker on the front: *Now a Major Netflix Series*. Frankie had already binge-watched it – it starred that British actress, Ruth something-or-other – but hadn't read the book yet.

'Do you want to go for a walk?' she asked.

Before he could reply, Ryan's mum, Connie, came out. 'Hey, honey,' she said to Frankie. She nodded at the Hollow Falls golf buggy parked outside the Andersons' cabin, which Vivian had arrived in. The staff drove them all around the site. 'Everything okay?'

Frankie told her about the ants.

'Holy shit. It's like Mother Nature is pissed with us. Ants. Dead rabbits.' She clapped her hand over her mouth. 'Oh, damn.'

Ryan rolled his eyes. 'Mom!'

'Dead rabbits?' said Frankie.

'Come on,' Ryan said, getting to his feet. 'Let's go for that walk.'

Halfway to the lake, Ryan groaned. His dad was coming up the path towards them, wearing a baseball cap and a Harley-Davidson T-shirt.

'Hey, guys,' he said, cheerily. He seemed excited about something.

'What are you grinning about?' Ryan asked.

'It's a beautiful morning! Why wouldn't I be happy?'

Ryan rolled his eyes again. When they walked on, he said, 'He's up to something.'

'Like what?'

'Who cares?'

Ryan was striding ahead so quickly that she had to jog to keep up with him. They stopped by the picnic benches, which were full of holiday-makers stuffing their faces or queuing for boat rides. Fleetingly, Frankie remembered that she and Dad were meant to be going for a pony ride that afternoon. More baby stuff. She'd been into horses and ponies back when she was a child. She wondered if she could get out of it, though she could picture his disappointed face.

'What was your mum talking about?' she asked. 'Dead rabbits?'

'Nothing.'

'Come on, you have to tell me.'

He exhaled. 'Okay, but don't freak out. We found a rabbit outside our cabin.' Seeing her take a deep breath, he hurriedly added, 'Almost certainly left there by a cat or a fox.'

'What did it look like?'

'I don't know. Like a regular rabbit. White fur. It was kinda bloody . . . Sorry.'

'White fur?' A horrible thought struck her. 'Did it look like Swifty?'

'I can't remember. Sorry, but most rabbits look the same to me.'

She pulled out her phone. Something had hit her. Something horrible. She began to read out the messages she'd first read yesterday.

'*Run rabbit run*. And this one. *Don't let the bed bugs bite.*'

It felt like the ants were swarming all over her again.

'What are you talking about?' Ryan asked.

She took a deep breath. 'If they looked at my Instagram, they would have seen all the pics of Swifty.'

She couldn't work out if Ryan was pretending not to understand what she meant.

'Don't you get it? *Run rabbit run*. Then a rabbit that looked like my pet was left out here. And *Don't let the bed bugs bite.* That's obviously a reference to the ants.' She stared at him, breathing hard.

'I think you're putting two and two together and getting a thousand,' he said. 'I mean, the rabbit wasn't even outside your cabin.'

'So? They could easily have got confused. If they followed us back here. Or have been watching us . . .' She felt sick. 'Or maybe they were trying to frighten *you*. I mean, you're the one who dissed them.'

'Frankie, seriously. It's just nature. A fox killed that rabbit and the ants got in on their own. We're in the middle of the woods. That's the kind of shit that happens out here.'

She wanted him to be right. She really did. Except she couldn't let it go.

'But what if it *is* the people we upset on Instagram? Trying to get their own back?'

Ryan's laugh wounded her, and it must have showed on her face because he said, 'Sorry. I'm not mocking you. It just sounds . . . unlikely.'

'It's not unlikely. I think we should apologise.'

'What for? Telling the truth?'

'You don't mean that. You were upset because of those weird kids.'

'What, you don't think Penance is a shithole?'

'Maybe it is. But how would you feel if someone said horrible things about your hometown?'

'Ha. I'd agree with them. I certainly wouldn't go around trying to get revenge. But . . . maybe you're right,' he said, suddenly changing tack. 'Not about them taking revenge or whatever, but about it not being nice. I get a little carried away sometimes.'

He plucked some grass from the ground with his fingertips. 'I should delete the post. Maybe make my account private.'

'That's a good idea.'

'Except we can't get online without going back into Penance.'

'Actually, maybe we can.' She stood. 'Follow me.'

She led him across the grass, towards the reception building. She felt a little reassured. Ryan was probably right. It was nature, that was all. No one had put ants in her bed.

She was hoping her guess would be correct: that if she got close enough, her phone would connect to the Wi-Fi without having to go inside.

There was a small shaded area around the back, with a couple of smelly dumpsters, and she headed for it, getting her phone out and checking the screen. Yes! It had worked. Her phone had remembered the password and she had a signal. She showed Ryan.

He got his own phone out. 'What's the password?'

She told him and he tried to connect but it timed out.

'I guess it prefers my old phone to your shiny new one,' she said. 'Here, you can log in to Instagram on my phone.'

She gave it to him and watched as he went through the fiddly process of logging out of her account and logging back in again.

He tutted.

'What is it?'

'WhatsApp notifications keep popping up. Whoa, Frankie, it's an avalanche.' He paused and a smile crept on to his lips.

She stiffened. Had a message come in from one of her friends? A message about him? Her whole body went hot and cold, and it took all her willpower not to snatch the phone from his hand.

'Are you logged in?' she said. 'I'm worried Greg will appear at any second and catch us.'

'Chill, Frankie. What's he going to do? Kick us out for stealing the Wi-Fi? He's probably too busy, sitting in there watching porn.'

'Oh, gross.'

He had the grace to look ashamed of himself. 'Sorry. Okay, here we go. I'm in.' He angled the phone so she could see it and navigated to the picture that had offended the residents of Penance. 'That's good. No new comments. A few likes from my friends back home. And . . . delete. There you go. Feel better now?'

She did. A little. She pointed at the top-right corner of the screen. 'You've got a new message.'

He opened it. It was from someone calling him or herself CC123456. A nonsensical, anonymous username. The message contained three words:

Go home or . . .

'Short but sweet,' Ryan said. 'Go home or what? Go home or stay here, the choice is yours? Go home or go hungry?'

He clicked on the avatar. CC123456 had a private account, which meant they had to approve follower requests, so it was impossible to see if they had ever posted anything. They had zero followers and didn't follow anyone. It seemed they'd set up an account just to send this message. This threat.

'Maybe we should tell our parents,' Frankie said. She felt utterly sick now.

'No way.'

'Why not?'

'My mom and dad act cool, like they're young and swag or whatever. But my mom's really strict. She'll ground me for a month if she finds out about this. For antagonising the locals.'

Frankie thought her dad would be okay about it. Freaked out but not angry. She hadn't really done anything wrong, anyway. It was Ryan who'd posted the picture. But she thought he might forbid her from seeing Ryan. That alone made her decide not to tell him.

'I've deleted the post now,' he said. 'They must know they've scared us. They'll stop now, I'm sure.'

She couldn't have looked like she agreed, because he put a hand on her shoulder.

'Trust me,' he said.

Ryan remembered that he had promised he'd go out on the lake with his mum, so they said goodbye and she watched him half-jog towards the shining water.

Frankie made her way towards her cabin. She wasn't sure what to think. Ryan was probably right. The rabbit thing was a coincidence, as were the ants and the bed bugs message.

Before they'd parted, Ryan had tried to reassure her again. 'I know it sucks getting weird threats like this, but I bet they're all bark and no bite. Don't worry about it. Now I've deleted the post I'm sure that'll be the end of it. Okay?'

'Okay.'

She was deep in thought, finally persuading herself there was nothing to worry about, when she heard footsteps behind her. She was so hyped up that her body reacted immediately, her heartbeat accelerating, stomach plunging. But another impulse, the desire not to look stupid or foolish, prevented her from running.

Keeping a steady pace, she slowly looked over her shoulder.

It was them. The teenagers she and Ryan had encountered in Penance. They were behind her, walking at the same pace as her, side by side. She caught the girl's eye and the girl's lips curled into a smile. Except it wasn't a real smile. It was the kind of expression an alien who was trying to imitate human emotion might make. The boy did the same, and now Frankie was certain they were twins. They looked like two dolls who had rolled off the same production line.

Frankie increased her pace, expecting the twins to do the same.

But when she dared to glance back again, they were gone.

Chapter 11

He and Abigail stand concealed by the trees, watching Frankie and Ryan as they slip behind the reception building. A moment later he hears a little cry of triumph and he realises what they're doing. Not making out. Not sparking up cigarettes. They're stealing Wi-Fi. It's kinda funny, and he goes to catch Abigail's eye, to see if she's smiling too, and she is, but at something else. There's a faraway look in her eye.

'What?' he asks, not moving his lips.

I was remembering, she replies. *When you were their age.*

She's moving away, slipping into the trees, away from the teenagers, and he has to hurry to keep up. It's easier for her, though he knows these woods like he created them himself. He's walked these paths for so long. She's moving down towards the lake, along the shoreline, and he knows where she's leading him. It's a hot day, and the mosquitoes are attracted to the heat of his flesh, to the stink of his sweat, and he swats at them as he goes. They don't bother Abigail, of course, and she aims a smile back at him as he flaps at the buzzing insects.

Sweetgrass, she says. *How many times have I told you?*

He nods. He has some braided and hung in the cabin – she knows that – but it's not doing him any good now, is it?

They reach the little cove by the edge of the lake, and she reaches out a hand towards his cheek.

You were always such a sweet boy, she says, and they both look out at the water, this corner of the lake undisturbed by boats, and all of a sudden it's 1998 again, he's lost but innocent, and the woman beside him is warm.

Warm and alive.

ϖ

He had never met anyone like Abigail and there was a good reason for that. Because there wasn't anyone like Abigail. Not in this town, anyway.

His mom worked twelve-hour shifts at the strip club out near the highway. Not one of the dancers – not these days, anyhow – but helping to manage the place, looking after the girls and the takings and the clientele. She was always asleep when he left for school, and by the time he got home she was at work, though she'd leave his dinner in the refrigerator with a note, always signed with a kiss and a smiley face. Her days off, she was usually too tired to do much except sit around watching TV. When he was younger he'd curl up with her on the couch and impress her by answering the questions on *Jeopardy!*. Now, though, he was too big for that, and besides, she was dating this loser she'd met at work and spent most of her free time at his place.

With no dad on the scene – no dad had ever been on his scene – he was left to look after himself. There was nothing to do in Penance. The youth centre had shut down after the guy who ran it was caught exposing himself to a pair of eleven-year-old girls. He wasn't into sports, and his only childhood friend had moved to Chicago after his dad got laid off. He had entertained himself playing video games and hanging out in chat rooms on the computer he'd guilt-tripped his mom into buying, discussing the bands he liked. Most of that time was spent on a board for metalheads, trading chat and gossip about Korn and Metallica and the Nordic death-metal groups he was getting into.

Until this summer, when he met Abigail.

He'd just turned fourteen, the summer was blazing, and their dial-up internet wasn't working right. He'd taken himself into the cool of the woods, thinking he'd go for a dip in the lake. He headed down to a small clearing he'd visited before. A good spot for swimming, well away from the campground and the out-of-towners that came and went throughout the spring and summer months. There had been times when he'd hidden in the trees and watched them, looking out for pretty girls, of which there were many. But not today. Today he wanted to be on his own.

Which was why, when he spotted the figure on the shoreline, a grown-up with her back to him, he almost left straight away. Except he must have made a noise, a grunt of disappointment maybe, because she whipped her head around like she'd heard a rattlesnake.

'Hey,' she said. There was a smile in her voice and on her face. Then she laughed. 'You look like a startled fawn.' Her smile grew broader as he gawped at her. 'You don't need to look so afraid. I don't bite.'

She had long golden hair that reached almost to her waist, shot through with purple and red streaks. Bare feet and a loose cream dress that he would later discover was called a tunic. She had lines on her face that made him think she might be somewhere around his mom's age – his mom had just celebrated her thirty-fifth birthday – but she seemed somehow both younger and older. She didn't have the under-eye smudges and the vampire skin of the night worker; but she seemed . . . wise. Maybe it was dumb to think that within seconds of meeting her, but there was something about her that reminded him of a teacher. Which, as it turned out, she was. Just not like one of the teachers at school.

'I'm Abigail,' she said.

He told her his name, approaching her slowly and warily, like a stray dog drawn by a piece of meat.

'It's beautiful here, isn't it?' she said in her soft voice. 'You planning on taking a swim?'

He nodded.

'Well, don't let me stop you.'

But there was no way he was stripping to his shorts in front of this woman.

'I ought to be getting back,' he said.

'No, why don't you stay? We were about to have a picnic.'

It took a few seconds for that 'we' to penetrate his brain. He looked around stupidly. There was no one else here. Just him and Abigail. He peered at the lake, in case there was someone out there, swimming, but the water's surface was flat and unbroken.

She said, 'Here they are.'

He turned back towards the path just as a boy and a girl appeared, carrying a cooler. They looked at him with clear suspicion. Like, *who are you and what are you doing here?* The boy was big and red-faced, with peach fuzz on his upper lip. The girl – well, the girl was pretty, with her hair cut short, kind of like Cameron Diaz in *There's Something About Mary*. She stared at him with eyes that were big and green and he realised he knew these kids. They were in the year above him at school.

Abigail was beside him. She shocked him by putting a hand on his shoulder.

The two older kids stopped on the path and let the cooler drop to the ground with a thud.

'This is Goat,' Abigail said, gesturing to the boy. Then she nodded at the girl. 'And this beautiful creature is Fox.'

ʊ

He snaps back to the present. He's standing by the shoreline, the toes of his shoes almost in the water, and Abigail has gone. He hears the drone of an engine, a speedboat across the lake, and grits his teeth. Somebody shouts and there's a screech of laughter that makes him flinch.

He feels something touch his shoe and looks down.

It's a Coke can, bobbing on the water's surface.

He crouches and picks it up, staring at it like he can't believe it's real. But of course it's real. This is why Abigail vanished. This is a . . . what's the word? He gropes for it. It's a word she taught him.

Affront.

It's an affront.

And a confirmation.

He crushes the can in his fist and stalks back through the woods, too angry to feel the mosquitoes, unable to think about anything except what needs to be done.

Chapter 12

Frankie had gone out while I was talking to Vivian, who had eventually agreed – with much huffing and tutting – to replace Frankie's mattress. I'm sure I heard her mumble something about 'goddamn city folk' as she stomped away.

It was only after Vivian had gone that I remembered what had happened immediately before Frankie had screamed. The 'inhuman' face at the window.

Ignoring the clothes and wet towel Frankie had left on the floor, I opened the blind in my bedroom and peered out. The room backed on to the woods, so all I could see were trees.

I went outside to take a better look. There was a clear space of about six feet between the cabin and the woods. The ground was clear. No footprints. No sign anyone had been there.

I was reassured. I must have seen my own reflection, and my imagination, fired up by a mixture of jet lag and Frankie's comment about the cabin feeling different, had done the rest.

I went back to the kitchen and made myself a coffee. I wanted to go out, to find Frankie and see more of the resort. Perhaps we could go for a drive somewhere. But I needed to see if Vivian would keep her promise, and as I waited for the coffee to brew my eyes fell upon the book Nikki had lent me.

I picked it up. *A Night in the Woods* by Jake Robineaux. There was Everett Miller's picture on the cover, peeking out beside a stock photo of creepy trees. This wasn't his yearbook photo: it showed him in full metalhead regalia, his hair loose and long, dark make-up around his eyes and a piercing through his lower lip. He was grinning at the camera. He looked genuinely happy, maybe slightly sheepish.

I opened the book and quickly became absorbed. It was a short book, around 150 pages, with the first section focused on Robineaux's stay at the camp – all the hijinks he and his friends got up to, with pen portraits of the other kids, including the locals he'd encountered.

One passage early on stood out:

> *There was a lot of crazy talk among the kids about the campground being cursed or haunted. Some things went missing from a few kids' tents. Someone had brought a radio with him, and one girl, Jenna Sankey, had brought along these expensive earrings. These disappeared along with some other stuff, like Brad Dion's secret stash of candy. There were a lot of accusations flying around, and the teachers, including Mrs. Fredericks, carried out a search. I remember Mrs. Fredericks making a little joke about how it was probably a good thing for Brad to go without candy for a few days. None of the missing items turned up, and Jenna spent the rest of the week crying about her earrings.*

> *Another time, we got back from a day kayaking and found that half our tents had collapsed. Someone had pulled out a load of the poles. Worse than that, one of the girls who shared with my friend Mary-Ellen—a*

cheerleader called Stacey—went to get in her sleeping bag and found it was soaking wet. I'll never forget her screaming, "Someone's peed in it!" She was totally hysterical. Of course, everyone thought it was hilarious, especially when Stacey tried to blame Brad, who had accused her of taking his candy.

I'm making out that it was funny and that we all coped in a typically teenage way, not taking anything seriously unless it directly affected us, but to tell the truth it was kind of scary. No, more than that. It was hard to get to sleep, especially after Mary-Ellen said that she'd been told by one of the rangers that the campground was haunted by a girl who'd drowned in the lake years ago. That rumor quickly morphed into one about a woman who'd been drowned in the lake hundreds of years ago, as part of the witch trials that went on around that time, and she had put a curse on the woods with her dying breath. Corey did a hilarious impression: "Anyone who—glub—treads upon—glub glub—this ground shall be—gargle—cursed to DIE!" which made everyone laugh until Mr. Daniels pointed out in his typical joy-killing way that there hadn't been any witch trials in Maine.

Still, as more and more creepy stuff happened, the more the rumors of ghosts and curses spread. One night, we heard a scream coming from Stacey's tent and Corey cracked a joke about how someone had peed in her sleeping bag again, but then Mary-Ellen screamed too and they both said they'd seen a figure standing in the woods, watching them.

"What were you doing out of your tent?" Mr. Daniels wanted to know, and everyone knew it was because they'd snuck out for a smoke. Mrs. Fredericks took a flashlight into the trees and came back reassuring everyone there was no one there and that we should calm down and go back to sleep. I thought they'd imagined it too, except Mary-Ellen—who wasn't the kind of girl who gets spooked easily and who had described The Blair Witch Project, *which a load of us had snuck into the theater to watch earlier that summer, as a dumb movie for scaredy-cat babies—had gone totally pale. When I asked her about it she said that they had definitely seen someone.*

"Or something," she said.

"What do you mean?" I asked.

She shivered and hugged herself. "It wasn't human," she said.

But she wouldn't say any more.

I stopped reading and glanced through the open door at my bedroom window. *Not human.* I forced a laugh and told myself not to be ridiculous. It was this place, that was all. The primal fear that dark woods bring out in all of us.

A long section was dedicated to the night Jake found the bodies. I read this with keen interest, trying to imagine what it must have felt like. How scary it must have been. The rest of the book was dedicated to Robineaux's 'philosophy of life', a series of almost comically clichéd motivational statements – *Live every day like it's the most important of your life*; *You don't need to chase a pot of gold—the rainbow is enough!* – accompanied by his deep thoughts about the meaning of everything.

There were several quotes from Sally's widowed, cuckolded husband too. Neal Fredericks. Robineaux had interviewed him for the book, and it seemed he'd been only too willing to talk, mostly about the inadequacies of the local police and their failure to find Everett Miller.

I was tempted to go searching those woods myself, with a shotgun, Neal Fredericks was quoted as saying. *Mete out my own justice. It's a disgrace that they let that kid get away. But I'll tell you one thing. I don't care if he's a pagan or heathen or whatever the heck you call it, Everett Miller is going straight to Hell. And thanks to the Maine police, that's the only time he's going to face justice.*

Neal Fredericks had been eager to speak to Jake. Maybe he'd be willing to talk to me too.

I put the book down with a heavy feeling in my gut. Jake Robineaux didn't seem like he'd been suicidal when he wrote his book, but perhaps the inspirational slogans were his way of putting on a brave face – because according to what David and Connie had told me, Jake had killed himself a couple of years after the book's publication. That was—

The front door of the cabin opened with a bang.

I almost jumped out of my chair. But it was just Frankie. She went straight into the kitchen and filled a glass of water, gulping it down.

'Are you okay?' I asked, rising and approaching her.

'Yes. I'm fine. Why wouldn't I be?'

I put my hands up in surrender. 'All right. Sorry. You seem tense, that's all.'

'I'm just hot. What are you doing? What's that book?' She went into the living area and picked up *A Night in the Woods*. She groaned. 'Not you too. Ryan says his parents never stop banging on about this shit.'

'Frankie!'

I very rarely heard her swear. But I decided to let it go. I was hardly a saint myself when it came to bad language, and yet again I had to remind myself she was almost grown-up now. There were far worse things than swear words. I'd just been reading about some of them.

She dropped the book and appeared to hesitate for a moment. Then, to my great surprise, she threw her arms around me and rested her face against my chest.

'Love you, Dad,' she said.

'I love you too.'

As quickly as she'd hugged me, she pulled away. 'Isn't it time we got going?' she said.

'Huh?'

She rolled her eyes. 'Aren't we supposed to be pony-trekking?'

Of course. I had completely forgotten.

I put the murders from my mind and headed out with my daughter.

Chapter 13

Before she'd moved to the States with her mum, I had taken Frankie for riding lessons every week, never missing them even when I was at my lowest ebb and my career and marriage were falling apart. It had been one of our things, a dad-and-daughter activity, although I hadn't ridden myself. I drove her there, sat and waited in the car while she had fun, and then, on the way back, we would stop for milkshakes and cake at a local café. I found it hard to think back on those days without getting emotional. I'd had no idea back then that my time with my family was so limited.

I didn't blame Sarah for leaving me. I knew I had become impossible to live with: grumpy and morose much of the time; filled with self-pity and hard to love. I was no longer the man she had married. I did blame her, however, for taking Frankie to America. I had never imagined she would do such a thing, and she claimed it wasn't something she had planned either, until a job opportunity came up that was too good to miss. I could have fought for custody. I might have been able to get a court order to stop her taking Frankie, who didn't want to go either. But I had no money to pay for lawyers and, well, I had no fight in me. That was part of the problem. And in the end I realised it would be better to go along with Sarah's wishes. I needed her to give me access to my daughter.

The situation became normal. We settled into a routine. My trips to the US were special. But it was on days like this – reminded of what we'd once had, and knowing that I was missing most of her adolescence – that I had to try extra hard to keep a brave face.

We gathered with a couple of other families on the edge of the resort, the horses still out of sight. Frankie seemed nervous.

'Are you okay?' I asked.

'Yeah. It's been a long time.'

I was a little nervous too. This was going to be my first time on horseback in years.

The instructor, a woman called Susan, had handed out helmets and was running through the health and safety instructions, and telling us about the route we were going to take. Through the woods for a couple of miles, which would take us close to Penance, then loop back to where we started.

'It will take about an hour,' Susan said. She was young and sturdy-looking, with brown hair cut in a bob. 'How many of you are experienced riders?'

A couple of women raised their hands and I nudged Frankie. Susan noticed.

'You know your way around horses?' she asked.

Frankie gave me her patented 'thanks for embarrassing me' look and said, 'I used to ride every weekend when I was a kid.'

'Well, in that case I've got a beautiful pony you can take out, honey.'

Susan went through a gate towards the stables, and over the next ten minutes she and another woman brought out the horses and ponies. They had already been saddled and they plodded along with their noses down, flanks shining in the afternoon sun.

'This is Magpie,' Susan said, giving Frankie the reins of a beautiful piebald pony. 'We only let more experienced riders take her. Is that going to be okay?'

'Why's that?' I asked. The pony kept hoofing the ground and tossing her mane. I was worried she might be skittish.

Susan smiled. 'Oh, Magpie is quite a character. But if you'd rather I fetched one of the quieter ponies . . .'

'No. I want Magpie,' Frankie said. It was love at first sight. The pony pushed its nose against her and she stroked its mane. It was like having the old Frankie back, even more so than when she'd hugged me.

Everyone was introduced to their mount. I had a grey gelding called Springsteen, who was considerably bigger than Magpie. He fixed me with a hard stare before allowing me to stroke his head. I put one foot in the stirrup and climbed up, my stomach lurching as the horse shifted and I saw how far I was from the ground. I'd forgotten what it felt like to be on such a powerful creature, but then I saw Frankie so at ease on top of her own horse and forced myself to stay calm.

'Now,' Susan called, 'the horses know where they're going so you don't need to worry about directing them. We're all going to walk at first, but when we get a little further in, those of you who want to trot will be able to do so, once I've said it's okay.' She continued with the brief, said, 'Any questions?', and then we were off.

As we started moving I was convinced I was going to fall, and I clung on tight, intoning 'Don't look down, don't look down' under my breath. But once I relaxed, I loved it. The trail, which led northwest through the woods, sun splashing through the branches, was only wide enough for the horses and ponies to walk in single file. Frankie looked over her shoulder and smiled at me, a sight that connected directly with my heart.

When the path widened, I found myself next to a woman who introduced herself as Madison, who was from New York. Her husband and teenage daughter were behind us. After ten minutes or so, we passed the clearing that David had taken me to, with the flat rock at its centre.

'Hey,' Madison said to her husband. 'That's the spot where it happened.'

'You're here because of the murders?' I asked.

'No. Well, not just that.' She chuckled. 'It's an added bonus, is all.'

'Did you hear about this place on some kind of dark-tourism website?' I had slipped into interview mode.

'Uh-uh. It was on a podcast.'

'Connie Butler's?'

'Oh, are you a fan too?' Her voice became hushed. 'I actually saw her and David yesterday. They said hello to me.' She said it as if she'd encountered Prince Harry and Meghan. She leaned towards me and said, with a conspiratorial air, 'David told me they've got a surprise for people who are interested in the case.'

'Really? Did he say what?'

'Nope. It wouldn't be a surprise then, would it? Hey, do you think they might have found out something new about the case? Maybe they've found Everett Miller. You know, the woman in the cabin next to ours thought she saw him.'

'What?'

'I know. Creepy, right? She was out for a walk, out behind the tennis courts, and she says she saw a shifty-looking guy just hanging around in the trees. Like he was trying to hide. When she saw him, she says he vanished like he was made of smoke.'

This was good material for my article, even if I didn't believe it could possibly be Everett.

'Did she say what he looked like?'

Madison hesitated. 'She was kind of reluctant to tell me, like I'd think she was crazy.'

'But?'

'She said he didn't look normal. She saw his face for a split second but she said she thought there was something wrong with it. Like – well, it sounds crazy, but like he wasn't human any more. As if the evil inside him had transformed him.' She cleared her throat. I was staring at her and I think she was regretting bringing up the subject. 'Like he was a demon or something.'

The path narrowed again and Madison and her horse fell in behind me. It was silent apart from the clip-clop of the horses' hooves on the hard ground and the low rumble of chatter among the riders. Susan was at the front, on a large chestnut gelding, then Frankie, then me.

'We're close to Penance now,' Susan called back to us. 'The path ahead forks. We're going to go left and start looping back to where we started.'

I was sure I saw Frankie's shoulders tense when Susan mentioned the town. Perhaps she was worried about her pony, Magpie, taking the wrong turn. But the animals knew which way to go and, one by one, we went left, the path widening again, another clearing just ahead. I could hear distant traffic and something else close by, a tinkling. Wind chimes? I saw Frankie turn her head towards the sound too, a frown on her face.

And then something went *BANG*.

It sounded like a gunshot, very close by. A crack, immediately followed by an echo. Everybody turned towards the sound, the horses jittery, one or two of them stopping, flaring their nostrils, backing away from the noise. Magpie was among those that had stopped. She skittered backwards a few steps, almost colliding with my horse. Frankie wore a look of intense concentration, trying to keep control of Magpie. Behind me, I heard someone cry out and turned to see one of the women at the back of the group struggling to stay on her horse, which had reared up. You could feel it: a wave of panic rippling between the animals. Ahead of me, Susan called, 'Everyone stay calm. These horses—'

There was another bang.

The wave of panic broke.

My horse went up on his back legs, and before I knew it I was on the ground. I hit hard and all the wind went out of me. The world flashed white and then I snapped back to reality, my inner red alert blaring, and I scrambled to get away from the hooves of the horses around me. Madison was thrown too, landing flat on her stomach and lying still for a moment, groaning. It was chaos, all the horses dancing on the spot, only one or two remaining calm. I couldn't see Frankie. I crawled over to Madison and helped her to the side of the path, worried we were both going to be trampled. Her husband was yelling, asking if she was okay, and Susan was calling out too, imploring people to remain calm, to soothe their horses. I had a throbbing pain in my hip but managed to get to my feet and take hold of the reins of my horse. Now I could see Frankie. Her pony kept rearing up, then hoofing at the ground, and I could see that Frankie was trying not to panic.

The gunshot came again.

This time, Magpie bolted.

Chapter 14

The pony crashed through the line of trees, branches scraping Frankie's back, and turned in a circle before bolting back the way we had come. Frankie screamed but clung on, her arms wrapped around Magpie's neck, unable to do anything to stop her. I was frozen for a moment. I looked at my horse. I wasn't experienced enough to ride after her. I had no choice. I ran.

I pictured the worst: Frankie thrown into a tree, Frankie with a broken spine.

Frankie dead.

I sprinted along the path, stumbling on the uneven ground. The sun was high and cruel, and little black flies swarmed around me like a bad omen. If Frankie was badly hurt it would be all my fault for bringing us here.

'Frankie!' I called when I reached the clearing.

And, like a miracle, she responded.

'Over here.'

I ran past the flat rock and found her beneath a malformed tree on the other side of the clearing, its trunk twisted and scorched as if at some point in the distant past it had been struck by lightning. It bent over her like it was protecting her.

She sat on the ground, a stunned expression on her face. Her pony stood nearby, nose to the ground, calmly chewing on a shrub as if nothing had happened.

I got down on my knees. 'Are you okay? Where are you hurt? Can you walk?'

She had dirty tear tracks on her cheeks and was mute.

'Frankie?'

'I'm fine,' she whispered.

'We need to get you to a doctor.'

'Dad, I'm fine!' She almost yelled it, which made Magpie glance over at us, as if we were bothering her. Frankie got to her feet and stroked each hand over its opposite shoulder, examining herself.

'I'm okay,' she said, and then she started to cry again.

'Oh, sweetheart.' I pulled her into an embrace.

'Ow!'

'Shit, sorry.'

She smiled through a wince and then looked over my shoulder. Susan was coming towards us on her horse.

'Everything all right?' she asked. 'Anybody hurt?'

'Dad, don't make a fuss. Don't start doing your "I want to talk to your manager" thing.'

'Okay, okay.'

Susan dismounted and Frankie explained that Magpie had stopped of her own accord.

'She's a good girl,' Susan said, stroking the pony's neck. 'Do you feel able to ride back?'

'They were gunshots, weren't they?' I said. It wasn't a sound I was accustomed to.

Susan nodded. 'Hunters, I guess.'

'That close to town?'

100

'I don't know. Maybe it was someone shooting targets. Tin cans or whatever.' She grew angry. 'Greg needs to talk to his buddies in Penance. If he wants the town and resort to coexist . . .'

'I know what it was,' Frankie said. 'It was a warning.'

Susan blinked at her. 'I'm sorry?'

But Frankie wouldn't say any more. As we led Magpie back across the clearing to join the others, Frankie remained silent.

ϖ

As soon as Frankie was settled in the cabin, I went off to find a first-aider. She needed painkillers and antiseptic cream for her scratches. As I passed the area with the picnic tables, I noticed a small crowd of around a dozen people gathered in a circle. At the centre, I realised, were David and Connie, surrounded by their adoring fans. I walked straight past. I wanted to talk to them, but now was not the right time.

I found Greg in reception. I swear I saw a flash of fear in his eyes – trepidation, at least – as I approached the desk. Perhaps he thought I might threaten to sue. The A/C was ramped up so it was almost chilly in the building, but Greg was still sweating.

'I'm so sorry,' he said, wringing his hands. 'Is Frankie okay?'

'She'll live,' I said. 'She's tough.'

If you'd asked me that morning if Frankie was tough, I wouldn't have been sure how to answer. Was she? But she'd got over the incident with the ants pretty quickly and I'd been impressed by how she'd acted since the pony had thrown her. Walking back to our cabin, she'd told me several times not to make a fuss, and she'd refused to answer when I asked her what she'd meant when she said 'It was a warning', telling me to forget she'd said it.

'You're very lucky,' Greg said.

'What do you mean?'

'She strikes me as a very capable, confident girl. A real credit to you.'

I looked at him. When had he formed this opinion of my daughter?

Seeing my confusion, he said, 'She was here yesterday. Has her water bottle showed up yet?'

'Sorry?'

'Her whatchamacallit . . . Hydro Flask? Is that it? She came here to check our lost and found box. *Has* it showed up?'

'No, I don't think so.' I didn't want him to think he knew something I didn't. 'Are you going to talk to someone about the hunters? In the woods?'

'Hunters?'

'I assume that's who was out there with a gun.'

'Oh, yes, of course. I'll deal with it.' He paused. 'Let me give you a couple of vouchers for the ice cream kiosk.'

I took the vouchers, the antiseptic cream and a box of Advil, and left.

I went back as quickly as I could, but was stopped in my tracks as I passed the cabin next to ours, where Donna and Tamara were staying. They were pulling up in their car, a red four-by-four, and Tamara waved at me as they got out.

'Been anywhere nice?' I called as I went past.

'Huh, not really. We had to go in search of a drugstore.'

I stopped walking. 'Oh. Everything's okay, I hope?'

'It will be.'

Donna stood on the other side of the car. She looked a little grey, like she was sick or in pain, and her forehead was creased with worry.

'We just have to avoid any excitement for a couple of days,' Tamara said.

Donna scowled. 'I'm sure you threw them away by accident.' She looked at me. 'She's always doing things like that. Tidying up. Not noticing what she's throwing out.'

Tamara gave an indulgent but weary smile. 'Come on, let's get you inside.'

They went in. What was all that about? I didn't have the mental space to try to solve any more puzzles, so I shrugged and moved on.

When I reached our cabin I found Frankie standing by the door.

'What are you doing?' I asked.

'I'm going to see Ryan.'

'But . . .' I held up the antiseptic cream and Advil. 'I brought you these.'

'I told you, Dad. I'm fine, okay? And I need to see Ryan.'

She moved past me towards the door.

'Is he your boyfriend?'

She winced. 'Oh, please.'

'Sorry. I mean, it's fine if . . .' I trailed off. This was one of the disadvantages of us living apart. I had no experience in this area. No idea what to say. Though maybe, probably, almost certainly, I would have been just as clueless if we did still live in the same house.

She huffed, 'Can I go?'

'Wait. Did you lose your Hydro Flask?'

'I . . . How did you find out?'

'Greg told me.'

'Ew. Weird Greg.'

I fought to keep my face straight. 'What makes you say that?'

'I don't know. He's just creepy. Can I go?'

'No. That Hydro Flask cost fifty dollars, Frankie. You promised me you'd look after it with your life.'

'I did!'

'Apparently not.'

I didn't really care about the cost of her water bottle, and knew how easy it was to lose things. But I was tired, still shocked by the events with the horses, and I had an uneasy feeling that I couldn't quite explain. Too many weird little things going wrong. So I didn't deal with the situation as I would have done if I were calmer and less exhausted.

'I knew you'd be like this,' Frankie cried. 'That's why I didn't tell you. I'll save up, okay? Give you my allowance and pay you back.'

ω

A little while later I looked out the front and saw David and Connie on their deck. There was a man with them.

Restless and thinking this might be a good chance to talk to them and get some more information for my article, I went over to say hello.

'Tom!' David said, effusive as always. 'You want a beer?'

'That would be great.'

He handed me one, the bottle cold and wet.

'This is Neal,' he said, nodding at the man sitting in the chair opposite Connie. He was, I guessed, in his fifties, with a bald head and the eye bags of a chronic insomniac. He rested a beer bottle on his paunch. Neal. Where had I heard that name recently?

'Hey,' I said. 'Are you another fan of Connie's podcast?'

David, who was now standing behind Neal, made a throat-cutting gesture at me.

'I'm not a big fan of true crime,' said Neal.

I was confused. Who was this guy?

Neal stood and said, 'I guess I'd better be going. See you tomorrow, David?'

'Sure.' David and Neal shook hands and David said, 'It was so good to meet you.'

Neal went down the steps and walked off in the direction of the lake. I waited till he was definitely out of earshot and said, 'Who is that?'

'You'll see,' said Connie.

'Wait. He's something to do with your big surprise?'

She gave me an enigmatic smile. This was interesting. If Neal was connected to the murders . . .

And that's when I remembered. Neal was the name of Sally Fredericks' husband.

'Don't tell me that's Neal Fredericks,' I said.

Connie and David both looked stunned. 'How did you know that?' David asked.

'I read Jake Robineaux's book.'

'You did?'

'Yeah.' I didn't want to tell them about my article yet, because I wasn't sure how they would react. They might think I was treading on their patch and clam up. 'I was intrigued after talking to you and visiting the clearing. But what's Sally Fredericks' husband doing here? I'd have thought it would be the last place he'd want to come.'

David and Connie exchanged a glance. They seemed annoyed that I'd figured out who Neal was.

'You'll find out more tomorrow night,' David said.

I nodded, thinking I wasn't going to wait that long. I wanted to talk to Neal Fredericks. He could be a pivotal part of my article. Speaking of which . . .

'Can I ask you something? In Jake's book he said a lot of strange stuff happened at the campground in the days before the murders. Do you think it might have been connected?'

'You really need to listen to our podcast,' Connie said. 'I guess you haven't been able to get online, but it's something we cover at length. Jake didn't make the link explicitly in his book and the police didn't either, apparently.'

'You think it is connected, though?'

'It has to be,' said David. 'We actually tracked down some campers from the weeks before Jake was here and the same thing happened to them. Hearing weird shit at night. Random items going missing. So it had to be someone local, and no one was ever caught or came forward to admit to it. We think it was Everett, and that's where he first spotted Sally and Eric.'

'And decided to target them,' Connie added. 'We think he was probably stalking them. Watching them. Maybe he overheard them making plans to sneak into the woods.'

'But why would he steal things? Pee in their sleeping bags?'

'Because he was a freaking nutjob,' David said with a laugh.

'I don't know,' I said. 'Surely there has to have been more to it than that.'

'I agree,' said Connie, shooting David a look that made him fall quiet. 'To me it always seemed like . . . like he was marking his territory.'

All three of us turned our heads towards the woods, and a sensation of dread trickled down my spine. A shadow moved in the trees. Shifting light. Wind stirring branches. But it was easy to imagine something else at work. Something alive and ancient that had lived among these trees since they were saplings.

Everett's territory?

Or the territory of something he worshipped?

Chapter 15

Frankie and Ryan sat beside each other on the swings. The scratches on her back from the tree branches were sore and her ant bites itched. Neither of those things really mattered, though. Not now.

At some point on the walk home her phone had pinged. She must have walked through a pocket of cell signal. She hadn't checked it until her dad had gone to reception to get the first aid stuff.

She showed Ryan now. It was another message received through Instagram. An image of a girl falling from a horse, accompanied by a message, blocky white letters on a crimson background: *Maybe next time you'll break ur neck*. That was followed by several crying-with-laughter emojis.

'The message arrived about ten minutes after I'd fallen.'

Ryan looked at the message, then at Frankie, then back at the screen. 'Did you see anyone?'

'No. But whoever it was must have been there. Following me.'

'Following you? Are you sure?'

He was annoying her. Why, for once in her life, couldn't some-one simply believe what she was saying? It was the curse of being a teenage girl. Everyone always questioned you. Everything was because of hormones or social media or just being young and being a girl. It was *infuriating*.

'I'm sure, Ryan. I think they fired the gun and then followed to see what would happen.'

She heard a groaning sound and realised she was making it herself.

'I'm scared they're going to do something worse,' she said. 'Like, next time they won't just scare the horses.'

'But why are they targeting you and not me?' he asked, visibly shaken by her words. 'It wasn't your post.'

'I don't know. Maybe they think I'm an easier target. And anyway, the rabbit was left outside your place. They're probably after both of us. They might be following you too.'

He blinked, his mouth forming a frown, like he'd remembered something.

'What is it?' she asked. 'Has something happened to you?'

'I don't know. It's just . . . a couple of times I've felt like I was being watched. Like, you know how you can feel it when there's someone behind you? That's happened two or three times but when I turned around there was no one there.'

Something else struck her and she jumped down from the swing. She raked her hands through her hair.

'What is it?' he asked.

'My Hydro Flask. I swear to God I usually watch that thing like a hawk. But it's possible I put it down for a minute and they took it when I wasn't paying attention.'

They were both quiet for a minute.

'Deleting that post clearly wasn't enough,' Frankie said. 'They might not have even noticed it. I think we need to talk to them.'

'What? You mean, like, DM them?'

'No. I think we should really talk to them, face-to-face. Apologise and get this over with.' Even as she said this, it sounded like a terrible idea. But what else was there to do?

He was chewing his thumbnail. She wanted to slap his hand, get it away from his mouth. His knee was bouncing up and down too, and she realised something: he was scared. Maybe even more afraid than her.

'Who are we going to talk to?' he asked. He poked a finger at the message on the screen. 'We don't know who sent this.'

'I think I do. I think it's those freaky kids,' she said. 'The ones who said we were trespassing.'

Whenever she pictured the boy, with his close-cropped hair and hollow eyes, a little chill rippled across her skin, making the hairs on her arms stand on end. The girl, surely his sister, wasn't much better.

'What makes you think that?' Ryan asked.

'Just . . . the way the threats are written. The stuff that was taken. It doesn't seem like the kind of thing adults would do. And did I tell you I saw them again?'

'Wait, when?'

'Yesterday. They were on the path behind me. Here, at the resort.'

He still didn't seem convinced. 'You're only blaming them because we haven't met any other locals.'

'Ryan, I'm sure it's them. But even if it's not, it's a small town. I bet they know the person or people who are sending us the threats. If we apologise to them personally maybe they'll spread the word, tell people to leave us alone.'

Ryan got off the swing. 'I don't know.'

'Why? Are you scared of them?'

'Those freaks? Of course not. I just don't think it's a good idea – going to apologise to these . . . freaks. If it really was them who scared the horses, they've got a gun, remember?'

'But they wouldn't . . .'

'Wouldn't what?'

'Shoot us in broad daylight in the middle of the street.'

'You think?'

He was confusing her. But surely it would be safe in public? If these kids really were murderous psychopaths, they wouldn't merely have fired a gun into the air to frighten the horses. They would have done more than leave a dead rabbit outside the cabins. She'd been walking alone when she'd seen them on the path yesterday. They could have attacked her then. They could have shot her when she was lying alone in the woods after falling from the pony.

'I can always go on my own,' she said, having no real intention of doing that. Even if she didn't believe they would hurt her on their own doorstep, there was no way she would go and face those two without Ryan beside her.

She took a step towards the exit, calling his bluff, and his hand shot out, catching her forearm. The swift movement made her gasp.

'You're not going alone,' he said. *Thank God.*

'Then come with me.'

He bit his lip. 'Maybe we should tell our parents.'

'No. We can't. I don't want my dad to know. He'll confiscate my phone. Stop us from hanging out together. I think this is the . . . the responsible thing to do.'

The way Ryan was looking at her, impressed by her maturity, made her feel the way she did when she went home with a glowing report card, except multiplied by a hundred because it was him and, unlike her parents, he wasn't predisposed to be impressed by her. She felt proud. Capable. At the same time, though, she was aware that her courage was built on the flimsiest of foundations.

'I want to go now,' she said. Before she lost her nerve.

'Now?'

It was seven o'clock. Still plenty of daylight left. 'I want to get this over with, Ryan. I won't sleep tonight if I have it hanging over me. I want to fix this so I can get on with enjoying my vacation.'

'Okay.' He shook his head. 'At least if I die I'll leave a beautiful corpse. And Glen Troiano might cry at my funeral.'

'Shut up. No one's going to die.' But she laughed.

Five minutes later they were walking fast along the same path they'd taken the first morning here. They passed the clearing where the murder had taken place. Ryan asked her to slow down, but she couldn't. She needed to get into town before she chickened out. Now they were actually doing this, she felt sick and cold inside. As they passed the spot from which the pony had bolted, the scratches on her back began to throb as if they remembered this place.

They reached Penance and stepped out of the woods, in the same spot as last time. The junkyard was down the road to their left. They headed right, just as they had before. She could hear the wind chimes she'd heard before, somewhere to the east.

They carried on in silence. Frankie wished it could be described as a companionable silence, but the tension between them was as thick as tar. She glanced at Ryan, at his long eyelashes, the fullness of his lips, his fringe flopping into his eyes, and she thought *Lucky Glen Troiano*.

'I'm wondering how we're going to find where they live,' Ryan said. His voice was jittery, agitated. 'Do you have a plan?'

She didn't have a plan. They had reached the entrance to the street where they had seen the twins before. Paradise Loop. There were two smaller kids playing on a front lawn. A man further up the road was doing something beneath the hood of his car. Tinny rap music drifted from the open windows of a house along the street. Frankie looked up at the sky. The sun was beginning to dip and the edges of the clouds were turning pink.

'Let's ask these children,' she said.

She walked purposefully up the street towards where the kids were playing. They stopped their game and looked up at her from the lawn. A boy and a girl, around six years old. They both had the

111

same shaggy blond hair and freckles, and she realised they were probably twins as well. She suddenly had an image of a town where everyone was a twin; a place where all the children were born in pairs, like something from some spooky science fiction movie.

'Hi,' she said. She intended her voice to be bright, but when it reached her ears she sounded like she was teetering on the edge of hysteria. 'Do you know a boy and a girl about my age who live around here? I think they're twins.'

The two kids stared at her, unblinking, not speaking.

'Do you know where—'

She stopped. The toys the children were playing with had caught her eye. They were dolls, the old-fashioned type, with realistic hair and staring glass eyes. They were coated in several layers of dirt, as if they'd just been retrieved from a dumpster. The dolls had been stripped naked, revealing their smooth, featureless bodies, and beside them was a hole in the lawn, dug with a pair of plastic spades. Both the children had soil-encrusted fingernails.

She started again. 'Do you know them?'

The children stared at her, mute, and she felt Ryan arrive by her side.

The boy pointed to a house across the street.

'Is that where they live?' Frankie asked.

The boy nodded.

'What are their names?'

'Buddy,' whispered the boy.

'Darlene,' said the girl. 'You shouldn't play with them.'

Frankie and Ryan exchanged a look. 'Why not?'

'They're mean.'

'They killed Milo,' said the boy.

It was as if the temperature in the street had dropped several degrees. Ryan was staring at the kids. 'Who's Milo?' he asked.

'He was our cat,' said the boy.

'And Buddy and Darlene killed him?' Frankie wanted to puke.

'They buried him. They told us they buried him while he was still alive. They sat on his grave until he stopped mewing.'

Frankie tried to speak but there was no saliva in her mouth.

Ryan looked as sick as she felt. 'Did you tell your parents?'

The girl shook her head. 'They said if we told any grown-ups they would bury us next.'

'Alive,' said the boy.

'They killed next door's rabbit too.'

Frankie felt all the remaining blood drain from her face.

'Took him from his hutch and carried him into the woods,' the girl said. 'We saw them.'

The children looked like they were going to cry.

Ryan tugged at Frankie's arm. 'We should go. I knew this was a bad idea. Buddy and Darlene are clearly complete psychopaths.'

'Wait,' said Frankie. 'Was the rabbit white?'

'Uh-huh,' said the girl. 'White and super cute.'

'And did they say what they were going to do with the rabbit?'

'No. But Buddy said if we told . . .'

'They'd take us to *him*.'

Frankie and Ryan exchanged a look. 'Who?'

The boy's voice dropped to a whisper, and his eyes flicked nervously in the direction of the woods. 'The man who lives in the woods.'

'In a secret cabin.'

'He's lived there a long time.'

'He killed people.'

'And if he catches you, he'll choke you or smash your head in with a rock.'

'Oh my God,' said Ryan. 'They're talking about Everett Miller.' He crouched on the ground beside the kids. 'He went away a long time ago. You don't need to worry about him.'

'No,' said the boy, with the fervour of a true believer. 'He's hiding.'

'He's still here,' said the girl.

'And if you're not good, if you tell tales,' the boy said before the girl joined him: 'He'll get you.'

Chapter 16

I'm fading.

The words are like a spear through his chest.

I don't know how much longer I can hold on.

'Abigail. Please don't say that. You have to stay. It's all—'

Fading, she says again, not letting him finish.

And it feels exactly how it did when he first realised he was going to lose her.

ϖ

1998. Summer turned to fall and fall gave way to winter. The cold weather forced them inside, to the house that Abigail shared with her husband, though he was hardly ever around – always on the road, Abigail said. Some kind of travelling salesman. It was strange seeing her in a house. Those first meetings and outings and picnics had always taken place in the woods or down by the lake. That was where she seemed at home, among the trees and rocks, with the animals and the wildflowers. From the day of that first picnic by the lake, when he had met Goat and Fox, he had become part of their group, their gang. He knew if he'd told his mom he and a couple of other kids from school were hanging out with a woman her age, she would have freaked. She would have wondered what this grown-ass woman wanted with a trio of high-school kids. Was she giving them drugs? Was she some kind of pervert?

His mom didn't understand that people could be pure and good.

Before they retreated inside, on a Saturday in fall, Abigail had taken them on a trip.

He'd had a vague idea that, right now, this time of year, was when tourists flocked to Maine to see the famous foliage. To him, the explosion of colour in September and October was normal – beautiful, yeah, but kind of boring. The way people talked about it on TV, though, made him picture the rest of the country and the world as a place that must be permanently grey and drab. Concrete and evergreen leaves.

He was fourteen. He really didn't give a damn about leaves.

But Abigail changed his mind.

That late September morning, as they drove north in Abigail's car, a 1984 Plymouth Voyager, pale brown with what looked like a wooden plank running along its sides, she talked to them about the history of this place and about the spirits that lived here, that resided in the trees, the earth, even the rocks. Fox sat in the front passenger seat and he sat beside Goat in the back, as they sped through the orange and gold landscape, Abigail talking so fast her words tripped over one another. Some of what she said went over his head – words with loads of syllables that he would never know how to spell – but the general gist got through. This land, the place where they lived, was sacred.

She thumped her hand on the wheel, her voice alive with passion. 'And we're allowing people to ruin it.'

She must have had a dry throat because she coughed and couldn't stop, even after drinking from the bottle of water Fox passed her.

He was worried she might have to pull over, but she finally got hold of herself and they drove on. Abigail put the radio on. A rock station.

'Oh, man,' Abigail said as a Led Zeppelin track came on, and soon they were all singing along. Next up was a track by Iron Maiden, 'Bring Your Daughter to the Slaughter', and Fox made them all laugh by screeching along, doing her best Bruce Dickinson impression. Then Bon Jovi came on.

'Urgh,' Goat groaned. 'This isn't real rock. This is pussy music.'

Abigail shocked him by saying, 'I love Bon Jovi. He's hot.'

Fox giggled and agreed.

And then they were all singing along to 'Livin' on a Prayer'.

They were his best friends. Even though, if he passed them in the school hallway, Goat and Fox would ignore him without even a glance. It hurt at first, but he figured he was new; he still needed to earn their trust. And he hadn't even been given a name like theirs yet.

Abigail hadn't yet discovered his spirit animal.

He looked at Goat. He was quiet, as always. Kind of passive but big and strong, with hormones exploding out of him in a riot of pimples and peach fuzz. His skin was pink and meaty, and he smelled of cheap deodorant. Goat lived with his grandparents in a trailer on the other side of Penance. There was a rumour that his dad had beaten his mother to death and was serving life for it.

Fox, on the other hand, lived in a nice house in the richer part of town, though nowhere in Penance was really rich. She was a rebel who claimed to hate her parents and she was pretty sure they hated her back. He wondered if there was something crappy going on in her house. If her parents were absent and neglectful like his mom, or if it was worse. She was always reading, usually books Abigail had given her, books about spirituality and history. Fox had a book of spells that she'd bought at the hippie shop in town, the one that sold crystals and incense sticks, and she would often have her pretty nose buried in it. He wondered if the book contained any love spells.

Because he would have done anything to make Fox fall in love with him.

As he thought this, Fox turned around like she'd read his thoughts, and his cheeks must have gone pink.

'What are you thinking about?' she asked.

'Just . . . I was wondering when I was going to get my name.'

'Soon,' Abigail said, smiling in the rear-view mirror, and then she coughed again, setting off a volley of further coughs, and he thought she was going to lose control of the car. Fox had to grab the wheel to keep it straight.

Abigail slowed the car and pulled over by the side of the road.

'Are you okay?' they all asked, and she nodded, trying to smile even though she could hardly speak.

'We're here,' she said. 'I mean, we have to go on foot the rest of the way.'

He looked towards the trees. Here they were. The pines that Abigail said had been here for over three hundred years. She got out and the others followed until they were all standing at the foot of the path that led into the forest.

'Come on,' she said.

He was used to living near trees, was bored by beauty, but today he felt different. The ancient woodland covered a hundred acres. At points the path was overgrown, thick with needles that had fallen from above. According to Abigail, the trees beneath the 130-foot pines were sugar maples, and their leaves were a dazzle of yellow and orange.

It was like walking into a fairy tale, the modern world disappearing behind them, the road silent and out of sight. He had the weirdest impulse to rip off his clothes – as if they were an insult

118

to this place that had barely been touched by humans – and run naked. Of course, he would never do that, especially with Fox here, but by the time they were a mile or two deep in the forest, he felt as if some great power, some great *dark* power, was coming up through the earth into his body, filling him up, his senses alive like they'd never been before. The taste of the crisp fall air, the scent of pine needles, the crunching beneath his feet, and all the colours, so vivid they burned his eyes. And the hum, like electric cables. Like the trees were speaking to each other. He wondered if Abigail had slipped something into their water bottles, one of the 'potions' she sometimes mentioned. For a moment, he experienced a flicker of fear, the suspicion that he'd been led into a trap. But then he looked at Abigail, her face turned upwards, bathing in the glow of the forest, and he realised the voice of doubt was his mom's. He pushed it away.

Abigail was good.

Abigail was pure.

He reached out and touched the trunk of one of the mammoth pines as he passed it. A warm, throbbing pulse rumbled through him, and for the first time in his life he felt truly connected to the planet, to nature, to the past and the future. That would sound like such bullshit to say aloud, but every bit of it was true. He understood how insignificant he was, a pine needle in the forest, but how important too: every needle, every life, was all part of this. He stared at Fox and Goat and saw that they were feeling it too. Their eyes shone, their faces were flushed.

Abigail stopped and stared straight at him. In that moment, framed by the trees, their glow upon her skin, she looked otherworldly, like she was one of the spirits she talked about, something eternal. A goddess. He experienced a rush of something he had never known before: love. Not the dizzying horniness he felt for Fox. Nothing like the weak love he still retained for his mom. It was the absolute knowledge that he would do anything for this woman. He would die for her. He would kill for her if she asked him to.

She gestured for him to come closer. But as he reached her she began to cough again. He stood helpless as she bent double, wet hacking noises echoing through the trees. At last, she recovered and stood straight.

'Are you—'

She shook off his concern and spoke, her voice raspy. 'I have it. Your animal. Your name.'

He stared. This was it. He would properly be one of them now.

'Crow,' she said, holding out her hands towards him while Fox and Goat looked on.

Later, he would look it up in one of her books. To have crow as your spirit or totem animal meant you had integrity, that you were willing to embrace change. More than that, it meant that once you knew your life's mission, you would follow it without bending or veering off course.

But he wasn't thinking about any of that. He was looking at Abigail, at her outstretched hands.

At the wet specks of blood on her palms.

ϖ

I'm fading, she says again.

He refuses to be afraid. He is Crow.

And when the crow knows its mission, it follows it without bending.

Chapter 17

I sat on the deck outside my cabin, an empty beer bottle in front of me. It was almost dark and Frankie hadn't come back yet.

I looked over to cabin twelve. David and Connie had gone inside a while ago. Maybe I should go and talk to them again, find out if they knew where Ryan and Frankie might have gone. Or perhaps I should go and look around the resort . . . except if they were just hanging around eating ice cream, I didn't want to seem like an overbearing dad. Frankie needed her freedom to hang out with boys or her friends or whatever.

Still, there were limits. It was getting dark and she hadn't told me where she was going. I decided I would give it another twenty minutes. If she didn't come back by then I would go looking for her.

I went inside to use the bathroom.

I paced around. Fifteen minutes passed. Eighteen minutes.

And then I heard a woman shouting outside.

'Help! I need help!'

I ran out of the cabin. David appeared outside his cabin too.

It was Tamara. She was on the deck of the cabin opposite mine. She had her hands in her hair, her eyes darting back and forth, almost breathless with panic. 'Please, help!'

David and I both ran across to her and reached her at the same time.

'It's Donna,' she said. She seemed like she was close to hyperventilating.

We followed her inside. Tamara was muttering to herself, something about medicine. 'I thought it would be okay. I didn't know.' She was babbling. I exchanged a look with David, both of us fearful of what we were going to find in the bedroom.

We went in.

Donna was lying on the floor on her back. She wasn't moving. One of her hands was clasped around the gold cross she always wore, her grip so tight I could imagine the metal cutting into her palm. Her expression was neutral, though, as if she were asleep.

I threw myself down on my knees beside her. She wasn't breathing. I grabbed the wrist beneath the hand that wasn't clutching the cross and felt for a pulse, not finding one. All the while Tamara paced the room behind me, making distressed noises and saying, 'Oh no oh no', over and over.

'Do you know first aid?' I asked David.

He shook his head. 'Do you?'

'No.' I was pretty sure that even if we were both trained paramedics, we wouldn't be able to do anything. She was gone.

Tamara was giving me the desperate look of someone who craves good news they know isn't going to come.

'I'll go and find someone,' David said, getting up and running out.

I got up too. 'Maybe we should go outside,' I said, gently guiding Tamara from the room and out on to the deck. I didn't want to be in that room with Donna's body, and I didn't think Tamara should be either. There was no sign of David.

I thought back to the scene earlier, when Tamara and Donna had returned from their trip to the drugstore. How grey and shaken Donna had looked.

'What happened?' I asked. 'Was it her heart? Is that why you'd been to the drugstore?'

It took a while for her to get the words out, and when they came they were wet, drenched in tears. 'She forgot her beta blockers. She had a heart attack last year that almost killed her and she's been on meds ever since, and she swore she brought them, accused me of throwing them out, but I swear I didn't.'

'So you didn't manage to get any at the drugstore?'

She shook her head. 'They said we needed to wait twenty-four hours for them to arrive. We should never have left the city. But I thought she'd be okay as long as she didn't exert herself. As long as her heart rate didn't get too high. And I wasn't there with her, at the . . . at the end. She'd been griping and blaming me for losing her pills and I got angry with her and went to take a shower. I didn't want to get out because I didn't want to fight with her again and then . . . when I came out, she was like that.'

I went inside and found some Kleenex, handing one to her. She wiped her eyes and blew her nose.

I thought about the cross around Donna's neck and the way she'd been clutching it as she died. Clearly a woman of faith. I wasn't sure if Tamara was religious too, but I said, 'She'll be in a better place now.'

Tamara stared at me. To my surprise she said, 'She thought she was going to Hell.'

'Sorry?'

'When she had her first heart attack, she thought it was a punishment from God. For the two of us. Being together.'

So they *were* a couple.

'It's how she was raised. Her father was the kind of man who chucks around words like "sin" and "fornicate" and "damnation" over breakfast. The kind of man who throws his sixteen-year-old daughter on to the street and tells her she's got a demon inside her, that she's going straight to Hell.'

I shook my head, unsure of what to say, letting Tamara talk.

'It never really left her. She'd be fine during the day, but at night it'd come out. These awful dreams, real as day. The Devil, *coming* for us. It was okay for a while – especially after she joined another church, one that was more liberal, more modern – but after her heart attack it was like she was that terrified, confused sixteen-year-old again. She thought everything her daddy warned her about was coming true.' Her lip curled. 'That bastard. If he wasn't already long dead . . .'

'That's awful.'

'She almost left me over it. Not just because she was scared for herself. She got so sleep-deprived that she honestly believed she was saving me from him.'

Eventually David returned. He had Vivian with him. I followed her into the bedroom.

'Oh, dear Lord,' Vivian said. She threw herself down beside Donna and examined her, doing what I'd already done. She shook her head sadly and went over to Tamara. 'I'm so sorry, honey.'

I left the room, found David and told him what Tamara had said. He sighed. Then he said, 'Wait a second.'

He gestured for me to follow him back into the bedroom. Tamara was sitting on the bed, weeping, and Vivian was using her walkie-talkie to speak to someone back at reception, relaying what had happened.

David crossed to the dresser and beckoned me over.

'I thought I spotted these,' he said.

He picked up a bottle of pills from the dresser and handed them to me. I read the label.

Beta blockers, with Donna's name on the label. The bottle was almost full.

Tamara saw us and got up from the bed. She snatched the pills from David's hand. 'Where did you find these?'

'They were right there. On the dresser. Are these the pills Donna lost?'

Tamara nodded, dumbstruck for a second. 'I looked here. I searched this whole room. This whole cabin.'

'I guess she must have found them just before . . .' David trailed off.

'But I searched the whole cabin,' Tamara said again; and, clutching the bottle of pills, she collapsed into a chair, sobbing.

Chapter 18

They reached the main road. Frankie couldn't stop shaking. She wanted to go home. Back to Albany. No, further than that. Back to England. Back into her childhood. It didn't really matter. She just wanted to get away from this place.

She was even more certain now that Buddy and Darlene were after her. It was them who had left the dead rabbit outside the cabin. A rabbit they had stolen from their neighbours and murdered. There was no doubt about it. Maybe they were responsible for the ants too. Her missing Hydro Flask. Maybe it actually had been them firing that gun in the woods.

What were they going to do? Abduct her and bury her alive, like they'd done with those kids' cat?

She could hardly catch her breath.

'Frankie.' Ryan's voice appeared to be coming from a long way away. 'Frankie!'

'I want to go back to the resort,' she said. She staggered, and Ryan caught her, kept her from crashing to the ground.

'You need some sugar. Remember we saw that minimart on Main Street? If you wait here I can run there and grab you something before we head back.'

'No!'

He took a step away from her. She had shouted.

'This is all your fault!' she yelled. 'If you hadn't put up that stupid Insta post and written all that crap they wouldn't even have known we existed.'

'No. We'd already met them, remember?'

She didn't care. 'It's your fault they killed that rabbit.'

'Come on, that's unfair.'

'No, it's not. Why did you do it? Why did you have to be such a twat?'

His face hardened. 'I showed it to you the moment I posted it. If you thought it was such a stupid thing to do you should have told me to take it down.'

'I hardly knew you. Jesus, I hardly *know* you. I was meant to be having a nice relaxing vacation with my dad, and instead I've been drawn into all this madness. Because of you. I wish I'd never—'

'Shut up!' Now he was shouting. He had his hands up by his ears, like he didn't want to hear her. 'Quit whining and blaming me.'

'I'm not whining!'

He put on a high-pitched voice. '*If you hadn't put up that stupid Insta post.* Fuck you, Frankie.'

She took a step back, as if she'd been struck.

'Get away from me,' she said. 'I never, ever want to speak to you again.'

She turned and, without another word, sprinted towards the entrance to the woods. She didn't think she had ever run as fast, even on sports day at school when she had come second in the hundred metres. Ryan called her name and she thought she heard his footsteps behind her but she was moving too fast to be sure, everything muffled by the sound of her heartbeat in her ears. She entered the woods, grabbing a tree to steady herself, and ran down the path that had led them into town – blindly, sure this was the way they had come.

It took a few seconds for her to realise how dark it had got. Dusk fell swiftly here and now the path was barely visible, the trees and shrubs black shapes against a grey backdrop. Suddenly, the woods weren't so pretty any more.

Fear forced her to stop running, to attempt to get her bearings. She had been following her instincts, her inner compass, sure she was heading back towards the cabins – but now? Now she wasn't sure. She expected to hear Ryan behind her, calling out her name, but there was nothing. He clearly didn't give a damn about her, and she didn't care. She really didn't care.

Except she was in the darkening woods. Not entirely sure where she was going.

They'd take us to him. *The man who lives in the woods.*

Once again, she thought she might be sick. *He's not real*, she told herself. *He's a stupid urban legend. The murderer disappeared twenty years ago.*

She took several deep breaths and forced herself to calm down, to take in her surroundings and work out where she was.

She could hear a gentle wind rustling the leaves on the trees. Just that and . . . scuffling? *It's the dead cat, digging its way out of the grave.*

Shut up! she yelled at her own brain. *It's birds, that's all. Nothing dangerous.* But the rational part of her brain was in danger of being shoved aside by the primal part. She took another deep breath, exhaled as slowly and calmly as she could.

She should turn around and head back, but she was still convinced she couldn't be too far from the resort. It was impossible to tell in the near-darkness. All the paths, all the trees, looked the same. She strained to listen and thought she could hear, very faintly in the distance, the hubbub of voices. The sounds of people enjoying themselves down by the lake.

She headed towards the noise, holding her phone out before her, trying not to think about the battery and how quickly the flashlight app drained it. She was only on 13 per cent. *Unlucky for some*, she thought, suppressing a hysterical giggle. Maybe she *should* turn back, look for Ryan, but how could she? Even if right now, scared like this, her conviction that she never wanted to see him again had weakened considerably, he probably wouldn't ever want to see *her* again. She was going to spend the rest of the vacation in the cabin. If Dad asked, she'd tell him she was sick. She'd tell him she wanted to go home.

She reached a fork in the path. Two options, left or right. Both looked exactly the same. Surely right would take her towards the cabins? Without stopping to think too much – fearful she would be paralysed by indecision – she went right. The path curved and quickly became overgrown, like she was heading off the track, deeper into the woods. Shining her phone's light into the trees, she couldn't see anything except the black bars of their trunks, the criss-cross of branches. This felt wrong. Again, trying not to hesitate, trying not to let the words *You're lost* enter her head, she retraced her steps, back towards the junction.

Except the junction wasn't there any more. The path kept going on, bending to the right and getting narrower. *Don't panic, do not panic*, she told herself, cursing the lack of reception here, seeing that her phone battery had drained to 7 per cent, and she walked faster, convinced that if she was determined enough, force of will would take her to the right place.

She tripped and went down, crying out with pain as she hit the ground.

It was a tree root, stretching across the path. She sat there for a minute, dazed, rubbing at her shin. 'It's okay,' she said to herself, her voice sounding very strange against the silence. She shut her phone light off, not wanting to completely kill the battery. She felt like Gretel, lost in the woods, but with no trail of breadcrumbs to follow.

Heading to the secret cabin in the woods . . .

She killed the thought and, as she got to her feet, checking she wasn't injured, she heard something.

A soft, high tinkle in the distance.

Wind chimes.

If she could hear wind chimes, she must be close to Penance. That was good. All she needed to do was follow the sound and she would wind up back in town. From there she should be able to find a taxi to take her back to the resort – Dad could pay when she got there.

Switching the flashlight app back on, and wincing when she saw she was down to 4 per cent, she stepped over the root and kept going along the path.

The chimes grew a little louder. She was heading in the right direction, though she had no idea how she had ended up so close to Penance. She must have taken a wrong turn early on. She kept going, walking fast, convinced that any moment now she would recognise where she was, even in the dark, and then she would see the lights of the town. She didn't even care that this was the town where people who apparently hated her lived. She just wanted to be out of these woods. The wind had picked up and, strangely, it was as if it were pushing her in the right direction, loose leaves and pine needles stirring at her feet.

As if the woods were telling her which way to go.

She found herself at another fork. The chimes were coming from straight ahead but the paths led left and right. She bit down on a scream. If she went left or right she was sure she would get lost again. She was sure the town was immediately ahead. As long as she went slowly and carefully, it should be okay. She just needed to go in a straight line. Follow the sound. Follow the wind.

Frankie left the path and pushed her way through the trees. The scratches on her back ached and the new bruise on her shin throbbed. She could hear things moving in the undergrowth and something else shifting in the branches above, and she increased her pace as much as she could, holding on to trees as she passed them, twisting her body this way and that, using the torch to illuminate the ground beneath her feet. Her phone was on 2 per cent now. She needed to reach the town before the battery died completely, and the wind chimes were loud. She was certain the town was on the other side of this patch.

Suddenly, there were no more trees ahead of her. She was in a clearing, one she hadn't seen before. Like a drowning swimmer with just a lungful of air left, she struck out for safety, a final push, running across the long grass, a circle of black trees all around her. She was sure Penance had to be just beyond the trees on the far side of this clearing.

Someone stepped out of the trees to her left.

She couldn't even scream. She stopped and turned. Her phone dropped from her grasp and she was so terrified she didn't stop to pick it up. In the clearing, the sliver of a moon provided just enough light for her to see.

Enough light for her to see two more figures standing before her.

Two ahead. One behind. They stood still and silent, watching her. And between the gulps of panic, the fear that flooded and threatened to shut down her system, she realised she couldn't see their faces.

They weren't human.

A scream ripped out of her and she ran, leaving her phone behind in the grass, running towards the trees and the woods, not thinking, not making any kind of rational decision. The figures – the inhuman figures – didn't move, didn't make a sound. They watched her.

She stopped at the tree line. There was a new voice yelling inside her head, telling her not to go back into the woods. Not without a torch. She felt hot tears burning her cheeks. What should she do? *What should she do?* She wanted her mum, her dad, someone, anyone. She wished they'd never come here, wished she'd never met Ryan, wished wished wished she hadn't fallen out with him. This was her punishment. These things, these creatures, were going to catch her, kill her, just like those teachers.

She gave up.

Turned back towards them, ready to accept her fate. Unable to run any more.

She opened her dry mouth to speak.

And a hand clamped down on her shoulder.

PART TWO

Chapter 19

The day after Abigail's funeral, on a spring morning in 1999, the three of them gathered at the spot by the lake where Crow had first met the others. They hadn't arranged it; it just felt like the right thing to do. Crow had worried, in the lead-up to Abigail's death, that without their leader the group would break apart, but her final words to them – the last time they saw her before she was admitted, against her will, to the hospital – had quelled those fears.

'The three of you,' she had said, 'you need to stick together.' Her voice had been weak but the humour, the wisdom, never left her eyes. 'Only you understand this place.' She looked at each of them in turn. 'You have to remember what I've taught you. Will you do that?'

They all nodded.

'This is a sacred place. Our sacred place. We—'

At that very moment, there came a noise in the trees. The sound of laughter, of teenage voices, and then the distinct smell of cigarettes. Kids from the campground. Abigail sighed but Crow's stomach clenched with anger, and he charged towards the line of trees to confront them, Goat and Fox backing him up, just as one of the kids crushed out a cigarette underfoot.

'Hey. Assholes. Pick that up.'

A fight almost broke out and Goat held Crow back, Crow's fists clenching and unclenching, the hatred hot in his veins. He yelled after the campground kids as they retreated, and it felt good to see the fear on their faces.

'That's right!' he yelled. 'Run back to your little campground.'

When they returned to Abigail, she looked weak. Even though they were young and ignorant, they knew she didn't have long. The sickness had done its work quickly.

'It's a full moon tonight,' she said. She had spoken to them at length about lunar cycles, their importance in nature, how pagans and believers in the old ways scheduled their lives around the moon. 'A good time to go.'

'Please, don't say that.' Goat had tears in his eyes.

She reached out to cup his face. 'I'll always be here,' she said.

'What do you mean?' That had been Fox.

Abigail had smiled, though it hadn't reached her eyes. Her voice was weak and they had to lean close to hear her. 'Why would I ever want to leave this place? I'm gonna stick around, kids.' She had attempted a laugh, then eyed the spot where the campground kids had been and shook her head. 'This place needs to be protected. Just know that whenever you hear the wind stirring the leaves, the lake lapping at the shore, when you trip over a rock . . .'

They had all laughed.

'That'll be me.'

Now she was gone, and the woods were silent. The water was silent.

And Crow, Fox and Goat were silent too.

They hadn't been to the funeral because nobody except Abigail's husband, Logan, knew she had been their friend. The three of them were aware of the questions that would be asked if they turned up. They all knew, too, that the funeral, a small Baptist ceremony, would have made them sick. It wasn't what Abigail had wanted or deserved, and she'd only agreed to it because it was what Logan wanted.

'What do you guys want to do?' Goat asked after a while, unable to bear the silence any longer.

Fox stood up. 'I need to get going.'

Crow, who was sitting on a rock, whipped his head towards her. 'Why? What are you doing?'

'I'm meeting someone,' she said.

'Who?'

She made an exasperated noise. 'Do I have to tell you everything?'

He found it impossible to argue with her. He was too afraid of upsetting her. Every time he looked at her he felt itchy and nauseous. When he wasn't with her, he longed to see her, like there wasn't enough oxygen in the air when she wasn't around. But when they were together he was no happier. He found it impossible to act natural; in fact, he had forgotten what natural felt like. He wondered if he was going crazy. Or maybe this was just what love felt like. It was horrible. But there was nothing he could do about it. He wouldn't be cured until she loved him too.

'Are you going to drop us, now Abigail's gone?' he found himself saying.

She tutted. 'Don't be dumb.'

'Then who are you meeting?'

'I don't have to tell you.'

His mouth was running away with itself. 'I just think it's disrespectful, is all. We came here to remember Abigail and now—'

'We're not even talking!'

'Then let's talk. I want to hear about the first time you met her.'

Fox hesitated, looked towards the path. Then she folded her arms and sat back down. 'Okay.'

Crow smiled to himself. He had won. And as he sat there, listening to Fox talk, Goat joining in, reminiscing about Abigail, something struck him. This group needed a new leader now. And as he thought this, he felt something. The breeze stirring around him. A ripple on the water. The hairs on his arms stood up and he felt something brush against his face.

Fox had been halfway through a sentence about the time they had all gone swimming right here, and the story – which brought back images of Fox in her bathing suit – would normally have captivated him, but now her voice had faded to a background hum.

Fox noticed. 'What is it?' she asked.

Goat looked at him too.

Crow could hardly speak. His throat felt too tight. He was, he realised, shaking.

'She's here,' he said.

'What?' Fox and Goat said together.

He lifted a trembling hand and pointed towards the trees. Abigail hadn't been lying. She hadn't deserted them. Hadn't left this place. It didn't matter that her body had gone, that she had been buried in a cemetery miles from here.

Fox and Goat stared, confused. They couldn't see her. That meant . . . that meant he had been blessed. He was special. Abigail's chosen one. He also understood that with that blessing came great responsibility. Enormous responsibility.

'Can't you see her?' he asked, as Abigail smiled back at him. 'She's right there.'

Chapter 20

There was a knock on the cabin door.

Frankie stood there, head down, wringing her hands. Her hair fell over her face, tangled and wild.

Beside her was Nikki. The woman from the bookstore.

'I found your daughter wandering around the woods in the dark,' she said.

Frankie took a step towards me, face still turned to the floor, and I gathered her in, putting my arm around her shoulders. It was a warm night, the air on the doorstep soft and balmy, but she felt like she'd just been taken out of the fridge.

'Wandering in the woods?' I repeated.

I had only recently got back from the neighbouring cabin, where I'd waited with David, Tamara and Vivian – who had proven herself to be both sympathetic and efficient – until an ambulance trundled through the resort and took Donna's body away. That, along with the beta blockers mystery, had been so distracting that I hadn't started worrying about Frankie again until I got back to the cabin.

Now, Frankie extricated herself and hurried inside. I followed, while Nikki hovered in the doorway. She was dressed all in black, dark hair falling into her eyes, and I couldn't help but notice again how attractive she was. Perhaps not classically beautiful, but she had that look. A woman from an indie band. My type.

Still, Nikki wasn't my focus right now. Frankie was. I had so many questions and was about to start firing them at her when I noticed she was shivering. I found her a blanket, wrapping it around her and settling her on the couch.

'What happened?' I asked.

She didn't reply. She seemed like she was in shock.

I turned my head towards Nikki, who had drifted into the room, closing the door behind her. In her black clothes and with her pale face, she looked like a vampire who had invited herself in. 'Where was she?' I asked.

'In the woods, close to town.'

I wondered what Nikki had been doing in the woods, and she must have anticipated the question because she said, 'I was looking for Cujo. He got out of the store and ran off towards the trees. He's not supposed to go out but those woods are like a buffet for cats.' She sighed. 'I'm sure he'll come home.'

'Was Ryan with Frankie?' I asked. 'A boy, about her age?'

'No. She was on her own.'

I turned back to my daughter. 'Frankie, where's Ryan? Why wasn't he with you?'

She looked up and the blankness of her stare scared me.

'They weren't human,' she said in a whisper, half talking to herself.

I sat beside her on the couch. 'Frankie, what are you talking about?'

She gave me that blank look again. Nikki was watching us intently.

'I want to go home,' Frankie said. 'I don't want to be here any more. Daddy, please.' She hadn't called me Daddy since she was six. 'I really want to go home.'

140

She started to cry.

'What happened, Frankie?' I thought about the face I'd seen outside the window.

'I can't . . . Please, Dad. I just want to go to bed.'

'Of course, in a minute. But you have to tell me – where's Ryan?' A dark thought entered my head. 'Did he do something to you?'

'No! Of course not.'

'Then where is he?'

'I don't know.'

I waited.

The next part came out in a rush. 'We got separated. I tried to find my way home through the woods but it got dark and my phone was dying and oh God I've lost my phone and then I was in the clearing and I was sure the man was coming to get me to take me to his secret cabin and then I saw them the creatures they weren't human and I want to go to bed *I want to go to bed*.'

She stood up, the blanket still wrapped around her, and left the room. She closed her bedroom door behind her.

I sat there, stunned for a few moments.

'Wait there,' I said to Nikki. 'Please.' I didn't want her to leave. Not yet.

I went outside and hurried across to the Butlers' cabin. Knocked on the front door.

Connie answered almost immediately.

'Has Ryan come home?' I asked before she had a chance to speak.

'Um, yeah?'

'Can I talk to him?'

She looked me up and down. 'He's taking a shower. Is everything okay?'

'Did Ryan say anything to you when he got back?'

'Just something about feeling scuzzy.' She came out on to the deck and pulled the door to behind her. Her eyes darted towards the cabin where Donna had died. 'What's going on, Tom? What's happened now?'

'I need to talk to Ryan. Frankie just got back and she's in a terrible state. She got lost in the woods. I want to know where the hell Ryan was.'

David appeared. 'What's the problem?'

Connie told him.

'Let me speak to your son,' I said.

David looked drunk. His eyes were bloodshot and he was swaying. I guessed he'd felt the need to blot out what he'd seen in cabin fifteen. 'Wait here,' he said.

He disappeared inside while Connie filled the front doorway, stopping me from entering. David reappeared. 'He's still in the shower. You'll have to come back in the morning.'

I knew I wasn't going to get past them. I wouldn't have let them in to demand answers of my kid either.

'Okay. Fine.'

I went back over to my cabin. Nikki was sitting out on the deck, smoking a cigarette.

'You don't mind, do you?'

'No. I'm tempted to have one myself.'

But I didn't. I went inside and opened Frankie's bedroom door a crack, peeking in. She appeared to be asleep. I went back out and sat opposite Nikki.

'Did you see anything?'

'No. All I saw was her, in the dark, looking scared and lost.'

I replayed Frankie's stream-of-consciousness ramble. 'She said something about a man. A secret cabin. What was that about?'

Nikki blew out a plume of smoke. 'It's a local myth. One that started about the time those teachers were killed. This nameless guy who's supposed to live deep in the woods. They say if he catches you he'll strangle you or bash your brains out. All the children and teenagers in Penance talk about it. They dare each other to go into the woods to look for his secret cabin.'

'Everett Miller?'

'Yup. Our local bogeyman.'

'And what about this secret cabin?'

She shrugged. 'It doesn't exist, of course.'

I mulled this over. 'So Frankie must have been talking to some local kids. Except . . .'

'What?'

'I don't know . . . I thought I saw something too. Or some*one*, I should say. But it looked more like . . . an animal. I feel slightly embarrassed telling you because I really don't believe in all this stuff, but I'm not the only one. A few people around the resort have reported seeing something – a figure that doesn't look human. Frankie said it too. And the more I think about it, the more it's coming back to me: what I saw outside, at the back of this cabin. It looked like an animal's head. Like, I don't know, a deer. Or a sheep.'

She had lit another cigarette. Her hand was trembling slightly. 'I've never heard anything like that.'

'Are you sure?'

She nodded.

'God,' I said. 'Maybe it's a sort of mass hallucination. Maybe some magic mushrooms got into the water supply.'

She laughed, though her hand was still shaking a little. She saw me notice and said, 'I'm cold.'

'Me too.' I rubbed my face. 'Jesus, what a day. I'd only just got back from that cabin over there when you got here. The ambulance had just gone.'

'What ambulance?'

I told her.

'And the beta blockers were just sitting there?'

'Yep.'

She tapped ash from her cigarette. She'd found an ashtray, presumably in one of the cabin's cupboards. 'I do things like that all the time. Spend half an hour searching for the TV remote then find it sitting right there on the couch.'

'Me too. But Tamara swore they'd both searched for the pills, and they were sitting right there in plain sight. I think . . . Maybe it sounds crazy, but what if the person who took them returned them? And Donna saw them come in and the scare triggered her heart attack.'

'That sounds . . . kinda far-fetched.'

'I suppose so, yeah.' But honestly, though it made no sense, I could see it all too clearly. The figure appearing before Donna out of nowhere to complete its errand. It was no more implausible than my seeing someone with the head of some horned animal, or Frankie seeing her 'creatures' in the woods. What shape had been taken by Donna's shocking visitor?

Then it struck me. Not an explanation yet, but maybe the start of one.

'Masks,' I said.

Nikki sat very still, waiting.

'Someone, or more than one person, wearing a mask. Donna was convinced the Devil was going to punish her.'

Nikki tried to interrupt but I waved a hand, asking her to let me finish.

'If she saw someone in a mask, with horns, in her cabin . . .'

I wished I'd managed to get a better look at the horned face at my window. Had it been a mask? I looked up to see Nikki regarding me sceptically.

'I think the Hollows are getting to you, Tom. You and Frankie. They do that.'

'What do you mean?'

'Just . . . You'll probably think this is mumbo jumbo, but there are people who think the woods have some kind of . . . power. An influence.'

'An influence?'

She sighed. 'Yeah, I know, it sounds like crazy-person talk, but . . . Okay, yes. *I've* always thought that. The woods make people do and see odd things. Make them act in ways they would never usually.'

Her words just hung there between us while we stared at each other for a long moment.

'The woods make people do things,' I said at last. 'Like . . . Everett Miller?'

'Yeah. I guess.' She picked up her cigarette packet and I thought she was going to light up again, but she placed it back on the table. 'Listen, the Hollows are old. Not as old as the ancient forest further north, close to Eagle Lake, but old. And even if you don't believe in all that supernatural stuff, you can't deny the power places like this have over our imagination, if nothing else. We all have images from fairy tales and horror movies in our heads. Add shadows and moonlight and teenage hormones, and suddenly your imagination is on steroids.'

'What about me? It's been a long time since I had teenage hormones.'

'Yeah. But you've got other stuff going on. You're grieving.'

I couldn't speak for a second. 'Grieving? I'm not—'

'Oh, but you are. I don't know your situation, Tom. I don't know where Frankie's mom is—'

'She's in Albany.'

'There are all kinds of grief,' she said. 'And I recognise it when I see it.'

I stared at her. I felt like she'd ripped me open and peered inside. I tried to formulate a response, a riposte, but she was right. I was such a stranger to myself that the realisation came as a shock. I was grieving. And maybe now would be a good time to talk about it, to tell this almost-stranger all about it. I wanted to invite her inside and, maybe I was mistaken, but it seemed like she wanted me to invite her in too. Despite the chill in the air and the topics we'd been discussing, there was a tension between us. A connection. She made me feel seen. She knew me. I wanted to know her too.

'I'd better get back,' she said suddenly. 'See if Cujo has come home. I'm worried about him.'

I tried to keep the disappointment off my face. 'Of course.'

We both stood at the same time. I felt awkward, unsure what to say. Then she gave me a quick hug and ran down the steps off the deck.

'Hey,' I called, but she didn't turn back. Within moments, she was swallowed by shadows.

Chapter 21

Frankie didn't wake up until eleven the next morning. It was frustrating. I was desperate to find out more about what had happened the night before, why she'd been alone in the woods, but I also wanted to let her sleep. I had already been over to the Butlers' cabin to talk to Ryan but they weren't there and their rental car wasn't in its spot. They must have got up and gone out early, left the resort.

When Frankie finally emerged I made her breakfast and poured her a glass of freshly squeezed orange juice.

'Are you feeling any better?' I asked in a gentle voice.

'I think so.'

She certainly had an appetite. She tore into the food I'd laid out for her. And while she ate, she told me everything that had happened.

Walking into Penance. Meeting the twins, Buddy and Darlene. Ryan's Instagram post in which he called Penance a shithole. That my ridiculous worry that she and Ryan were an item was dumb because, *duh*, Ryan was gay and she wasn't interested in boys anyway because they were all idiots. Back to Instagram and the angry, threatening messages she'd received. Because she'd lost her phone she was only able to give me a summary of what they said, and I suspected they were even worse than she told me.

She went on to explain her conviction that the dead rabbit, the shots fired during the horse ride, maybe even the ants in her bed, were an attempt at revenge. Finally, she told me how they had gone back into town intending to apologise. Met a couple of weird little kids. The argument with Ryan.

I was stunned. All this had been going on without me being aware of it? I'd heard many people say over the years that you never really know what's going on in your kids' lives, especially once they're teenagers, and with the Atlantic Ocean separating us that was true on a basic, everyday level. But this was the first time I had become aware of it happening right under my nose.

I couldn't help it. I lost my temper.

'Why the hell didn't you tell me?'

'I was embarrassed.'

'I'm not surprised! You can't go around slagging off where people live. I'm not surprised you pissed them off.'

'It wasn't me!'

'No, but you went along with it. And then the two of you went sneaking around, trying to put it right. Putting yourselves in danger. I'm shocked, Frankie. I thought you were sensible. You keep telling me that you're not a little kid any more and then you go and do this . . .'

I was on my feet, pacing around the table. At the back of my head, a voice was telling me to calm down, to stop yelling at her. I knew this explosion was partly caused by my own tension. But I was angry with her too. It *had* been stupid. And it played on something I had long worried about. We give kids access to these new online tools, like Instagram, but they don't always have the emotional maturity to use them. I had thought

Frankie was mature enough. I didn't even know she'd managed to get online.

She got up from the table too. 'I knew you'd be like this. That's why I didn't tell you.'

She ran to her bedroom and slammed the door behind her.

I wanted to slam something too. And Ryan, who had started all this, and then allowed Frankie to run off into the darkening woods on her own, was the obvious target. I went outside to see if the Butlers were back, but their rental car was still gone.

Back inside, I rapped lightly on Frankie's door.

'Leave me alone,' she said.

I pushed the door open.

She was lying on her bed, facing the window. As soon as I opened the door she rolled to face me. Her eyes were red and tears streaked her cheeks. 'I said, leave me alone!'

She screamed it and a wave of contrition went through me. I was the adult here. I should have been handling this better. But I also knew that now was not the time to talk. I had to wait for us both to calm down. I left, closing the door behind me, and heard the click as she locked it.

ϖ

She eventually emerged two hours later, thirsty and needing the bathroom. When she came out she had washed her face and tied her hair back.

'What is it?'

I realised I had been staring at her. She looked so much like her mother, so grown-up. But I knew from experience that if I told her that, she would groan and roll her eyes.

'I'm sorry,' I said instead. 'I shouldn't have yelled at you.'

'It's fine,' she said, slumping on the couch.

I went over and sat beside her. 'I understand why you didn't tell me. But from now on, I want you to know you can tell me anything. I won't blow up again. I promise. Okay?'

'Okay.'

'Can I ask you about last night?'

She huffed. 'I guess.'

I didn't want to upset her again, but I needed to know what was going on. For the past couple of hours I had been replaying my conversation with Nikki. Maybe my grief and Frankie's teenage hormones, combined with the imagination-stoking power of our surroundings, had led us to see things that weren't there. But I hadn't mentioned what I'd seen outside my window to Frankie. And I still thought my theory about what might have happened to Donna, though outlandish, needed to be examined.

'When you said they didn't look human, what did you mean?' I asked.

'Just . . . their faces. They looked like animals.'

'Like they were wearing masks?'

She thought about it, then nodded.

'Can you remember what kind of masks? I mean, what kind of animals? Was one of them a deer or a sheep?'

She squeezed her eyes shut, trying to see it. 'Maybe a sheep. And I think, yes, one of them was some kind of bird.'

'And the other?'

'I don't know.'

'But there were definitely three?'

'Yes. I think so, anyway. It was dark. Confusing.'

But whether there were two or three, I felt reassured that I wasn't imagining things – and neither was Frankie.

Had Donna seen one of these masked figures too, and thought it was the Devil coming to punish her? Who were these people sneaking around in masks?

Everett Miller, said a little voice in my head. But surely, even as dark and thick as they were, he couldn't have been hiding in these woods for twenty years, could he?

I decided to move on to the more important topic: the teenagers Frankie and Ryan had apparently upset. Buddy and Darlene, those were their names. In a way I didn't blame them for being angry. I'd probably have felt aggrieved if I were them, living in a dying town, a couple of tourists coming along and calling it a shithole. But if the little kids Frankie had spoken to had been telling the truth, Buddy and Darlene had gone way too far. Killing a rabbit. Could they really have buried a cat alive? It seemed likely they had boasted about it to scare the small children without actually doing it, but even if they weren't sociopaths, they still sounded like a couple of delinquents. Frankie and Ryan had chosen the wrong kids to make enemies of.

'Do you want to leave? Go home?' I asked.

'What? No.'

'Are you sure? We could cut the vacation short, go back to Albany.'

She shook her head. 'No, Dad. I want to stay here with you. And Mum's not even there.'

This was news to me, but I would come back to that. 'Maybe we could find a hotel.'

'No! You came all the way from England. I don't want something stupid I did to mess up our holiday.'

'I don't know . . .'

'Please, Dad! I want to stay.'

'Even though you've fallen out with Ryan? And even with everything else that's happened?'

'Yeah. I'll just hang around the cabin with you.'

That sounded great to me. It was what I'd wanted all along. The circumstances certainly wouldn't allow me to feel any great glee, but

I was glad for the result. And as for my article, well, that could wait. Maybe I could come back and research it properly later, after I'd taken Frankie home. Find somewhere cheaper to stay in Penance.

I would think about that later.

'We still need to deal with Buddy and Darlene,' I said.

Frankie looked nervous. 'What do you mean?'

'What do you think I mean? We need to stop them harassing you.'

'You want me to try to apologise to them again? After what they did to that rabbit?'

'No, I'm not saying that. I'm going to talk to Greg. Tell him what's going on.'

Frankie cringed.

'It's okay, Frankie. He's not going to want any trouble between the town and the resort. I expect he'll know who they are, know their parents.'

She nodded but looked miserable.

'What about Ryan?' I said. 'Do you want to talk to him?'

She stared at the floor. 'No.'

'He should never have left you in the woods. I ought to go next door and give him a piece of my mind.'

'No, Dad, please! You can't do that.'

'Why not? He was a jerk. Why did he tag you in that post? If he wanted to make himself a target, that's fine. Whatever. But to get you involved. What the hell was he thinking? And then to let you go off on your own.'

'He didn't know.' She winced, like she couldn't believe she was defending him.

I calmed down. Ryan was only fifteen, after all. A child. I was so happy we hadn't had social media when I was that age to show the world proof of my immaturity and stupidity. It had taken years for me to gain the wisdom to realise I didn't know everything.

'Can I go to my room?' Frankie asked. 'I'm so tired.' She hesitated. 'Will you go and look for my phone?'

'Of course. But first I'm going to talk to Greg. I'll come back and check on you in a bit.'

'Okay.'

She shuffled off to her bedroom and did what teenagers do. She went back to sleep.

ω

Greg was at the front desk. He looked stressed, a pile of paperwork in front of him. I guessed the death of a guest, even by natural means, must cause all sorts of headaches for the manager of a place like this. Well, his headache was about to get worse.

'Mr Anderson,' he said with a smile. He didn't just look stressed. He had dark circles around his eyes, as if he hadn't got much sleep. As usual, he was sweating too, though with the A/C turned up high it was chilly in the office.

'Can I have a word with you?'

'Is this about Miss Capello?'

I assumed that was Donna.

'No.' I told him as much as he needed to know, from Ryan's unfortunate Instagram post to the messages Frankie had received. I told him about the rabbit but left out the part about the cat, as I still wasn't convinced that was true. Greg got increasingly sweaty as I spoke. By the end he was dabbing his brow with a handkerchief.

'Who are these local teenagers?' he asked.

'I don't know their surname but their first names are Buddy and Darlene.'

He stared at me. 'Ah.'

'You know them?'

'I do.'

His voice had gone flat. I guessed Buddy and Darlene already had a reputation.

'I don't really want to get the police involved in this,' I said. 'Frankie and Ryan obviously provoked them and I don't want Frankie to have to be interviewed by the police.'

'I can understand that,' he said.

'So far it's just been a load of horrible messages and a dead rabbit. I'm sure it's just teenage drama. In my day we would shout at each other or send notes, and none of it ever came to anything. Now they all have phones it's a thousand times easier to make threats, and probably even less likely to end in actual violence. But I will get the police involved if the threats don't stop. And I'm sure nobody wants that.'

'Of course. I'll deal with it. You have my word.'

'Good.'

The conversation was over. I went back to my cabin and looked in on Frankie. She was still asleep and I didn't want to disturb her. I left her a note, telling her not to leave the cabin, which I was sure she wouldn't do anyway.

I was going to try to find her phone.

ω

The problem was, I didn't really know where to look. A clearing, somewhere close to town. That was as much detail as Frankie had been able to give. That and the wind chimes.

As I got closer to Penance, I listened out for them but all I could hear was the incessant chatter of unseen birds. The faintest hum of traffic in the distance. I scoured the ground at my feet and, managing to get a slight signal, tried phoning Frankie's number several times, but the phone had been on low battery when she lost it and it went straight to voicemail. I couldn't use Find My iPhone either because the phone was dead.

I wanted to find it. It would be expensive to replace, and I could imagine how Sarah would react when she heard Frankie had lost it. I really didn't want Sarah to know about any of the creepy stuff that had happened this week. I also wanted to see the messages Frankie had received on Instagram. But this was hopeless.

There was someone who could help, though. Nikki. She might not know exactly where Frankie had dropped it, but it seemed likely she could identify the correct clearing.

Except, when I got into town, the bookstore was shut.

I peered through the front window. All the lights were off. I thought I saw a movement inside then realised it was the cat, Cujo. At least he was safely home.

I looked around. Wyatt, the homeless guy I'd seen the first time I came here, wasn't in his spot beneath the statue. In fact, there was absolutely no one in sight. Unsure what to do next, I headed down the street to the minimart and, happy to find a living person behind the counter, bought a bottle of water, a notepad and a pen. I tore a sheet of paper out of the pad and wrote a note for Nikki, asking her to come and see me. Then I went back to the bookstore and put it through the letterbox.

'They not open?' said a voice behind me.

I turned. It was the guy who had taught us archery. The young Walter White, with his bald head and goatee. What was his name?

'Hey,' he said. 'It's Robin Hood. How's Katniss?'

I laughed. It appeared he couldn't remember our real names either, but his had come back to me. Carl. 'Frankie? She's okay.'

He peered past me at the door. 'She was meant to open two hours ago.' He tutted. 'I was supposed to pick up a book. Oh, Nikki, you're going to go broke if you don't manage to get yourself out of bed in the morning.'

'You know her?'

He grinned. 'Hey, have you seen the size of this town? We all know each other.'

He was a local. Maybe he could help me.

I told him what had happened last night: just the part about Frankie losing her phone in the woods. I didn't want to get into the whole story.

'She says it was in a clearing quite close to town. She could hear wind chimes nearby.'

He stroked his chin. 'I think I might know where you mean. I'm heading back to the resort. I can help you look if you like.'

'That would be great.'

We walked down the street together, back towards the woods.

'So you know Nikki, huh?' he said as we stepped into the trees.

'Yeah. Well, I've been to her store. And she found Frankie in the woods last night. That's why I was going to see her this morning.'

'Ah, I see.' He appeared to be smirking.

'What is it?'

'Nikki's cute. A total mess, but very easy on the eye.'

I didn't like his tone. 'What do you mean by that?'

I must have sounded aggressive because he said, 'Hey, I'm sorry if I've offended you, if you're, like, in love with her or something.'

'I'm not in love with her!'

'I mean, I wouldn't blame you. Like I said, she's hot, and a lot of guys are into screwed-up women.'

'I'm not—'

He laughed. 'I'm messing with you, man. To be honest with you, I don't know her that well. But she was always one of the smartest kids at school. Why she didn't get out of Penance the minute she had the chance, I'll never know. She never even went to college. A waste, if you ask me.'

'You didn't get out either,' I pointed out.

'True. Not many of us do. But I like it here.' He stopped and looked around him. 'I mean, look at it. I bet I could travel the whole world and not find anywhere as beautiful.'

We had so far been following the path back towards the resort. Now we turned on to a new path, where the trees were thicker and the ground beneath our feet was less well trodden. I could hear wind chimes.

'So what do you do back in England?' Carl asked.

'I'm a music journalist.'

'That's cool. A lot better than being a true-crime journalist, anyway.' He shook his head, the disdain evident.

'You're not a fan?'

He grunted. 'Dark tourists, is that what you call them? Fucking ghouls, that's what *I* call them. It's good for business, though, I guess. Hollow Falls would be half empty if it wasn't for them.' He laughed. 'Hollow *Falls*. I don't even know why they called it that. There aren't any goddamn waterfalls for miles. Guess it sounded good to the marketing people, huh?'

The wind chimes were louder now and, all of a sudden, we were in a clearing.

'This could be it,' he said. 'The place where your daughter dropped her phone.'

I looked around. If he was right, this was the place where Frankie had seen the masked figures.

'What was she doing out here anyway?' he asked.

'She got lost.'

'Is that right?'

I could tell what he was thinking. A teenage girl, in the woods at night. She must have been up to no good. A boy, cigarettes, drugs.

We searched the clearing, walking in straight lines, scanning the ground. I was grateful to Carl for helping, though he didn't seem to be looking particularly hard.

'You got insurance?' he asked. 'Because I really don't think we're gonna find it.'

He was right.

'Where are those wind chimes coming from?' I asked.

'I don't know,' he said. 'It's weird, isn't it? I think they must be tied to a tree but I have no idea who put them there.'

I sighed. Then I had an idea. I wasn't going to actively work on my article over the coming days, but I was here with Carl, a local.

'You know how I said I'm a music journalist? I'm actually planning a change of direction. I'm writing a piece about Hollow Falls and what happened here.'

He looked at me, his hands on his hips. 'Are you now?'

'I'd like to interview a few of the people who lived here back then. Maybe you could give me your email address so I could send you some questions? I also want to write about the dark-tourism angle. It would be great if I could quote you. What you said earlier, about it being good for business.'

He laughed. 'Get out of here. You want me to get fired?'

'It could be anonymous.'

He shook his head. 'Sounds like it would draw even more rubberneckers here. All the way from the UK.'

'I don't think that would happen. Besides, like you said, no matter how distasteful you find it, it's good for business. Good for your job.'

He appeared to think about it. 'Nah,' he said. 'Sorry, man. I don't want to get involved. Greg was going on about it at our last team meeting. We don't want this place to be famous because of the murders.' He paused. 'I really don't think we're going to find this phone. What made her drop it anyway? Did something scare her?'

'What makes you ask that?'

'Hey, I'm aware of all the rumours. About Everett Miller still lurking in these woods. All bullshit, of course.'

'Did you know him?'

I knew exactly what he was going to say. 'Everyone knew him. He was the town freak.'

'Nikki said he was all right. That he wasn't a "freak".'

'Really? She . . . Hey, did you hear that?'

'What?'

'I thought I heard someone. In the trees.'

He walked quickly towards a spot near the edge of the clearing. I expected someone wearing a sheep or bird mask to step out at any second.

'Hey,' Carl called. 'Is someone there?'

Silence.

'Come on. Whoever it is, help us. Come out and help us look for this phone.' He laughed and winked at me.

More silence.

'I guess I imagined it,' Carl said.

I was sure I could feel it, though. Someone there, watching us. Listening. But all I could hear was the ringing of those hidden wind chimes.

Chapter 22

Walking back, I couldn't shake the feeling that someone was following me. I kept hearing noises. Footsteps. But every time I stopped and turned around, there was no one there.

It's not real, I told myself. It was hardly surprising that my imagination was so overstimulated. It was as if I'd hooked it up to a caffeine drip.

Back at the cabin, Frankie was still asleep. Trying to relax while I waited for her to wake up, I kept coming back to the same question.

Could Everett Miller really have been living around here for twenty years without being found?

I thought about what the children had said about a secret cabin and a 'him' who was supposed to live in the woods. Could this secret cabin be real? Was that where the sound of the wind chimes was coming from? And had Everett been living there all along?

As unlikely as it seemed, I let myself run with the idea. I imagined that Everett really had retreated into the woods after the murders and hadn't fled to Canada. Somewhere in this vast wooded area, between the town and the lake, was a cabin. Everett could have lived there, surviving on wildlife that he trapped. Sneaking out at night when there was no one around, maybe going into town and rifling through the garbage. A hermit. It wouldn't be the first time it had happened. There had been numerous cases of people, even whole families, who had retreated into the American wilderness, living off the land, hiding from society. In Everett's case, hiding from what he'd done.

For twenty years, these woods had been almost empty. He would have had them to himself.

And then the construction workers had come. The resort was built. Suddenly, Everett wasn't alone any more. There were strangers in the woods. Pony treks. Foot traffic between the resort and the town. His lifestyle, his very existence, was threatened. He couldn't roam around now. He might be spotted. His freedom would be taken away.

What would I do in his shoes? I could think of only three options.

One: cower and hide.

Two: run away. Finally head for the border.

Three: try to make things how they were before.

But how, exactly, would he achieve that?

Chapter 23

A month had gone by since Abigail's body had left the earth, but Crow felt closer to her than ever. Whenever he came to the woods, she would fall into step beside him. She talked to him. Carried on her teachings. He had a book that she'd given him before she died, and they would talk about it, discussing the history of the Hollows. He re-encountered the words that hadn't sunk in when she had first used them. Words like 'animism'. That was the most important one. She helped him understand how the world worked, how humans and nature and animals were connected.

Best of all, she showed him secret paths.

On a day in late May, when the ground was still damp and black flies swarmed in the air, she had taken him deep into the woods, a secret tangle of undergrowth and firs, the trees crowded together so closely that there wasn't even room for a bird to fly between them. It had rained heavily the week before and the ground squelched underfoot, sucking at his soles as if it were trying to hold him there, prevent him from going deeper. The sky was blue but it was cold here, in this place the sun never reached. He could sense animals watching him, hostile but afraid.

Follow me, Abigail whispered.

And there it was. The cabin.

He had, of course, shown Goat and Fox right away. Up to that point he wasn't sure they believed that he could see Abigail, that she was still with them, but when he led them to the cabin and told them Abigail had brought him here, he finally saw it on their faces. Belief.

'I can feel her here,' Goat said.

'She decided to show herself to you, now you've finally shaved that dumb peach fuzz off,' Crow laughed.

'What about you?' Crow asked Fox, and she nodded, dumbstruck. She was as awed by this place as he was. It was so close to Penance, but nobody knew it was here.

They began to spend all their time there. It became their true home. Crow created a kind of altar to Abigail, with a photo they had stolen from her house, along with candles and rocks from the lake shore, a pine cone, and a perfectly preserved skeleton of a mouse that Goat had found in the woods. They hung wind chimes on the porch.

They got together every day after school, shooting the shit, listening to metal on Fox's old boom box, getting high. Abigail had shared joints with them sometimes, telling them it would make them feel closer to the earth, and she had been right. Whenever Crow smoked and went out into the woods, he felt like he had that day they'd gone to the ancient forest. The power of nature thrumming inside him. It made him feel like an animal, flooded by smells and sounds, reading shadows like they were words in a book.

Only one cloud hung over his life: his feelings for Fox. He still didn't know who she hung out with when she wasn't with him and Goat. He hadn't seen her talking to any other boys at school, but he couldn't help but worry. What if she found a boyfriend? That would be the worst thing that could ever happen. She was supposed to be his.

Be brave, Abigail said. *Tell her.*

But he couldn't. Not yet.

ω

A month after Abigail first brought him to the cabin, Crow had a surprise for them.

'Abigail's not happy,' he said.

Both Fox and Goat looked alarmed.

'It's the campground. All those asshole kids tramping around, treating the woods like they don't give a shit. I saw this boy carving his initials into a tree yesterday, and this boat spilling gas into the lake, and this dumb group of girls were starting a fire near the flat stone, and . . .'

He ranted on for a while, listing all the ways the idiots at the campground were spoiling the Hollows. Polluting Abigail's woods. *Their* woods. He was aware that his voice got kind of high and that his face turned pink, and that Fox wouldn't find that hot, not one bit, but he couldn't help it. They were being besieged by outsiders. Invaders.

As leader, it was up to him to do something about it.

'Abigail and I have come up with a plan,' he said, getting up.

He had been sitting on one of the rickety, half-rotten chairs that had been in the cabin when he'd found it, along with a bed that stank of mould, and some rusty old tools that he'd been attempting to clean up.

He picked up the plastic bag he'd brought with him and reached inside, taking out the first rubber mask. He handed it to Goat. 'That's yours.'

Goat turned it over in his hands. 'Whoa,' he said.

'Cool, huh? This dude my mom is dating works in a factory that makes Halloween costumes. I asked him to get these for us.'

He tried to swallow the lump in his throat as he turned and extended the ginger fox mask.

'And for you, Fox,' he said.

Goat had already put his on and was feeling his new face. 'How do I look?'

'Like you ought to be hanging out with Satan,' Crow replied.

Goat chuckled while Fox examined her mask and said, 'This is awesome. Did you get yourself one?'

'Of course.'

He pulled the crow mask from the bag and, using both hands, pulled it over his head. It stank of rubber and made his face hot and uncomfortable. But when he wore it, he felt himself change. He was no longer merely called Crow. He *became* Crow.

'So what are they for?' Goat asked.

Crow grinned, even though he knew they couldn't see his mouth beneath the rubber. 'We're gonna scare those campground kids out of our woods.'

Chapter 24

Frankie leaned back, adjusted her sunglasses and let out a sigh. We were in a rowing boat, somewhere close to the centre of the lake. The water was placid, just the gentlest breeze keeping us cool. 'Maybe we should stay here forever,' Frankie said.

I stopped rowing, letting the boat drift to a slow halt. 'At Hollow Falls?'

'I mean right here in the middle of the lake, away from all the weirdos in masks and the rabbit-murdering twins.'

I laughed. It was great to see her sense of humour surface, even if she did flinch when she mentioned the rabbit.

On the way out of the cabin, we had bumped into David and Connie.

Connie had immediately said, 'Oh, Frankie, are you okay? Ryan's so worried about you.'

'He could have come over to tell us that,' I said. 'Maybe—'

Frankie shot me a look telling me to stop.

'He wasn't raised that way, I can assure you,' David said. 'I'm really sorry, man. I'll make sure he comes over to apologise to you and Frankie. He's gone for a walk but I'll talk to him as soon as he gets back. He really was worried, Frankie.'

I saw her face soften. But before I could say anything, we were joined by the man I'd met briefly on the Butlers' deck. Neal Fredericks. The husband of Sally, the woman who'd been killed with her lover years ago. The top of his bald head was pink like he'd caught the sun.

As though he'd noticed me looking, he touched the tender-looking skin and grinned. 'Guess I left home without a hat.'

I smiled, nodded. An odd, rather pitiful guy. I still didn't know what to make of his presence here. But for the second time since I'd sworn not to pursue my article while I was here with Frankie, I found myself thinking about it. Neal would be the perfect person to talk to. But I couldn't say anything while I was standing here with Frankie, David and Connie. I didn't even want to let on to Neal that I knew who he was.

The three of them walked away and I noticed that David and Connie were flanking him like he was a celebrity. What exactly were they up to?

ω

The water lapped gently around the boat. Frankie had brought a book with her and she opened it and read for a while. I knew how annoying it was when someone tried to talk to you when you were reading so I didn't interrupt. I gazed towards the shore, where there was a lot of industry happening. Of course, tonight was the big barbecue event. Greg had sold us tickets earlier in the week.

Frankie closed her book and smiled at me. She looked so grown-up. I felt a pang, realising we only had a few days left together.

'Are you going to come to England for Christmas?' I asked. I'd been meaning to broach this subject all week. I was going to have to find some money to pay for her airfare, but was sure I'd manage it somehow.

'I don't know. Mum was talking about going to Aspen.'

'Aspen! How is she going to afford that?'

'Bill,' Frankie said. 'The guy she's gone away with this week.'

'Your mum has a new boyfriend?'

'He's hardly a boy. He's, like, a proper boomer. Not a Gen Xer like you. He's got totally grey hair. Mum's friend Karen said he's a silver fox.'

Why did I feel so wounded by this? We had divorced three years ago. I no longer had any feelings for Sarah.

'Is it serious?' I asked. 'Where did she meet him? Are they going to move in together? What do you know about him?'

'Whoa, Dad, relax. Mum says it's just a fling.'

'But she's going skiing with him at Christmas? And taking you?'

'I don't want to go. I want to come to England.'

'I'll talk to her,' I said. I was sure Sarah would be fine with it. I didn't think she'd want a teenager cramping her style when she was on the slopes with her 'silver fox'.

I realised, then, it wasn't myself I was worried about. It was Frankie. Would she get on with this Bill guy? Would he try to replace me? He was obviously wealthy. And he was here. In America.

'Are you all right?' she asked. 'I know it must be weird.'

'Huh? I'm fine.'

'Especially as you don't have a girlfriend.'

'Rub it in, why don't you?'

She laughed. 'Hey, what about that woman from last night? She seemed nice. It makes me want to throw up saying this, but I think she's into you.'

'Really? What makes you say that?'

'Don't know. Just a vibe.'

'You're so grown-up sometimes.'

I began rowing us slowly back to the dock.

'Have you thought about moving to America? Then we could see each other all the time. You could move here, to Maine. I bet you could sell your flat in London and buy a huge house in Penance. Then you and Nikki could be a couple and you could write a memoir about all the pop stars you've met.'

I laughed. 'That's not going to happen, Frankie.'

'Why not?'

'Firstly, I think Nikki would be shocked to hear you making plans about her life and this great love affair she's about to have. Secondly, it would be hard for me to get a visa right now.'

'Oh yeah. Shame you're not still married to an American.'

Her smile came and slipped away quickly.

'I'm sorry,' I said. 'I know how hard it must be for you.'

'It's better than it was.'

I couldn't tell if she was on the verge of tears. I felt a little like crying myself. I missed her so much. Was dreading getting on the plane home. Going back to my empty flat. Only seeing the digitised version of my daughter. Next time I saw her she would practically be an adult.

'Listen,' I said. 'In a few years, you'll graduate high school and you'll be able to come back to the UK. Maybe you can go to university in England. I'd love it if that happened.'

'But Mum's talking about me applying for Harvard or Yale.'

'What about Oxford or Cambridge?'

She put her palm against her forehead. 'Dad, this is making my brain hurt. Can we not talk about it right now?'

'Of course. Sorry.'

We lapsed into silence, just the gentle sound of the lake lapping against the sides of the boat. I clenched my jaw, trying not to let the tears come. Frankie looked like she was fighting her emotions too.

Then she chuckled.

'What is it?' I asked, surprised.

'I was just thinking about the end of *Friday the 13th*. You know, the first one? When Jason comes looming out of the water and grabs the woman in the boat?'

'Um . . . Is that your way of saying I should row faster?'

'Yep,' she said.

ᛒ

We reached the dock and got out of the boat. It took me a minute to get my land legs back, then we got an ice cream from the kiosk, using the coupons Greg had given me. I was surprised he hadn't offered me more today.

'What do you want to do now?' I asked.

'Hey. Frankie.'

The voice came from behind us. We both turned. It was Ryan.

I stepped in front of Frankie. 'She doesn't want to see you. Not after what happened last night. You left her on her own!'

'Dad . . .' said Frankie. But seeing Ryan had reminded me how I'd felt when Nikki had brought Frankie back.

Ryan hung his head. 'My folks ripped me a new one over it.'

'I'm glad to hear it,' I said.

'I came to apologise. Frankie, I'm really sorry. I just . . . You went off so quickly and I couldn't catch you. And then I didn't think you wanted to talk to me. Plus I was angry too.' He flicked a glance at me.

'I've told him everything that happened,' Frankie said.

'Ah. Cool.'

'That's right,' I said. 'And I understand you were both angry and upset but you should never leave a girl to walk home on her own in the dark.'

'I think that's slightly sexist,' he said. 'With all due respect.'

'Let me rephrase, then. You should never leave my daughter to walk home on her own in the dark. Come on, Frankie. Let's go.'

170

I took a couple of steps before realising Frankie wasn't following.

'Frankie?'

'He's right. I did sprint off.'

'She's way faster than me,' said Ryan.

That was easy to believe. Frankie had always been a fast runner. She had the medals in her bedroom to prove it.

'Let me just have a quick chat with him,' she said.

'But . . . Are you sure?

'Yeah. I want to talk to him. I want to hear him grovel.'

I wasn't sure. But then I didn't want to stand in the way of this friendship; and, of course, I wanted her to be happy. It would be better if they did make up.

'All right.' I spoke to Ryan. 'But do not leave her on her own. When you've finished talking, come back to the cabin together. All right?'

'I think he wants you to salute and say, "Yes sir",' said Frankie.

I walked back to the cabin, hoping I was doing the right thing.

To my surprise, there was someone outside the cabin, their back to me. It was a woman, peering through the front window.

She turned, her mouth forming an O of surprise – and guilt? – when she saw me.

'Nikki?' I said. 'What's going on?'

For a moment, I thought she was going to run away. Her body was tense, poised. But then she appeared to relax, and smiled.

'You want to come in?' I asked.

'I don't know.' Her eyes darted around nervously, like she was afraid of someone seeing her. 'I ought to . . .'

But I wasn't going to let her get away without telling me why she was here.

'Come on,' I said, and I steered her inside.

Chapter 25

'Do you want to go for a walk?' Ryan said, after her dad had gone.

'Sure. I guess.'

They walked along the lake's shore. Neither of them spoke at first. It was around six thirty in the evening but the sun was still high and strong, and Frankie took some sunscreen out of her bag and rubbed it on her arms.

'Do you want some?' she asked.

'I'm good.' An awkward pause. 'Are you going to the barbecue later?'

'Barbecue?'

'Yeah, the big campfire thing. Pretty much everyone here is going, I think. Mom and Dad have some mysterious surprise lined up for it.'

'What is it?'

'They won't tell me. They said they can't risk it leaking. Like I'm gonna run around talking to all their weirdo fans as if I actually give a shit. I think it's something to do with that bald dude they've been hanging with.'

They had entered a lightly wooded area. A path continued to follow the perimeter of the lake.

'About yesterday,' Ryan said. 'I really am sorry.'

She wrapped her arms around herself, creating a shield. Now she couldn't look at him. 'It wasn't only your fault. I shouldn't have got so mad and I definitely shouldn't have run off.' She felt very adult saying this. 'I thought I'd be able to find my way back but it got dark quicker than I expected.'

'So what happened?' he asked.

She told him.

'Whoa. This place is messed up. What the hell were they doing?'

'Just standing there.' She giggled even though it wasn't funny. 'Like they were communing with nature.'

'Shit. Maybe they were Devil-worshippers. Or pagans. You know about the symbols that were painted in those teachers' blood.'

'Please. Don't.'

'Sorry. But it really is freaky around here. Next time, get your dad to bring you to California. We'll go to Big Sur. Do you surf?'

'Oh yeah. We're all big surfers in Albany.' She smiled. 'Parkour and surfing? You got mad skills, bro.'

'You're being extra funny today,' he said.

'I think the stress has broken my brain.'

'Anyway.' He stuck out a hand. 'Still friends?'

She went to shake his hand but then he withdrew it and said, 'Why are we acting like we're doing a business deal? Come here.'

He pulled her into a hug. It was nice. All the tension inside her melted away, the knots coming loose. It was one of the best hugs she'd ever had.

They walked on.

'Can I ask you a question?' she said. 'Have you come out to your parents?'

'Ha. I could bring a boyfriend home and I doubt they'd notice. I guess it will dawn on them someday, but they're so wrapped up in their stupid serial-killer shit they barely notice anything I do.'

'What about the boy you like? Glen, is that his name? Do you have a plan for how you're going to snare him?'

Ryan found that hilarious. 'Snare!'

They carried on like this for a while, coming up with a plan for how Ryan was going to ask Glen out. For the first time on this stupid holiday, Frankie felt properly happy. Properly herself.

The path had taken them up a little hill so they could see the lake behind them; it now ran downhill, towards another part of the lake. The trees here were spaced out, letting the sun through, so she didn't feel creeped out or afraid. They talked for a while about Ryan's parents and how one day Ryan would be grown-up and they would regret neglecting him, and Frankie talked about her parents' divorce and how hard it had been at first, especially moving to a new country, and it was one of the best conversations she could remember having. She felt like she could really be herself with Ryan, more so than with any of her friends back home, and way more than she could be with her mum or dad. It was all going so well.

And then they heard the voices.

Ahead of them, the trees ended and gave way to a flat area on the edge of the lake. Frankie wasn't sure what to call it – a cove? – but it was a pretty spot, secluded and quiet.

Ryan and Frankie stood concealed by trees. Over in the cove, two people were sitting on a large rock and another was standing beside it. They all had their backs to where Frankie and Ryan stood.

Then the one who was standing turned to the side and walked around the edge of the rock. From his body shape it became clear it was a man. The two who were seated turned their heads to watch him.

Frankie gasped and clutched Ryan's arm.

They were wearing masks.

'What the fuck?' said Ryan.

'It's them,' she said. 'This is who I saw last night.'

They were too far away for her to make out the details of the masks, but they were clearly animals. One was a black bird, most likely a crow. Yes, a crow. Frankie squinted. The other sitting figure's mask was, what? A dog or a fox. The one who was standing wore a greyish-white mask. It wasn't a sheep, though. She saw that now. It wasn't a devil either. It was a goat.

Frankie's insides had turned to jelly. She wanted to turn and run. But she also wanted proof. Something to show her dad or the police.

Because the clothes two of these masked figures were wearing were familiar. The goat was wearing a black track top with stripes up the sleeves. The fox had on a faded orange T-shirt with cream piping around the neck. The first time she'd seen the T-shirt, it had stuck in Frankie's mind because it looked like something from a nineties fashion museum. The kind of thing her mum had worn before she had Frankie.

This was what Buddy and Darlene had been wearing the first time Frankie and Ryan had encountered them. The goat was Buddy and the fox was Darlene.

There was no doubt.

'Have you got your phone?' she whispered to Ryan.

He nodded and pulled it from his pocket. It was, as she already knew, one of the newer iPhones. He did exactly as she'd hoped, zooming in as far as he could go. Frankie looked over his shoulder and examined the image on the screen. They looked like rubber masks, the kind that covered the whole face.

Ryan took a photo. The phone made the camera-shutter sound. And the person wearing the crow mask whipped his head round to face them. Buddy, the goat, and Darlene, the fox, did the same. It was so quiet here that the sound of the shutter must have carried across to them. Or maybe the crow had sensed something.

Frankie found herself transfixed, unable to move. The phone clicked. Ryan had taken another picture. She stared at the masked figures. Buddy and Darlene were on their feet now. Then they stooped . . . What were they doing?

It only took a moment for her to realise.

They were picking up rocks.

'Run!' Frankie said.

Chapter 26

Nikki looked terrible, like she'd been awake since I'd seen her last night. There were shadows around her eyes and worry creases on her forehead.

'What's going on?' I asked. 'Why were you looking in the window?'

'I just wanted to see if you were here. Check you're both okay after last night. Where's Frankie?'

'She's with Ryan.'

'Oh. They made up? That's cool. That's really cool.'

She took a seat but didn't relax. She leaned forward, her elbows on her knees.

'Do you want a drink?' I asked. 'Coffee? Wine?'

'Water would be great.' She took her cigarettes out of her bag and was about to light one until she remembered where she was.

'You want to go out on the deck?'

'No!' she said. 'I mean, no, I'm good.'

I filled a glass of water and handed it to her. There was very clearly something wrong but I didn't think I'd get very far if I demanded to know what it was. She would clam up.

'I came by the bookstore earlier,' I said, 'but it was closed.'

'Sorry about that. I overslept. Were you coming as a customer or . . .'

She met my eye then looked away.

I momentarily forgot what we were meant to be talking about.

'Tom?' she prompted.

'Oh. I was hoping you might be able to show me where you found Frankie, so I could look for her phone.'

'Ah.'

'But it's okay. I bumped into Carl, the archery teacher here, and he helped me look. With no success. Also, I spoke to Greg and told him about last night and everything that's been going on with Buddy and Darlene. Wait, did I already tell you about that?' I was rambling. 'I hope he sorts it out. I really don't want to have to get the police involved. Do you know him?'

'Who?'

'Greg. He's about your age, I think.'

'Yeah. Everyone knows—'

'—everyone round here. I get it. So I guess you know Buddy and Darlene too?'

Nikki stared at me like she hadn't been listening. 'What?' Then, to my surprise, she stood, went over to the window and peered out, then drew the blind.

'What's going on?' I asked.

She turned to me and smiled. 'Nothing. The sun was in my eyes.'

I was confused. She was staring at me and seemed nervous. Had she shut the blind because she was about to try to seduce me? I wasn't sure what I would do if she did. I liked her. She was gorgeous. But Frankie could be back any minute and Nikki was acting strangely, pacing around in front of the window and chewing on her thumbnail.

'I like you, Tom,' she said.

'I . . . I like you too.'

Were we going to kiss? I waited, so out of practice I wasn't sure what to do. Make a move? Wait for a sign?

'I think you should take Frankie and leave,' she said.

I hadn't expected *that*. 'What? Why?'

'Because I don't know . . . I don't know if it's safe.'

'Okay, now you're scaring me.'

She exhaled, a kind of shuddering laugh with no mirth in it. 'Bad things happen here, Tom. I have . . . I just have this feeling that it's going to happen again. If I were you I would pack up and get out of here. Take your daughter as far from the Hollows as you can. There are things going on . . . things that go back a long way.' She trailed off, as if she'd said too much. 'I really like you, Tom, and I don't want to see you get hurt. Frankie too. Please, pack up the car and go.'

She went back to the window, parted the blinds and peeked out. When she turned back I saw that her face had gone white. She seemed terrified.

I got up from the chair. 'What are you talking about? Are you saying we're in danger from Buddy and Darlene?'

She looked like she was about to cry. She fumbled with her bag, taking the cigarettes out again. 'I can't say any more. No one can know.'

'No one can know what?'

She shook her head. She had pulled a cigarette from the packet and was holding it close to her lips. Her hand trembled.

'I have to go,' she said. 'But please, Tom, you should go. Take Frankie home.'

She opened the front door and went to leave. I caught her arm.

'Has someone threatened Frankie?' I said. 'Threatened me?'

'Let go of me. That hurts.'

She pulled her arm away and I shrank back as she ran down the steps, feeling bad for hurting her, for grabbing hold of her. But I was desperate. If my daughter was in danger . . . Had I been stupid? Underestimated Buddy and Darlene?

Oh God. Frankie. I needed to find her.

Nikki had already vanished from sight. Trying not to panic, I headed down towards the lake.

The resort was a hubbub of activity, with pretty much all the staff building a campfire and preparing for the barbecue, which was taking place on the lake shore close to where the picnic tables were. People in red Hollow Falls polo shirts rushed around. There was a man who appeared to be in charge, barking orders at his underlings. I assumed he was the chef. He rushed over to yell at a young woman who was struggling to carry a large cooler. She dropped it, the lid opened and a lobster fell out on to the ground.

There was no sign of Greg. Hiding in his office, I expected, while everyone else did the work.

I was about to head along the shoreline when I spotted David. I hurried over to him. He seemed excited, shifting from foot to foot. He was handing out flyers to passers-by. He gave one to me. It was handwritten.

> *Tonight! 9pm at the Archery Ground. A Big Surprise you won't want to miss! Spread the word.*

It was seven thirty now. 'Have you seen Ryan and Frankie?' I asked.

'Oh, are they friends again? That's cool.'

'So you haven't seen them?'

'No. Why, what's up?' He handed out two more flyers.

I shook my head. I didn't have time to explain. I didn't even know what I'd say. But before heading away I said, 'What's the big surprise?'

He grinned. 'Oh, it's something special for our fans.'

'It's related to the murders?'

He winked at me.

I didn't have time for his teasing. Where would Frankie and Ryan have gone? I knew they sometimes hung out at the playground, and headed in that direction. They weren't there. I was pretty sure they wouldn't go into Penance, not after Frankie's scare last night. I ran back towards the ice cream kiosk, which was where I'd last seen them, and spoke to the young woman behind the counter.

'I'm looking for my daughter,' I said. 'Have you seen her?'

I described her and Ryan.

'I think I saw them heading that way,' she said. She pointed to the path that snaked around the lake towards a wall of pines.

'Thank you.'

I jogged in that direction, though there were so many people around that I had to keep slowing or stopping.

I deeply regretted coming somewhere that had no phone signal. How easy it would be if I could phone Frankie right now – except she had lost her phone, hadn't she?

My heart was beating hard and my mouth felt dry. Nikki had said 'bad things happen here', but I knew she wasn't just worried about the history of this place. To be that jittery, to tell me to pack up and leave, she must have known something concrete. Something that meant Frankie was in danger.

The path ahead of me cleared, and I ran towards the trees.

Chapter 27

Frankie and Ryan ran up the slope, back the way they had come. The ground seemed rockier and hillier this time, and when they reached the top, Ryan stopped where the path split into three.

'Right,' Frankie said.

'Are you sure?'

Now, scared and on the cusp of panic, she was doubtful. Scarred by her recent experience in the woods near Penance, Frankie had no confidence in any of their decisions. She turned to look back at the lake, shimmering in the near distance. If the lake had matched her mood, its surface would be churning, mist rising from it. The water would be black.

'Yes, go right.'

When they were a little further along, she asked, 'Who's the man with them? The one with the crow mask.' But Ryan shook his head.

They reached another crossroads. Left led up a gentle slope and right would take them deeper into the trees. Her inner compass told her the resort was to the right, but she had no memory of walking through such thick woods on their way here.

Who was the crow? Thinking about him made her feel nauseous and cold. The way his masked face had turned towards them. The aggressive way he had stooped to pick up a couple of rocks. Maybe she was being stupid, but she was certain she could feel loathing emanating from behind the mask.

'It could be their dad,' Ryan said. 'And this is their idea of a great family day out.'

Despite everything, she laughed. But the laugh got caught in her throat. Because she could hear them, not far behind. Two young voices.

'This way,' said Buddy.

'You sure?' asked Darlene.

Then a man's voice. 'Go right.'

'But—' Buddy began.

The man spoke over him. 'We have to get that phone. I'll go left. You two go right. If you spot them, shout. Okay?'

'Okay,' said Buddy.

'Hurry,' Frankie urged.

But Ryan didn't move. 'It's just Buddy and Darlene coming our way. Maybe we should stop. Reason with them.'

'Reason?'

They're going to bury us alive. No one will ever find our graves. She was starting to panic again, her legs turning to rubber, the breath sticking in her throat.

Ryan was still trying to be rational. 'Come on, you were the one who wanted to talk to them. This is our chance.'

She could hardly believe she was hearing this. 'That was before we realised what psychos they are.'

But he still didn't move. 'I'll just apologise, get it out of the way. Say sorry for badmouthing Penance.'

'No! That won't work. They're not normal. They're evil.'

'I don't think—'

'Ryan! Please. We can't reason with them.'

She could hear the other two coming down the path towards them.

'Oh God,' she said. 'Ryan, please.'

'No. I want to straighten this out. I want us to be able to enjoy the last few days of our vacation without having to look over our shoulders the whole time.'

She realised then what he was doing. He was trying to make up for last night. His dad had probably given him a lecture about being a man, and here he was trying to be macho and show her he wasn't the kind of guy who let weirdos in masks scare him.

She tried to take his hand, to pull him away, absolutely sure this was another mistake, but then it was too late. Both Buddy and Darlene appeared on the path, about twenty metres behind. They were still wearing their masks. Frankie eyed the bulging, lumpy pockets of Buddy's tracksuit top warily, knowing they were full of rocks.

'Hey, guys,' called Ryan. 'Let's talk.'

He took a step towards them. They didn't move. Frankie thought she might throw up.

'I don't care what kind of weird games you're playing,' Ryan said, projecting his voice. 'I want to make peace. Okay? Buddy? Darlene?'

They turned their masked faces towards one another, like they were surprised that Frankie and Ryan knew who they were. She had a feeling Ryan had just made things even worse. She was convinced they were going to start shouting to the man, letting him know they'd caught up with their quarry. At least then she would know who he was, assuming they called him 'Dad' or his name. But they stayed silent.

'Oh, come on,' said Ryan. 'Are you just gonna stand there like a pair of creeps?'

He couldn't help himself, thought Frankie, as Buddy and Darlene stepped forward and shortened the distance between them.

She tugged at Ryan's arm. 'Please. We need to go.'

What if they had knives? Or the gun that they had, she was now certain, used to frighten the horses? All she could hear was what those children had said about them burying a cat alive. Anyone who was capable of doing something like that had to be a psychopath. She needed Ryan to shut up.

But now he was set on doing the opposite. So much for apologising. 'What, you guys celebrate Halloween early around here? Planning on going trick-or-treating later? Come on, take off the masks and let's talk.' He held up his phone. 'You really don't want anyone seeing these photos, do you?'

The way Buddy and Darlene stood completely still was making Frankie's blood run cold. They had been exactly the same last night when she'd seen them in the woods, before Nikki had found her. They both held their arms straight down by their sides. She was sure they knew exactly what they were doing, that they understood this stillness made them scarier, more intimidating.

And then, as if they were communicating with their minds, like they had that mythical twin link, they both lifted their arms, and Frankie saw the rocks clutched in their fists, and she grabbed Ryan's T-shirt and tugged at it. 'Come on,' she urged.

Finally, *finally*, as two rocks came arcing through the air towards them, Ryan turned and the two of them ran.

One of the rocks struck a tree beside Frankie and ricocheted off it, missing her by inches. The other landed somewhere nearby. She glanced over her shoulder. Buddy and Darlene were running too. They both had more rocks in their hands and Frankie experienced a spasm of fear in her gut. The ground was dry and rough and it was difficult to run without tripping. Another rock flew past her, so close it skimmed her ear, and she tried not to think about the damage it would have done if it had hit the back of her head. There was a sob somewhere deep inside her, trying to get out, but she needed all her breath. She increased her speed as another rock whizzed by, and then, beside her, Ryan cried out and went down, flat on his belly.

Frankie skidded to a halt as Ryan tried to scramble to his feet. 'Did one hit you?' she demanded and he shook his head. He must have tripped. But as Ryan got into a crouching position, another rock flew towards him, and as he twisted his body to dodge it he fell back on to the dirt.

Buddy and Darlene stopped ten metres from where Frankie stood, Ryan finally getting to his feet beside her.

Buddy pulled back his arm. He was clearly aiming at Ryan and, without thinking about what she was doing, acting on instinct, Frankie stepped between them.

'Please,' she said. 'Stop.'

Buddy froze for a second, his arm still pulled back, then he took a couple of steps to the left so he had a clear shot at Ryan. Again, Frankie moved to cover her friend.

'We'll delete the photos,' she said, her voice high and strange in her ears. 'We won't tell anyone we saw you. Whatever you're doing, we don't care.'

Ryan had his phone out again and held it up for the other teenagers to see. He seemed a lot more contrite now. Or maybe just scared.

'Look,' he said. 'I'm deleting them. I'll empty the trash too.' His phone clicked as he did it. 'They're gone.'

He held the screen out so they could see, even though they would have needed incredible eyesight to make anything out from where they stood.

'We're going to go now,' Ryan said. 'Okay? I'm really sorry about what we said. What I wrote.'

They were both doing that weird standing-still thing again.

Ryan reached out and took Frankie's hand. He nodded at her, a look that asked if she was okay. She nodded back, even though she was very far from okay, and as they turned to go she heard movement behind them, a scuffing sound, and Frankie's heart was skittering like Swifty's when she held him, so fast she feared she was using up a lifetime of heartbeats.

She dared to look back and saw both Buddy and Darlene had raised the rocks they held, and were bracing to throw them. And again like her pet rabbit, she froze, bracing herself. Beside her, Ryan did the same.

'Hey!' said a voice from further down the path. 'Hey, what the hell?'

For a second, Buddy and Darlene didn't react. She thought they were going to throw the rocks anyway. But then they had one of those weird moments of silent communication and, simultaneously, dropped the rocks and retreated up the path.

'Are you guys okay?'

Frankie had no strength left. She fell to her knees. She couldn't remember the last time she had been so pleased to see her dad.

Chapter 28

I watched the two masked figures run away up the path. Should I pursue them? No, it was more important to make sure Frankie was okay. She had fallen on to the path, and I knelt beside her and pulled her into a hug.

'Are you all right?' I asked.

I felt her nod against my shoulder. Her heart was beating rapidly against my chest. Gradually, it slowed and returned to normal. Ryan sat on the ground close to us, arms wrapped around his knees, looking like someone who'd just got off an unexpectedly terrifying rollercoaster.

'That was Buddy and Darlene? The masks they were wearing – were they the same ones you saw last night?'

Frankie nodded. 'Buddy had a goat mask and Darlene's was a fox.'

'There was a man with them too,' said Ryan quietly. 'He was wearing a bird mask. A crow, I think. They split up to look for us and he went the other way.'

The two of them took turns to explain what had happened.

'Please don't tell me you actually deleted the photos you took?' I said.

Ryan groaned. 'I did.'

I knew that, in the moment, it had been the sensible thing to do, but it was still bloody frustrating.

'Wait here,' I said.

Frankie sat up, alarmed. 'Where are you going?'

'I just want to see if they're still around.'

'You can't leave us here,' Frankie pleaded. 'I want to go back to the cabin. Please, Dad.'

But I needed to know who this person was, this crow, even though I knew they were dangerous. Nikki's warnings rang in my ears. I ought to take Frankie straight back to the cabin, load up the car and get out of here.

But I couldn't. I wasn't thinking about my article. I didn't care about that right now. I was thinking about justice. I was certain these kids were responsible for killing Donna. They had attacked my daughter. I wanted them caught and punished. And I needed to know who the guy with them was.

Could it actually be Everett Miller? Suddenly, having witnessed this attack, seeing these masked figures in the woods with my own eyes, it didn't seem so impossible.

I picked up one of the rocks Buddy and Darlene had dropped before they ran. It wouldn't make a great weapon but it was better than nothing.

I hurried up the path, telling Frankie and Ryan to stay where they were. It only took two minutes to reach the point where the path split in two. I listened for voices, for movement in the woods, but heard nothing except the distant noise of motorboats on the lake. Buddy and Darlene, and the mysterious man in the crow mask, were long gone.

☡

I took Frankie back to the cabin. The sun had gone down as we walked back and the resort was bustling now, the barbecue ready

189

to go, and a band was setting up on a makeshift stage. A large bon-fire had been constructed beside the lake, ready to be lit. I saw a few of David's flyers discarded on the ground. Seeing the barbecue and all the food in metal containers lined up made my stomach growl, and I realised I hadn't eaten since breakfast. I was running on adrenaline and stress.

We said goodbye to Ryan outside his cabin. I had asked him to come in with us but he was insistent: he wanted to be alone for a while. Probably it was the only way he could process what had just happened. There was no sign of David or Connie and I assumed they were busy elsewhere, setting up whatever their surprise was.

'Are you sure you're going to be all right on your own?' I asked him.

'Yeah. I'll be fine.'

'Lock the doors, just in case. If you need anything, you know where we are. Okay?'

We went inside. Frankie was shivering. She sat on the couch where Nikki had sat not an hour before. Outside, I could see people walking past the cabin, heading towards the festivities. I wondered how many of them had been drawn to this place by its dark past. How thrilled they would be to think that Everett Miller might still be here. That he'd been hiding out for twenty years and was now getting ready for his comeback.

But I wasn't going to mention that to Frankie.

'Right,' I said. 'We're getting out of here.'

She blinked at me. 'What do you mean?'

'I'm packing up the car. We're leaving. Right now. I'm going to drive to Houlton, talk to the police or the sheriff.'

'But you just told Ryan we would be here for him if he needed us.'

I paused. She was right.

'We should wait for his parents to come back.'

I was torn. I didn't want to leave Ryan on his own, but I didn't think David and Connie would be coming back to the cabin any time soon. They had their big surprise planned. They would be busy with that, whatever it was.

'All right. We'll go and find David and Connie. Tell them what happened and that they need to come back to their cabin. Then we leave. Okay?'

'I want to stay here.'

'Frankie . . .'

'Please. I'll be fine. You're not going to be long, right? And I can start packing.'

Reluctantly, I agreed. I would be quicker on my own and there was the risk we'd get separated in the crowd. 'All right, but lock the door behind me, okay? I won't be long.'

As I reached the door, I added, 'We'll find a hotel in Portland and spend the rest of our holiday there. Far away from the woods.' I'd have to put it on my credit card, but I could worry about that later.

'That sounds great.'

I opened the front door and was halfway through when Frankie said, 'Dad.'

I turned back.

'I don't think we should have left Ryan on his own. Can you ask him to come over here?'

It was a good point. And they'd be safer together.

'I'll send him over.'

I left the cabin, looking around to make sure there was no one watching me, no masked figures lurking in the dark, then crossed to the Butlers' cabin. I knocked and waited. There was no reply. I knocked again. Maybe he was in the bathroom. I agonised for a moment then made a decision. I'd go on. I didn't want to leave Frankie alone for a moment longer than I had to. I would find

David and Connie and make one of them come back with me. We would be out of here by midnight. Later, I would try to get my money back from the resort. I still intended to come again on my own, without Frankie, to research the rest of my article – and, hopefully, to see justice done. I was now convinced that Donna had died because she'd seen either Buddy or Darlene, perhaps both, in or around her cabin. I was also certain the face I'd seen outside the window had been Buddy in his goat mask. This had gone way beyond teenagers acting out. Someone had died. And the way the twins had been chucking rocks at Frankie and Ryan, they could have been killed too.

And then there was the question of the man in the crow mask. I kept coming back to the big question: was it Everett Miller?

I didn't have the answer. And as much as I would have loved to be the one to uncover the truth, Frankie's safety was more important. I would let the police sort it out.

I hurried on. As I walked, more and more people came out of their cabins and headed down towards the lake. Most of them were dressed up: the women in summer dresses, the men in button-down shirts. I overheard someone say to his partner, 'What do you think it is?' They were presumably talking about David and Connie's surprise.

The spot beside the lake was crowded now. Dozens of people were lined up at the barbecue and many more were gathered around the bar. The bonfire hadn't been lit yet, but there was a party atmosphere – kids running around, people sitting on the grass holding plates that were piled high with food. The air was thick with the smell of cooking meat and barbecue sauce. I saw a young girl eating a hot dog while a golden retriever looked at her with pleading eyes. A young couple sat kissing beneath a tree, their legs intertwined. Over by the dock, the band were tuning up. I glanced in the direction of the woods where Frankie had been attacked. They were shrouded in darkness and I thought again about how scared Frankie must have been, how badly she could have been injured. I increased my pace, threading my way through the growing crowd.

Where were David and Connie?

I tried to question a couple of passers-by but they shook their heads at me, intent on getting to where they were going. Perhaps I should follow them, but what if they weren't going to the Butlers' big surprise?

A guy in a red polo shirt passed by. It was Carl. I stepped into his path.

'Hey, Robin Hood. Sorry. Is that joke getting old? How's Katniss? Did her phone turn up?'

I gave him a tight smile. 'Have you seen David and Connie Butler?'

He frowned. 'Sorry, I don't know who they are.'

Shit. 'What about Greg? Do you know where I can find him?' Surely the manager of this place would know what the Butlers' surprise was and where it was taking place.

'Sorry. I'm sure he's around somewhere, though.'

It was so noisy that I could hardly hear what he was saying. And then the band started playing. It was a cover of Prince's 'Let's Go Crazy'. A number of people rushed towards the stage.

'David and Connie have some big surprise planned,' I said. 'They were handing out flyers earlier.'

He put his hand behind his ear and leaned forward. The band were very loud. 'Sorry, dude, I didn't catch that.'

'Don't worry about it,' I said. 'I'll find them.'

He nodded like he still hadn't heard what I was saying, then vanished into the throng.

I looked around. It seemed that everyone at the resort was here. Perhaps I should go back to the cabin, find Ryan and hole up with him and Frankie until David and Connie came back. I would have one last look for them.

I pushed my way into the crowd, the smell of burgers and hot dogs and onions setting off a series of rumbles in my stomach – and then someone grabbed my arm.

'Whoa! Chill, man. I didn't mean to scare you.' It was David.

I realised I had my fist drawn back, ready to punch him. He looked alarmed.

I let my fist drop.

'I've been looking for you,' I said.

'Cool. And I've been looking for you. Come on, follow me.'

He began to walk off.

'No, wait, David.'

But he was walking fast, threading his way through the crowd, and the band had switched to an even louder song, 'Born in the USA', so he couldn't hear me pleading with him to stop.

I had no choice but to follow.

Chapter 29

I hurried along in David's wake. We went past the reception building towards the area where the tennis courts and playground were located. The crowd didn't thin and I realised that, along with all the vacationers, there must be a lot of people here from Penance. I guessed this event was intended to forge a connection between the town and the resort.

The lights that were strung between the branches of the trees that lined the path helped illuminate the way. Every step took me further from Frankie, but David wouldn't slow down. We kept passing people who were obviously his and Connie's fans. There were a lot of high fives.

'Here we are,' he said at last, a little out of breath.

We were in the archery field. A large tent had been set up, a dark shape squatting on the far eastern edge of the field. A couple of people with flashlights showed visitors where to go.

I wondered if this had been done with the blessing of the resort or if it was some kind of guerrilla event. A bit of both, I guessed. It seemed to me that, despite what Carl had said, Hollow Falls was happy to accept the dark tourists' money and didn't want to upset them, but they didn't want to blatantly encourage them either. I could imagine Greg turning a blind eye to this, giving himself plausible deniability in case he was ever accused of exploiting the deaths of two people for commercial gain. I felt a flare of anger towards him. Maybe he hadn't had time yet, but he clearly hadn't done anything about Buddy and Darlene despite his promise.

I was still trying to get David to listen to me, but he was too busy greeting people, and I found myself following him into the tent. It was well lit, a generator humming in the corner. Plastic chairs, presumably borrowed from the resort, had been arranged in lines. All, apart from a couple at the back, were occupied; I estimated there were around forty people here, with more coming in all the time. A makeshift stage had been set up at the front, with a microphone stand at the centre. Connie stood behind it, smiling at the audience.

'Take a seat,' David said, gesturing to the unoccupied chairs in the back row. 'It's about to start.'

'David, I need to speak to you. It's about Ryan. He's not—'

But he had gone.

That was it. I needed to get back to Frankie. But when I turned I found that dozens of people had crowded into the tent behind me, blocking the exit. I tried to push my way through, but an enormous man wearing a Chicago Bulls cap blocked me and wouldn't, or perhaps couldn't, move enough to let me pass. I was going to have to get across to the other side of the tent, which was blocked by all the rows of chairs. I began to pick my way along a row of tutting people. At the same time, onstage, Connie stood up, leaning on her stick.

'Ladies and gentlemen,' she began, speaking into a microphone. 'Thank you for coming here. I know how hard it must have been to tear yourselves away from that barbecue, but I'm assured all that delicious food will still be there when we're finished.'

'Sit down,' an elderly woman hissed at me. 'I can't see a thing.'

Everyone in my immediate vicinity was staring at me, shooting daggers. At the end of the row was a woman in a wheelchair. To get past I would either have to climb over her or ask her to move.

'Hey, buddy,' said a man with a red face. 'Sit the hell down.'

Feeling I had no choice, I shrank on to the nearest empty chair.

Onstage, Connie was saying, 'All right, I'm not going to keep you in suspense any longer. Many of you came to Hollow Falls because you wanted to visit the place where a terrible crime occurred twenty years ago. I know you wanted to pay respect to the victims, Eric Daniels and Sally Fredericks. I don't know about you, but seeing how beautiful and peaceful this place is makes the crimes seem even more heinous. How could something so terrible happen in such a lovely setting?'

I was desperate to leave, to get back to Frankie, but I was trapped. Meanwhile, Connie had the audience enraptured. This was my first proper view of how famous she was in her world. 'Many of you listen to my podcast and other true-crime podcasts because you are fascinated by puzzles. Perhaps you are drawn to the darker side of human nature and want to know what makes murderers and other criminals tick. Maybe you long to see justice done. But let me tell you what drew me to this area.'

Money and fame? I thought, only realising I'd spoken it aloud when the woman beside me gave me a filthy look.

A grey-haired lady in front of me jabbed her companion with an elbow and said, 'I wish she'd get on with it.'

But Connie was still doing her introduction. This was her stage and, for now, she wasn't going anywhere.

'I'm doing this to remember the victims. To honour them. How many victims of crime remain nameless? I bet I could point to any member of this audience and you could give me the names of ten serial killers.'

The woman next to me actually started mouthing their names.

'We all know Ted Bundy and John Wayne Gacy and Jeffrey Dahmer. But how many of the poor innocent women and men they murdered can we name?'

The woman beside me shut her mouth.

'I do hope,' Connie said, 'that when you hear the name Everett Miller you also think of Eric Daniels and Sally Fredericks.'

A murmur rippled through the audience.

'Their lives were snuffed out right here, less than half a mile from where we sit. A little more than twenty years ago, they ate their last meal, smiled their final smile. They breathed their last breath. Who knows what they might have achieved, or what they'd be doing now, if they hadn't attracted the attention of Everett Miller?' She paused, letting the emotion swell through the tent like she was conducting an orchestra.

'Tonight, we are going to honour one of those victims in particular. Sally Fredericks.'

I noticed there was a large screen behind Connie. Sally's face appeared on it.

'And we have a man who is going to tell us about her. The man who knew her better than anyone else.' She paused again. 'Ladies and gentlemen, please welcome to the stage Sally's widowed husband, Neal Fredericks.'

Neal walked on to the stage, his pink scalp shining beneath the lights. Connie gave him a hug while the audience applauded, then he shuffled up to the microphone. He held a sheet of paper in his hands and was clearly nervous. The applause died down and I wondered if the people here were disappointed. The victim's husband? The man Sally had been cheating on when she was killed? A lot of the audience shifted uncomfortably in their seats. *This* was the big surprise? Maybe he had some new information to share. Once again, I failed to understand why he, the cuckolded husband, would want to put himself through this.

He said something that got lost before it left the stage.

'Talk into the microphone,' yelled the grey-haired lady in front of me.

'Sorry.' His voice finally became audible. 'Is that better?'

'Yes, honey.'

'This isn't easy,' he said, clearing his throat. 'Coming to the place where my wife – where my darling Sally was killed. When it happened, I couldn't bring myself to visit this place. I didn't want to see it. And I can imagine what some of you must be thinking. It must have been extra hard knowing she was cheating.' He cleared his throat again. The crowd was hushed. 'I'm not gonna lie. It was difficult to cope with for a long time. To lose the person you love most in the world and then discover she was in the arms of another man when it happened . . . Yeah, it was hard.'

This was agonising to watch.

'But then I realised something. I was being selfish. Thinking only about myself. Of course, no man likes to think of his wife being made happy by another man, but wasn't her happiness the most important thing? Some people said if she hadn't been screwing around – pardon my French – she'd still be alive today. And yeah, maybe that's true. But I realised something else. To be able to mourn her, I needed to forgive her. Once I did that, I was able to miss my wife. The woman I'd hoped to have children with. This place took my Sally from me. But tonight I'm here to celebrate her life.'

There followed a slideshow of pictures of Sally and Neal, with him narrating, describing the photos, telling stories about their time together. There were photos of Sally holding her baby nephew. Pictures from their wedding day. At first it was awkward and fumbling, but after a few minutes Neal hit his stride. Soon he had the audience both eating out of his hand and crying into their Kleenex. It was weirdly moving – and effective. I realised what he was doing. Not only turning her into a flesh-and-blood woman in front of this audience of dark tourists, but reclaiming her. She wasn't Eric Daniels' lover. Nor was she Everett Miller's victim. She was Neal's wife and also her own person. All around me people sniffled, including the woman who'd mouthed the serial killers' names and the older lady who'd yelled at Neal to talk into the mic.

I watched Connie. She had a peculiar look on her face throughout Neal's talk. Almost smug. And I understood why this was such a big deal for her, why she and David had arranged this. True-crime podcasters like her were often criticised for fixating on the puzzle and glorifying the dark crimes they talked about, forgetting about the victims. I'd had the same prejudices myself. By inviting Neal along, she was forcing her audience to think about Sally and Eric and their families, and I guessed that was why he'd agreed to do it.

Neal finished talking, and in the silence I heard someone say, 'Dad.'

I looked around. It was Frankie, beckoning to me. She was near the exit. Her eyes were wide and she looked a little sick.

I stood up. The show was over and the people in the row behind me weren't so grumpy about pulling back their chairs so I could get by. I ran over to Frankie.

'What are you doing here?' I asked. 'I told you to stay at the cabin.'

She gave me a look of defiance. 'You said you were going to fetch Ryan but you didn't. So I came looking for you.'

'Frankie! What the hell?'

'It's fine. There are loads of people around.'

I sighed. The path to the exit had cleared a little, so I motioned for Frankie to leave the tent.

'Come on,' I said once we were outside. 'Let's get you back to the cabin. I've given up trying to get David and Connie to listen to me.'

'No. I need to show you something first.'

'Frankie, we should get back—'

'Dad! Listen to me!' She yelled it. 'Sorry, but just come with me. Let me show you.'

I followed her across the field, back down the path towards the barbecue. The music grew louder as we got closer. There was a small group of people standing behind where the food was being served. One of them was Greg, chatting to Vivian and another woman in a Hollow Falls polo. Beside Greg, with unhappy, sulky faces, stood two teenagers.

'That's them,' Frankie whispered. 'Buddy and Darlene.'

'What? Are you sure?'

'Of course I'm sure. They haven't spotted me but I've been following them.'

I waited.

'They've been here with Greg for the past five or ten minutes. I heard him introduce them to those women. Guess what he said?'

'What?'

'"Meet my kids".'

I stared at her, then turned back to look at Buddy and Darlene and Greg.

He was their dad.

'It must have been *him*,' Frankie whispered. 'The man in the crow mask. It was Greg.'

Chapter 30

Greg hadn't seen us staring at him. He was too busy chatting with Vivian and the other woman. Instinctively, I took a step towards him, but Frankie caught my arm.

'Dad,' she said. 'Maybe it's better if he doesn't know we know.'

I stopped. She was right. He was surrounded by people. If I marched up to him and accused him of creeping around the woods wearing a mask, of being involved in a rock-throwing attack on my daughter, he would act like I was crazy. It would *sound* crazy.

'I always thought there was something weird about him,' Frankie said. 'I told you, didn't I?'

I thought about what Frankie had seen, twice now. The crow, the goat and the fox. I had thought that perhaps the crow was Everett, but Greg – who hadn't been missing for two decades – was a far more likely candidate. What exactly were they up to? Was Greg involved in the teenagers' revenge plot against Frankie and Ryan? Was that what this was all about? Greg joining his children in taking vengeance against two kids who had bad-mouthed his hometown on social media?

It made little sense. I could understand a pair of teenagers doing that. But a grown man? One who was the manager of the local resort? Surely not.

There had to be something else going on.

Something connected to the murders?

I thought about the symbols painted in Eric Daniels' blood. The pagan symbols. Were Greg and his family pagans? Were the masks part of some sort of weird ritual?

Had Greg been involved in the murder of those teachers?

'Dad,' Frankie said. 'We should go. Let's take Ryan with us, go to the police.'

For a moment I was confused, still lost in my thoughts. *Tell them we think Greg might have been involved in a murder committed twenty years ago?* No, she meant the threats, the rock-throwing, the dead rabbit, the break-in that had killed Donna.

'Wait,' I said. I needed to think.

However crazy it seemed, there was something big here. Much bigger than what we knew Buddy and Darlene had done. I was sure of it. Before, I had intended to tell the police about what had happened with the teens, then leave and let them get on with it. But now . . . I felt like I was close to something. A revelation about this place and its twisted history.

'Dad,' Frankie prompted again. Greg was still chatting with Vivian. He seemed cheery and less sweaty than usual. Buddy and Darlene stood, sullen and bored, beside him.

What would the police say if I went to them with my new suspicions?

Greg was the manager here. That made him a respected member of the community. He could easily say that I was imagining everything or making it up. There was absolutely no evidence that Donna hadn't misplaced that bottle of pills herself. And without Ryan's photos, we had no proof that the masked figures existed.

Did we have anything? Any proof of wrongdoing at all? All we had were the Instagram messages, which could be retrieved by logging in to Frankie's Instagram account on any phone. They had been sent from anonymous accounts, but at least it was evidence of something. It might be enough to make the police talk to us.

'Do you remember the Wi-Fi password?' I said.

Frankie nodded. 'Hollow321. Capital H.'

It was the kind of weak password I would come up with. 'Great. Show me where you got a signal.'

It wasn't far; just on the other side of the reception building. We hid beside the dumpsters and I typed in the password. My phone didn't have much charge and it took a while to connect to the signal, but soon I was on.

I downloaded Instagram, which took far longer than it should have because of the poor broadband connection, then handed my phone to Frankie so she could log in. She fumbled the password then tried again, successfully.

'Oh, what?' she said.

She handed me the phone.

'They've all been deleted.'

'You're kidding.'

But she was right. Her inbox was empty.

'They must have found my phone when I dropped it, and unlocked it.'

'Is your passcode easy to guess?' I asked.

She frowned. 'It's my date of birth.'

Which I'd had to give when I booked this place, along with my own. Frankie looked crestfallen, like she'd done something very stupid. But I couldn't be angry with her. My passcode was my wedding anniversary. I'd been meaning to change it since the divorce but had never got round to it, even though it caused a flicker of pain every time I tapped it in.

We went back to near where Greg was standing, and just as we got there he started to move, heading in the direction of the unlit bonfire, Vivian and the other staff member following. Buddy and Darlene trailed behind.

They both turned their heads, looking back at us in tandem. Staring at me and Frankie. It sent a chill through me.

It was fully dark now and I realised Greg must be going to light the fire. I watched as people in red polo shirts moved through the crowd, directing people towards the spot on the shore where the bonfire had been built. Then the band finished the song they were playing and didn't resume another. A hush fell across the resort. At the same time, people who had been at the tent listening to Neal began to file back. I couldn't see David, Connie or Neal among them, and guessed they must still be at the tent.

'Dad,' said Frankie.

I was so deep in thought that I didn't hear her at first.

'*Dad.*'

'Sorry. What?'

Frankie nodded. There was a woman standing in front of us, smiling at me.

It was Nikki.

'Hey,' she said.

I blinked at her. She seemed completely different to earlier. She looked like she'd showered, washed her hair. She was wearing lipstick. And she was smiling. There was no denying it: she was beautiful. But this was all very disconcerting. It was as if our conversation earlier hadn't happened. As if she were a different person.

'What are you doing?' I asked.

'What do you mean? I didn't want to miss the party. Also, I thought I'd take your advice and spread the word about the bookstore.'

'But . . .'

'Hi, Frankie,' Nikki said. And that's when it started to make sense. She was putting on a show for Frankie. She didn't want to frighten her. But Nikki knew something. Something that had made her tell me we were in danger. Something connected to Greg? Something I could go to the police with?

I needed to talk to her alone. And from the way she was looking at me, I was sure she wanted to talk to me too.

I couldn't take her back to the cabin because it would be impossible to talk there without Frankie listening in. There was only one solution.

'Nikki, can you wait here? I'm going to walk Frankie back to our cabin. Then I'll be right back.'

'Sure.'

'Frankie, come on.'

She trotted beside me. 'What are you doing? What's going on?'

'I think Nikki might know something about Greg. Everyone knows everyone around here. That's what they keep telling me. Maybe she'll even come to the police with us.'

'What, and you don't want me there when you talk to her?'

'Frankie . . .'

'Fine. Whatever.'

We reached the cabin. 'You'll be safe here,' I said. 'Greg and the twins are by the bonfire. I'll keep an eye on them. Lock the doors and windows and wait for me. I won't be long. I promise.'

I hurried back along the path.

As I approached the spot where I'd left Nikki, I heard a whoop of excitement from down by the bonfire. They were about to light it. Greg was standing there with a flaming torch in his hand, a large crowd gathered before him. With the flames illuminating his face he looked very different. Powerful. Sinister. I could just about make out Buddy and Darlene among the throng.

'Let's find somewhere to talk,' I said when I reached Nikki. The smile she'd worn in front of Frankie had vanished.

Now, she looked afraid, staring at the ground. People jostled us, continuing to flow down towards where the bonfire was lit. The air smelled of smoke and cooking flesh. A flake of ash landed on Nikki's face and she wiped it away with the back of her hand. It left behind a grey mark, like she'd been kissed by Death.

I took a step closer to her. I could feel heat coming off her body. 'Nikki, do you really like me?'

'What?'

'I asked if you really like me. Because I like you and I need you to help me before . . . before somebody else dies. You said it yourself. My daughter and I are in danger. It's even worse now. Buddy and Darlene saw Frankie and me looking at them. They know we've figured out that Greg is their father. They also think that Ryan might have photos of them.'

'Oh God.'

'I need you to tell me what you know about Greg.'

'What kind of thing?' She had gone completely pale, her eyes darting about. I thought she might throw up.

'Like, could he have been involved in the murders.'

I could see the conflict raging behind her eyes. Then, before she could reply, a great cheer came from down by the lake. The bonfire was ablaze. Flames danced and licked at the air and smoke poured towards the stars, blotting out a section of the sky. Greg stood before the fire, a silhouette, his arms raised. He appeared to be making a speech, though I couldn't make out what he was saying.

'Okay,' she said.

'Thank you.'

'But first . . . first, I'm going to need a drink.'

Chapter 31

Frankie sat on her bed beside her packed suitcase. It was quiet here, the voices and music from the bonfire muted.

She was worried about Ryan. She hadn't seen him at the tent or anywhere around the resort. And her dad had said Ryan hadn't answered when he'd knocked on the Butlers' cabin door.

Was he in the cabin now, hiding? Too afraid to come out?

She desperately wanted to tell him what she'd found out, about Greg being the twins' dad. She also wanted to make sure he was okay. Surely it would be better if they were together. It would be safer.

Her dad was taking ages. What exactly did he want to talk to that Nikki woman – who he clearly fancied – about, that she wasn't allowed to overhear? Yet again, he was treating her like a little girl. He and her mum had been exactly the same when they were going through their break-up, always hiding away, talking in low voices, not asking her what she thought.

She made a decision.

She was going to go and get Ryan. Buddy, Darlene and Greg were by the bonfire. Her dad had said he'd keep an eye on them. Her urge to check that Ryan was okay overrode her fear.

She took a knife from the block in the kitchen – just in case – then grabbed the keys and locked the door behind her. The band had started up again and smoke rose above the tree line. The lights were out in all the cabins. Everyone else was down by the lake, having fun. But Frankie didn't care about that. All she cared about was the following, which she could see playing out before her like a movie she'd seen before: finding Ryan and telling him everything; waiting at the cabin with Ryan till her dad came back; then getting the hell out of there.

She could picture them driving out of Hollow Falls. Frankie would turn and show the rear window her middle finger, and her dad would laugh and put some rubbish music on. Then the end credits would roll.

She couldn't wait to get to that moment.

She reached the Butlers' cabin and knocked on the door. The lights were off. The windows were black, opaque. Now she was outside, Frankie had a horrible bubbling sensation in her belly. Maybe he *had* gone out. She didn't believe that Ryan would be asleep at this time, or sitting in there in the dark. Unless he was afraid. Too afraid to open the door.

'Ryan,' she called. 'It's Frankie. I need to know if you're all right.'

She banged on the door. No response. No sound from inside.

I should go back and wait for Dad, she thought.

But what if something had happened to Ryan?

What if he was hurt? What if, before going to find their dad, Buddy or Darlene had come looking for Ryan's phone? What if they'd got in and—

And what?

Killed him.

She reminded herself that the twins were by the bonfire now and went round to the back of the cabin, to where she knew Ryan's room was. She rapped on the window, then put her face right up to the glass. She was almost convinced something awful had happened to him. That he was dead. She had only known him a few days but she couldn't bear it. Last night, she had hated him. Never wanted to see him again. But after what had happened earlier, she was sure they would be bonded forever. They would keep in touch by WhatsApp and FaceTime, and when they were older they would meet up and he would show her California, take her surfing, teach her to parkour. Introduce her to his boyfriend, Glen, and give her advice about the boys she liked. But now, if he was dead, none of that would happen. All she would have was a hole in her life where Ryan ought to be. A sadder future.

She went back to the front of the cabin and peered down the path. There was still no sign of her dad. Should she go back, find him, look for David and Connie and beg them to come back here and open the cabin? *Now* she felt paralysed by indecision.

She went up on to the deck and put her face to the front window.

The room was dark. But she could see a darker shape on the floor.

She almost cried out.

It was a body.

Chapter 32

I followed Nikki to the bar, which had been set up close to the picnic tables. We stood in line, silent. All around us, people were having fun, drinking, laughing, sprawling on the grass or dancing to the music.

Nikki asked for a large glass of wine and, needing something to calm my own nerves, I bought myself a bottle of beer. We took the drinks over to an empty patch of grass and sat on the ground. Even though we were a fair way from the fire, its heat touched my face and the flames flickered in Nikki's eyes as she spoke. I could still make out Greg in the distance, and was sure his offspring must be with him.

'Okay,' Nikki said. 'Greg.' She heaved a sigh. 'He and I were friends when we were kids. We were at the same school, except we didn't become friends there. It was outside the classroom . . .'

She shook her head like she was struggling to organise her thoughts.

'I was a total loser back then. I mean, even more than I am now.' She gave a self-deprecating laugh. 'A loser and a loner. None of the other girls in my class liked me at all. The popular girls thought I was weird because I wasn't into all the bullshit they were into. I was, like, so introverted it was unreal. I wasn't interested in clothes or boys or sleepovers. All I cared about was reading and animals.'

'A bit like Frankie.'

'Maybe. Though Frankie's way cooler than I ever was. She's much more of a city girl. I was a total country bumpkin. I just wanted to hang out in the woods. I was building camps and climbing trees way past the age when you're supposed to stop being into that shit.' She gestured around us. 'This is where I used to hang. And it's where I met Abigail.'

'Abigail?'

'Yep. A local hippie woman. Actually, she wasn't from around here originally. She married a guy from Penance, Logan his name was, but she never really assimilated. The first time I met her, she was collecting mushrooms.'

'What, magic mushrooms?'

She laughed. 'Ha, no. Regular mushrooms. She was on her hands and knees, wearing this long skirt that was just dragging in the mud, all this wild blonde hair around her face. I'd never seen a grown woman – she was in her forties – do anything like that before, and I was entranced. When she saw me watching her I nearly ran off but she called me over. Showed me what she was picking. How to tell the poisonous fungi apart from the edible ones. And I guess that's when we became . . . well, "friends" isn't really the word. It was more like guru and student. I started meeting her after school most days, and she'd show me stuff, teach me. I worshipped her. My mom and dad were distant, working all the time, kinda strict. They didn't get me. But Abigail really did. Said I reminded her of herself when she was younger. But then, after a little while, it wasn't just me and her any more. It turned out Abigail enjoyed collecting misfits and strays.'

Now I saw where this was going. 'Including Greg?'

'Yep. He was another outcast like me. A boy with no friends. He became her student too. Her acolyte, I guess you could call it. He loved Abigail as much as I did.'

'Okay. But how does this connect to the murders? And to what's happening now?'

She took a sip from her drink. 'This is where it gets a little weird. Are you ready for this?'

'I think my time here has prepared me for weird.'

A couple walked past us, hand in hand, giggling like they'd just been doing something naughty in the woods. They probably had. Nikki waited till they were out of earshot.

'Much of what Abigail taught us came from this book that she'd got from some garage sale. It was called *A Sacred Space: The Secret History of the Hollows*. I can remember it like I can remember what I had for breakfast this morning. It was brown, with an old black-and-white photo on the cover, of a woman wearing this long white robe and standing in the woods. The pages were all stained a kind of nicotine yellow and it stank like an ashtray. But there was something so cool about it, especially the way Abigail taught it to us, like it was a holy text or something.'

She took a pack of Marlboros out of her pocket and lit up. 'Want one?'

'I'm good.' I was impatient for her to tell me how this all connected. 'What was in the book?'

Now she was into the flow of her story she seemed less nervous. 'It was about the history of this area. Penance was founded in the early eighteen-hundreds by a pastor named George Levett. He built the church where most people here still worship. Ask anyone in Penance about George Levett and they'll be able to tell you the official version of his biography. That he and his wife and their dozen children moved here from a logging town further south and founded the community. He used to carry out baptisms right here, by the lake.' She pointed towards the water.

I tried not to let my impatience show.

'According to the book, there was a hidden side to George Levett. A secret side. He had a deep love of nature. A respect for it. I guess you could call him an early environmentalist. On top of that, he had respect for the Native Americans the Europeans had stolen this land from. There were actually one or two Native Americans within the community. I guess you know that the settlers here tried their hardest to convert the indigenous people to Christianity? That included the Baptists. According to the book, Levett brought a Native American woman into his flock. They became friends. And she told him how all this was sacred ground.'

I must have looked dubious because she said, 'I'm not talking about haunted burial grounds and all that horror-movie stuff. It's about the Hollows being a sacred space. Hallowed ground. They believed in this essential harmony between people and nature. It's called animism. The belief that humans, plants, animals, even mountains and lakes and trees, have a spirit. And it's all part of the greater soul of the universe.'

'Are you saying that Levett came to believe in that too? Animism?'

'No. He was a Christian pastor. But he respected that belief. And he made it part of his mission to protect these woods and this lake. It's something that was handed down through the generations. Even though there would've been money in it, the people of Penance resisted attempts to log the area. Later, they fought off building factories that might've polluted the lake.'

'That's . . . great. But I still don't understand how that connects to Greg and all the stuff that's been going on.'

'Bear with me. I want you to understand that we were under Abigail's spell. We lived in a shitty town. Everyone at school hated

214

us. Our parents were mostly absent. We thought Penance was the worst place on earth, a nothing place in the woods that had just gone to hell because no one cared about it. That was our hometown. That was *us*, in a way. But then this book, reading about this area being sacred to the Native Americans and Levett honouring that and the townsfolk buying into it, at least for a few generations, treating the Hollows as a special place – undeveloped and unspoiled – it really got to us. It made us feel like the place where we lived wasn't a total shithole. That it was special and, by extension, so were we. And when Abigail died—'

'She died?'

Nikki stared at the ground like she was still deeply affected by the loss. 'Lung cancer. It was awful . . . She was too young, and we'd only known her for, like, a year. But this is the weird part – don't say I didn't warn you – after she died we didn't believe she'd gone.'

A beat passed before I spoke.

'You mean you thought her ghost was still around?'

'Her spirit. She loved the Hollows so much that, before she went, she told us she was never going to leave. And she didn't. Or so I believed at the time. I mean, *I* never saw her, but I felt her. I really thought she was still here. And that made this place even more sacred. It was Abigail's home. Her eternal home.'

'So you believe in all that stuff?'

She stubbed out her cigarette and put the butt in the box. 'I did. That's what's important. *We* did. And animism isn't some kooky belief, Tom. Most religions and belief systems around the world are based around this idea of nature spirits. Go to Japan, South East Asia, Africa . . . Look at Buddhism or Shinto or Hinduism. It's actually rarer for human beings to believe in just one God. And we were all about rejecting what society wanted us to believe. It was much more interesting to believe in this stuff. For me, it was fun, kind of cool.'

'I get that,' I said. I was wrapped up in the story but still aware that I needed her to hurry up so I could get back to Frankie. I motioned for Nikki to continue.

'So yeah, we believed Abigail's spirit was still here, in the Hollows. And we became obsessed with trying to protect it for her, because it was outrageous what was going on. The woods were full of garbage. People would party out here and just trash the place. There was a lot of hunting going on – in season, out of season. Pretty much a bloodbath. People dumped all sorts of crap in the woods. And to us, the biggest culprit was the campground and the people who stayed there. Whenever we ran into someone from the campground, dropping trash or whatever, we would tell them off, not that it did any good.'

I sat up straighter. A passage from Jake Robineaux's book had come back to me. Something about Jake and Mary-Ellen sneaking off for a cigarette and being confronted by some local kids.

'That was you?' I asked. 'In Jake's book?'

'Huh. Yeah.'

Something niggled. 'Hold on, I'm sure Jake wrote that he was told off by a girl and two boys. Who was the other one? Everett?' Everett Miller had only been a few years older than Nikki and Greg at the time. Surely it had to be him.

'Let me finish,' Nikki said. 'We tried to start a local campaign, to get the other kids at school and their parents interested in making the Hollows a protected area, but nobody wanted to know. The campground brought in a decent amount of money, and money always wins, right? Look at this place. Hollow Falls.'

She said it with contempt.

'No one cared. And that's when we decided to take things into our own hands.'

Now I understood. 'All the pranks, the weird goings-on at the campground. That was you?'

216

There was, I was surprised to see, a hint of pride in her eyes. Defiance, perhaps. 'We thought we could scare them off. Make them think the place was haunted. We'd sneak on to the campground and pull up tent pegs, move stuff around, or creep around at night so the kids would see shadows moving past their tents. We wanted to really scare the crap out of them.'

I shook my head.

'What? We never caused any real damage.'

'You took stuff, though. Peed in people's sleeping bags.'

She winced. 'That wasn't me. And it was towards the end, when we were getting desperate, starting to realise it wasn't working. That no matter what we did, the campers weren't going away.'

She lit another cigarette. She had finished her wine. I would have offered to get her another but I didn't want her to stop talking.

'And what happened when you realised that?' I asked.

She didn't answer straight away. She tapped ash on to the grass, flinching as she did so, as if she felt guilty about soiling the ground. This hallowed ground.

'That's where it all went wrong.'

Chapter 33

Frankie stared at the figure on the floor of the cabin. Ryan, oh Ryan. Was this all her fault? She should have insisted earlier that her dad bring him over to their cabin. Or maybe he was already dead at that point.

Maybe if they'd been together, they'd both be dead.

'I'm sorry,' she whispered, her breath fogging the glass. 'I'm so—'

The figure on the floor moved.

Frankie let out a scream. And the figure on the floor sat up and turned towards her, then stood, went to the wall and switched on the light.

She banged on the glass. 'Ryan. Let me in.'

He came to the door and opened it and she threw her arms around him. 'Oh my God, I thought you were dead. What were you doing?'

'I was listening to music.'

He held out a hand to show her a pair of AirPods. Wireless headphones.

'Why the hell were you lying on the floor?'

He shrugged. 'I always do that. Do you want to come in?'

She wanted to punch him.

'Yes. I mean, no. I have loads to tell you. You'll never guess who Buddy and Darlene's dad is.'

'Satan?'

It wasn't that funny, but she was so relieved he was alive she laughed anyway.

'It's Greg.'

'What? You're kidding.'

'No, I'm not. And I'm pretty sure it was him wearing the crow mask earlier. And my dad and me tried to retrieve my messages on Instagram so we'd have something to show the police – because you actually deleted those photos – and my whole inbox has been wiped.'

'Shit.'

'Yeah, shit. And now my dad's talking to that woman from the bookstore and trying to find out more about Greg before he goes to the police.' She glanced over her shoulder, hoping to see her dad coming up the path, but there was still no sign of him. 'So yeah, I do want to come in because I think it would be safer if we were together, you and me, but Dad is going to expect to find me at our cabin, so . . .'

'You want me to come over there.'

'Yeah. Is that okay?'

'Of course. Let me just grab my phone and a jacket. It's gotten cold out here.'

He went back inside and reappeared a minute later with a jacket on. Ryan locked the door of his cabin and they walked across to hers.

'We're going to have so much to tell our friends about when we get back to civilisation,' Ryan said.

'I know, right.' She paused. She didn't want to sound needy. 'Do you think we'll stay friends when this is all over?'

'Yeah, of course. You're going to come to California to learn how to surf, remember?'

She smiled.

'I'm so glad you're not dead,' she said, and they both laughed.

'Me too.'

Frankie opened the front door and they went inside.

Buddy was sitting on the couch facing them, his goat mask in his lap.

Frankie and Ryan saw him at the same time. She grabbed Ryan's arm and let out a little gasp. Ryan gasped too, and they both scrambled to turn and get the hell out of there.

But there was nowhere to go. Darlene – who had been standing beside the door – stepped into their path, shutting the door in their faces.

Frankie backed away from her, realising the kitchen knife she was still carrying would be of no use whatsoever.

Because Darlene was holding a gun.

Chapter 34

'So what did you do?' I asked Nikki. 'How did you step things up?'

She didn't reply. She lit yet another cigarette and I saw that her hands were shaking.

'I never thought this would come out,' she said. 'Not . . . not after all this time.'

She seemed nervy again now. It was clear that it was hurting her. That this had weighed heavily on her for a long time.

'What are you going to do with this information?' she asked. 'Because I'm scared, Tom. Scared of what's going to happen to me.'

I liked her. I really did. But I wasn't a priest listening to a confession. I couldn't absolve her of her sins, and I couldn't stay quiet if she had done something terrible.

'It depends what you did,' I said. I glanced around, ensuring nobody could overhear. We were concealed by shadows on the edge of the lake. The closest people were twenty metres away. 'Whatever it was . . . you were a kid.'

She sucked on her cigarette. 'That's what I've been telling myself for twenty years. I was a kid. A dumb kid. But it doesn't mean I don't deserve to be punished.' She swallowed and coughed, like she was choking on the words. 'I've had to live with myself ever since.' With what seemed like an enormous effort, she pulled herself straight. 'But maybe it's time it all came out. You know, I've been scared of being punished for a long time. But this secret . . . it's like a tumour, you know? I've been letting it grow inside me. Maybe it's time to cut it out and face the consequences.'

'Tell me what happened,' I said.

She met my eye and seemed to make a decision. 'I will. And I can give you evidence. You're going to need it. Greg's a highly valued and respected member of this community. His family has lived around here for generations. And the tale itself, even though it's the truth . . . Well, without proof I think they might laugh you out of the police station.'

I took this in. 'So you do have evidence?'

She paused. 'Yeah. It's at the bookstore. If you come with me now, I'll show you.'

I hesitated. 'I need to check on Frankie first.'

'Of course.' She stood up. 'Come on, I'll show you a shortcut.'

She began to walk away from the bonfire, in the direction of the area where I'd found Frankie and Ryan earlier.

'Are you sure this is a shortcut?'

'Yeah. I know these woods a lot better than you, Tom.'

We walked up a slope on to higher ground. Nikki stopped for a moment and looked towards the lake. 'That's where we used to have our meetings. Our secret cove.'

'The two of you? Wait – the three of you. You mentioned some-one else.'

'Goat, Fox and Crow,' she said. Of course. 'Crow got the masks for us. I think some guy his mom was dating worked in a factory that manufactured Halloween stuff. We loved them. We thought they represented our spirit animals.'

'Which one were you?' I asked, although I was sure I already knew the answer.

'Fox.'

222

It was so dark that I was finding it hard to follow the path. Nikki, however, was like a real fox, walking confidently, as if she had perfect night vision. As long as I stayed close behind her, I wouldn't lose my way.

'And Greg was Crow?'

She didn't reply.

'Who was the third person?' I asked for the second time. 'Was it Everett?'

I thought she was going to tell me but she said, 'I'll show you when we get to the bookstore. After you've checked on Frankie.'

'Show me?'

But she didn't reply.

'You and Greg,' I asked. 'Were you an item?'

She laughed at that. To be honest, she sounded a little hysterical, or on the edge of it anyway. 'An item? No. Not Greg.'

'But you and . . . Goat?'

She didn't reply.

'What about Greg now?' I asked. 'What's his family situation? I don't remember noticing a wedding ring on his hand.'

'That's because his wife left when the twins were toddlers.'

'Really?'

'Yeah. She was nice. A little too meek for me, but sweet. She went to school with us too. Greg started dating her when they were both twenty-one. Six months later they were getting married.'

'Because she was pregnant?'

'Yep. Have I mentioned how old-fashioned it is around here? Then she was gone, shortly after Buddy and Darlene turned two. I heard she went to Chicago. Maybe Seattle. Nobody's sure. She doesn't have any contact with Greg or the kids as far as I know.'

I couldn't understand that. I lived thousands of miles from my daughter, but the idea of not having her in my life was incomprehensible.

'Why did she leave?' I asked.

Nikki stopped walking for a moment. She looked like she was trying to decide whether to tell me.

'She said they were evil.'

'The twins?'

But she walked on without saying another word.

'Is it much further?' I asked, scrambling to keep up. I had no idea where we were. I couldn't see any cabins.

'No. We need to cut through here.'

She led me through a thicket of trees. The sounds from the resort fell away so I could no longer hear the band. I was starting to regret my decision to follow Nikki and wondered if I should go back the way I'd come, to follow the path I knew. But I wasn't even sure where we were, and I'd come this far already.

We crossed a path that led east to west.

'This feels familiar,' I said. It was hard to tell in the darkness but I thought we were on the other side of the resort, near the clearing with the flat stone.

I could hear wind chimes, faint, somewhere in the distance, deep inside the trees.

Here in the woods, the trees didn't feel like the benevolent, beautiful spirits that Nikki and Greg and Abigail had loved so much. They seemed hostile, as if they were stretching out their branches and trying to block us from where we were going. Their silhouettes were twisted, grotesque, like shadow puppets in a surrealist nightmare. And the distant wind chimes weren't light or tinkly or melodious. They sounded discordant, jarring. Like the forest was laughing at us.

Nikki picked up the pace, striding forward determinedly. She had cast off her nervousness and seemed resigned to whatever fate awaited her.

And then, with little warning, we were out of the woods. I felt like I'd stumbled out of a maze, disoriented and confused, but I knew where I was. We were indeed near the flat stone, and the path led back towards the cabins.

Soon, we passed the Butlers' cabin and reached mine.

I went to walk up the steps but Nikki put out an arm to stop me. Her mood had changed again. She was trembling and had gone pale. The ash smudge was still on her cheek. I stared at it for a second. Then, to my great surprise, she took a step towards me, took hold of both of my arms and kissed me.

We broke apart. 'What—' I started to say, but she put a finger to my lips.

'I wanted to do it,' she said. 'While I still had the chance.'

I didn't like where this was going. There was a voice in my head telling me to get out. But I had to ask. 'What do you mean?'

'You need to go inside, Tom.'

My entire body had gone cold.

'What are you talking about?'

She wouldn't meet my eye. She turned away. She was shaking. Was she crying?

'I'm so sorry,' she said.

Chapter 35

They walked in a kind of diamond shape. Buddy at the front, then Frankie and Ryan side by side, with Darlene behind, gripping the forbidding-looking black handgun.

'Follow me and don't say a word,' said Buddy.

'We will kill you,' said Darlene.

'Bury you alive,' said Buddy, clearly delighted by the idea.

'They say it's one of the worst ways to go,' his sister said. She sounded like she was reading from the world's dullest textbook, one she was being forced to read aloud in class. 'Fighting for breath. Mouth packed with dirt. Panicking. Gasping. Knowing there's no way out.'

'We won't bury you together, either,' said Buddy. 'You'll be all alone.'

'You're freaks. Psychopaths.' Ryan looked like he wanted to spit in their faces.

'I said shut up,' said Buddy. 'I don't want you to speak again until you meet Crow.'

Frankie was glad of the silence. Their voices were making her sick and she was scared, so scared. She reached out and found Ryan's hand, squeezing it. She could hear wind chimes close by again, and was sure they were near the clearing where she had got lost last night. But there was no Nikki here to save her now.

Buddy had a flashlight that illuminated the path – the spidery, black patterns of the branches connecting directly with some primal part of Frankie's brain. Something moved near her feet and she jumped backwards, letting go of Ryan's hand.

'Get a grip,' hissed Darlene.

They reached the clearing. The wind chimes were louder now. It sounded like the forest was laughing at them.

'We're going to be okay,' Ryan whispered to her.

Darlene laughed and told him to shut his mouth.

They reached the other side of the clearing. The wind chimes were clear and close. Buddy stopped and scanned the dense vegetation with his flashlight, searching for something. Then he pulled aside a low branch to reveal an overgrown path.

'Follow me,' he said. 'Don't do anything stupid.'

Branches reached out to claw at her as they pushed their way through, thorns catching on her clothes, something clinging to her hair. Frankie sucked in a breath as Buddy bent another branch out of their way. And then they reached the end of the path.

The flashlight revealed a cabin, the wood rotten and covered with what looked like moss, as if it had some terrible skin disease. Wind chimes hung from the porch roof, twisting slowly in the gentle breeze. The front windows were broken, most of the glass fallen away. The front steps up to the porch had rotted too.

The cabin was surrounded on all sides by trees. Abandoned. Long-forgotten. Protected by the woods. Looking up at it, Frankie found herself swaying and she had the first sharp stirrings of a headache. The diseased facade of the cabin appeared to shift, as if it were alive.

She couldn't take it any more. She turned and threw herself at Darlene, hitting her with her shoulder, convinced she would hear a gunshot at any moment. But that would be better, wouldn't it, than being taken to the man they called Crow – presumably their

227

dad? Better than being buried alive, dirt in her mouth and up her nose, centipedes and ants crawling all over her, feeding on her . . .

Darlene had hit the floor and Frankie was running, straight into a wall of vegetation. Where was the path? She tore at branches, came away with handfuls of leaves, but there was no gap, nowhere to go.

She was yanked backwards by her hair and Darlene stuck the gun in her face.

'I'm going to kill you,' Darlene hissed, and Frankie braced herself. This was it.

'What the fuck is going on?'

Darlene lowered the gun and Frankie turned.

There was a man standing on the porch. It was so dark she could hardly see him, though she could just about make out the shape of his mask. She knew it had to be Greg.

'Take them inside,' he said. 'Now.'

The path to the cabin was almost blocked by a tree that looked like it had fallen a long time ago. Buddy and Darlene forced them to clamber over it, then followed. The man – Crow, Greg – had vanished, presumably inside the cabin.

The twins made Frankie and Ryan walk up the porch steps.

'Careful,' Buddy said. 'Keep to the left.'

She did as he said, clinging to the handrail. She reached the top of the stairs and staggered.

'For God's sake,' said Buddy. 'Stay on your feet.'

Frankie wiped her brow. Her face felt wet and her sweat was cold and thick.

The front door stood open and darkness spilled from within. She didn't want to go inside. She really didn't want to go inside. But her legs were carrying her forward, Ryan holding her hand again, and Darlene was behind her with the gun. She had no choice.

The front door opened straight into what must have been the living room. In the dim light, she could make out a sofa and an armchair. A dresser in the corner with a photograph propped on a shelf and, what were they – candles? Piles of rubbish on the floor and the smell of something sweet and rotten. It was noticeably colder in here too, like summer hadn't reached inside this place.

She heard the front door shut behind her.

All she could hear now was her own breathing.

'Take them to the basement,' said Crow. She could see his mask properly now. He stood in the doorway on the other side of the room; a doorway that led deeper into the house. With his mask, he looked grotesque – a demon. Something otherworldly. Something from another time, when the world was ruled by super-stition. When people believed in dark gods.

Buddy grabbed hold of Frankie's arm and tried to pull her further into the room. She resisted. Not the basement. She didn't want to be taken to the basement. She stamped on Buddy's foot and he cried out.

'Jesus,' said the man. 'I'll do it.'

He moved towards her. She could smell him, the sour-sweet-ness of body odour, and he took hold of her arm, his grip hard, digging into her bicep. He was strong. He dragged her towards the doorway. Towards the basement. Behind her, she heard Darlene hiss to Ryan, 'Follow.'

The crow-man – surely Greg – pulled her through the doorway into a room that was even darker.

He let go. She couldn't see anything.

And then he turned on a flashlight and reached down to grasp something at his feet.

Lifted a hatch in the floor.

She backed away. 'No, please, no.' But Buddy was behind her, and he took hold of her, stopped her from getting away.

The man got up and turned towards her. She could see the whites of his eyes through the holes in the mask.

'Do it,' he said, his voice muffled by the rubber mask.

Buddy shoved her.

She fell through the hole in the floor.

PART THREE

Chapter 36

I ran up the front steps of our cabin, fumbled for my keys, dropped them. I finally got the door open and pushed it so it banged against the inside wall. Behind me, Nikki melted away into the darkness.

I went inside. 'Frankie?' I called.

I ran into her bedroom, then my bedroom, the bathroom. I stood in the living area and looked around, stupidly, hopelessly, mind racing and whirling. Where was she?

Why had Nikki said she was sorry?

Sorry for what?

And then I saw it, on the couch. A white envelope.

I approached it tentatively, as if it were a bomb, or like it might be filled with anthrax, and opened it. Inside was a single sheet of paper, folded in half. A note, written in a lurching scrawl.

Frankie is safe.

Do not call the police.

Do not talk to anyone.

Ignore these instructions and you'll never find her body.

More instructions tomorrow.

I read the note three times, ten times. I turned the paper over, searching for more words, but there were none.

I think I was in shock, unable to take all this in. Oh God, why had I left Frankie on her own? Why had I trusted Nikki? I had told Frankie to lock the door, but then it struck me: Greg had keys to all the cabins. That was how Buddy and Darlene had got into Donna and Tamara's. They must have let themselves into my cabin and waited for Frankie. Why hadn't I thought about that before?

But even as I tormented myself with regret, I realised something else. Something more important. This was no time to go to pieces. Frankie needed me. I had to stay strong. Strong and calm.

Which wasn't easy.

You'll never find her body.

Somebody banged on the door and I almost hit the ceiling. *Nikki?*

Then a male voice.

'Tom? Are you there?'

I rushed to the door and opened it. It was David.

'Oh, hi man,' he said. 'Is Ryan in there?'

I shook my head.

'Huh.' He turned to look back at his cabin. I could see Connie on the porch, with someone else beside her. Neal Fredericks, I realised. A few people were walking along the path, heading home from the party. Most of them looked happy and drunk. I was finding it hard to remember what happiness felt like. I wanted to be able to rewind time to the point where I had left Frankie alone here.

'Is he not in your cabin?' I asked.

'No. Can you ask Frankie if she's seen him?'

234

'She's not here.' I said it without thinking.

'Oh.' I could see the thoughts running through his head. Like he was trying to decide how worried he should be.

Really fucking worried, I wanted to tell him. *Terrified*.

Did the person who had Frankie have Ryan too? My first instinct was that they must be together, but had David and Connie not received a note like mine? Ryan hadn't been in their cabin earlier, when I'd knocked.

'Is he not there?' Connie called.

'No,' David called back. He returned his attention to me. 'What's that?' he asked.

'Huh?'

'In your hand.'

I realised I was still holding the note.

Do not talk to anyone. The last word had been underlined.

'It's nothing,' I said. Could I act any more suspicious? 'Just some notes for an article I'm writing.'

'Ah. Okay. So . . . any idea where they might be?'

As he asked this, Connie came down the steps from their cabin and walked over to us. She was leaning heavily on her stick like she was in considerable pain. When she reached us, David said, 'Tom hasn't seen Ryan, and Frankie's not here either.'

'You think they've gone off together?' Connie said, though I wasn't sure if she was addressing me or her husband.

'They must have,' said David. He seemed to find this amusing. 'That's my boy.'

Did he not know that his son was gay? Didn't Connie know either? It wasn't my place, right now or ever, to tell them.

Connie checked her watch. 'It's just past eleven.' She seemed far more worried than David. 'He knows he should be back by now.'

'I guess they lost track of time,' David said.

Connie looked up at me. 'What about Frankie? I assume she has a curfew?'

'Yes . . .' My mind was racing like I was playing a game of speed chess, trying to figure out my best moves. But there was something I badly needed to know. 'Are you sure he didn't leave you a note?'

They looked at each other. 'I don't think so,' said Connie.

'Why, did Frankie leave you a note?' He looked directly at the piece of paper in my hand.

'No,' I said.

'Maybe I should go check.' Connie made her way back over to her cabin. If whoever had Frankie – and I only had one suspect – had left the Butlers a note too, it would make my life a little easier. We would be in this together. I was scared they might ignore the instructions and go straight to the police, but at least I'd be able to be open with them.

David and Connie headed back towards their cabin. I hesitated. What if the person who'd left the note was watching? I peered into the trees opposite.

'Are you coming?' David asked over his shoulder.

The note had told me to wait for instructions tomorrow, but hadn't expressly told me to stay in the cabin until then. And I'd be able to see my cabin from the Butlers', anyway. I could run back over if someone came with word for me earlier than promised. But what if I was being watched, and Greg – surely it was Greg – thought I had already told the Butlers what was happening? It was impossible to think straight but I needed to know if the Butlers had received a note too. I hurried across.

I had tucked the folded note in my front pocket, afraid David would ask me about it again. I nodded hello to Neal, who was sitting at the table on the front deck, a tumbler of what looked like whisky in front of him. There was an electrical charge coming off him, presumably the after-effect of being onstage, his system still awash with adrenaline, but when he spoke, his voice was bland, betraying none of the excitement his body radiated.

'Kids, huh?' he said. 'I'm glad Sally and I never had any.'

I made a non-committal noise – I didn't need to hear this guy talk at all, much less about his dead wife – and then Connie came back outside. 'Nope. No note.' She looked properly scared now. Her eyes glistened and she wiped at them with the back of her hand.

'I'm gonna kill him,' David said. 'Making us worry like this.'

'They're teenagers,' said Neal. 'They think they're grown up and don't—'

The look Connie gave him made him shut his mouth, and he raised his hands apologetically.

'We need to search for him,' she said.

'Both of them,' said David, looking at me, and I had no choice but to nod.

'When did you last see Frankie?' Connie asked.

I decided there was no harm in being honest about this. As long as I didn't say anything else. 'She came and found me while Neal was giving his talk. Then I walked her back to our cabin before popping out again.'

'What time was that?'

I had lost track. 'Just before ten, I think. Maybe nine thirty.'

They didn't know what had happened that afternoon with Buddy and Darlene. I had been trying to talk to David earlier but he hadn't stopped to listen. Did they know anything at all about what had been going on this week? Were they aware their son had upset the locals with his Instagram post? I didn't think so, and they certainly wouldn't know about the masked people in the woods. Wouldn't know that I was sure one of them, the man in the crow mask, was Greg. This explained, I realised, why Greg, or his children, had left a note only for me. I was the only one who had some idea of what was going on. The only person who would suspect Greg and his kids of being responsible for Frankie and Ryan's disappearance, who could damage Greg's plan – whatever the hell it was – by going to the police.

'You seem really freaking agitated,' David said to me.

'Huh?' I snapped out of my thoughts. They were all staring at me. 'I *am* agitated.' I turned away from them, sure they would be able to see that I was hiding something. The note burned in my pocket.

'I'm going to look for them,' David said.

'I'll help,' said Neal, hauling himself to his feet with a grunt of effort, like he had bad knees.

'Connie,' David said. 'You stay here, in case they come back.'

'Listen,' I said. 'Why don't you two search the resort, and I'll go check the woods.'

'Maybe I should come with you, Tom,' said David. 'It's better if two of us look in the woods between here and Penance.'

I shook my head. 'No. Honestly. You guys search the resort. The tennis courts, the playground, down by the lake . . . Look behind reception too. They go there sometimes to use the Wi-Fi.'

'I didn't know that,' said Connie.

'Frankie told me earlier. And I'll meet you back here in an hour, okay?'

'You sure you don't want to call the police now?' said Neal.

'No.' I probably said it too effusively. 'I mean, if they've just snuck off to . . . do whatever teenagers do, we don't want to waste police time, do we?'

'I agree,' said David. It seemed to me that he was convinced his son was doing the kind of thing David had done when he was fifteen. Connie was more concerned. Maybe she knew about Ryan's sexuality but was reluctant to tell her husband, at least not yet. And

David was pretending to be worried for his wife's sake. There were so many layers of deceit here that it was hard to keep up.

'Do you have a flashlight I can borrow?' I asked. 'The woods are dark.'

'Sure.' David fetched me one.

'All right,' I said. 'I'll see you back here in an hour.'

They headed off towards the centre of the resort, and I went back over to lock up my cabin. I leaned against the door and took a few deep breaths, looking at the spot where Nikki had kissed me.

She had delayed my return to the cabin so Greg could take Frankie – and, presumably, Ryan too. The sickening thing was that she had tried to warn me. Even tonight, she had given me a final chance to get out of here. What was going on? Was she being threatened or blackmailed? Could she still help me?

Connie was watching me from their deck, no doubt wondering why I hadn't already gone into the woods. I was torn. Again, I hadn't been told to wait in the cabin all night. Instructions weren't due until tomorrow. But what if they changed their minds, appeared with some new demand? I couldn't stay here without arousing Connie's suspicions, though, which would surely be a worse breach of the note's demands. I'd have to risk it. I needed to *do* something – to go search the woods for my daughter.

But first, I needed to talk to Nikki. To demand answers. With a final glance over my shoulder at my front door, I ran into the woods.

ꞷ

Every movement in the trees, every shadow, made me jump. I was convinced that someone was going to leap out at me, that Buddy and Darlene would appear in their masks, motionless on the path before me. On top of that, Nikki's words about spirits kept coming back to me. *These woods are haunted*, I thought. *Everything is alive.* After that I was unable to shake the sensation that the trees and the rocks and all the dark spaces in between were watching me. Conspiring against me.

Soon I was back in Penance, running along the road to Main Street. The homeless man, Wyatt, was back in his spot beneath the statue. He raised his head as I passed but I ignored him and went straight over to the bookstore and the door to Nikki's apartment.

I pressed the buzzer. Held my finger down on it and listened to it rasp within.

Nikki didn't come to the door so I did it again.

'Hey.' It was Wyatt. 'She's not there.'

I crossed the street to him.

'She went out,' he said.

'What time did she go out?' I demanded.

'Hey, chill,' he said. 'You look like you wanna kill someone. What happened? Did she sell you a book with the last page torn out or something?'

I took a deep breath. My sense of humour had vanished along with my daughter. 'What time?'

'Jesus, man. I'm not an information kiosk.'

Gritting my teeth, I said, 'Can you please tell me what time Nikki went out?'

He shrugged. 'Hours ago.'

'And you've been sitting here all this time?'

'Yep.'

So Nikki hadn't come back here. That meant she had to be wherever Frankie was, didn't it?

But where?

Where was my daughter?

Chapter 37

Frankie landed on something soft, then immediately rolled off it on to hard concrete. The side of her head banged against the floor, sending a shower of sparks through her vision. A moment later there was a thump and a cry as someone landed beside her.

Above her, the hatch was slammed shut, plunging her into pitch-darkness.

'Ryan?' she said.

He groaned.

'Are you okay?' She was whispering, though she wasn't quite sure why.

'I think so,' he said, and his voice sounded much louder than it should have. She couldn't see him; couldn't see her own hand when she held it close to her face. This was utter darkness, the kind that your eyes never adjust to.

Gingerly, Frankie sat up and examined herself, patting her limbs and feeling her head. It throbbed but she couldn't feel any blood. Nothing was broken. Nothing physical, at least. Right now, she felt like there was something broken inside her, as if she were a piece of elastic that had been stretched beyond its limit.

She was going to have to stop thinking like that. Better to think that she didn't yet know where her limits were.

Better to hope she would never find them.

Ryan groaned again. She reached out and realised they'd both fallen on to a mattress. She guessed it had been placed there to break their fall, which was a good sign, surely. It meant he hadn't wanted them to die.

Not yet, anyway.

'Was it Greg?' Ryan asked. 'The guy in the mask? Was it him?'

He sounded like he was on the verge of a panic attack. She reached out for him and found him.

'Stay calm,' she whispered.

'I'm trying.' She heard him suck in a deep breath. 'Jesus, it stinks down here. The air tastes bad.'

He was right. It was damp and stale, like rotting vegetation. It made her think of earth and worms; how she imagined the inside of a grave to smell.

'Was it Greg?' Ryan repeated.

'It has to be. Right?'

Ryan didn't reply for a few moments, then he said, 'Sorry, I nodded. I forgot you can't see me.' He laughed, except it came out strangled, like a hiss. 'I'm cold,' he said. 'It is cold down here, right? It's not just me. Is it cold?'

It was a little cold. Certainly more so than above ground. But Frankie wondered if Ryan was going into shock. She thought back to the meditation classes they'd had at school. Some hippie woman had come in and taught them all about mindfulness and visualisation techniques.

'Ryan, I want you to close your eyes and imagine you're in a large space. A stadium.'

'What? What are you—'

'Just do it, okay? Trust me. Are you with me?'

Silence, then: 'I'm with you.'

'Good. Now, the stadium walls stretch as far as you can see and the ceiling is high and domed. Can you see it?'

'I think so.'

'Okay. You stay there, keep your eyes closed, keep imagining it.' She guessed he nodded again.

Carefully, she got on to her knees and felt in front of her, sweeping her arm slowly left and right. She had no idea how close they were to the walls or how big it was down here. Was there anything here? Anything they could stand on to reach the hatch? Any other way out? She needed information, even if it was just to keep her busy, to stop her from panicking. Also, she was trying to avoid thinking about it, but she needed to pee. The man in the crow mask had thought to put down a mattress. Was there a bucket too? She'd watched a lot of horror movies at sleepovers. There was usually a bucket in places like this.

She crawled forward, continuing to sweep her hand left and right.

She felt something. Something made of plastic. She grabbed it and pulled it against her, praying it was what she thought it was.

A flashlight. He'd given them a flashlight!

She found the switch and flicked it on.

Ryan made a distressed noise, a groan that came from deep inside.

'Keep your eyes shut,' she said. 'Picture that stadium.'

But now, with the flashlight illuminating the space around them, Frankie felt a shudder of claustrophobia herself. Four concrete walls, no doors or alcoves. It was hard to tell how big the room was. Maybe twenty feet squared?

She stood and pointed the flashlight at the ceiling. Frankie was five foot six. She stretched one arm upwards. The hatch was at least six feet out of reach. There was no ladder. Nothing to climb or stand on. The walls were smooth.

She forced herself to stop looking.

They were trapped.

'Frankie,' said Ryan. Again, he was whispering.

She pointed the beam of the flashlight towards him. 'Close your eyes.'

'No. It makes it worse. At least if I keep—'

'What's that?'

She blinked, once, twice, hoping it was a shadow, a hallucination. But it was real. The flashlight's beam had revealed something lying on the floor in the space behind Ryan.

'Ryan.' Now she was really whispering. 'Don't look.'

But of course he had to look. 'What is it?'

Frankie tried to convince herself it was a pile of old clothes. Some bags of trash. Broken furniture. But she knew she was kidding herself. The smell – that graveyard stench, of earth and decay – was coming from that part of the basement.

She knew she should stay away from it. But she found herself on her hands and knees, crawling towards the dark shape, the bad smell.

'Frankie?' Ryan said.

She got closer. The flashlight's beam reached it before she did. And now she could see. There was no doubt.

She had been mistaken back at Ryan's cabin, thinking he was dead.

But this time, it actually was a body.

Chapter 38

Crow glances over at Nikki, huddled miserably on the old couch, her arms wrapped around her knees, head down. She believed too, once upon a time. She wore the mask, took part in the pranks and, later, the ritual. She hated the campers, and believed in the need to protect this place. He wishes she still believed. But in the absence of faith, fear would have to do.

'If I'm caught, you'll be caught too,' he told her earlier that day.

At first, he had been incensed by her growing closeness to the British guy. All the old feelings of jealousy came flooding back, even though he hadn't thought about Nikki in that way for a long time. But then Abigail had whispered to him that they could use it to their advantage. Use Nikki to lure Tom, get him out of the way so they could get their work done. He had considered bringing Tom here too, but he was worried if both he and Frankie went missing it would draw the attention of the police, spark a manhunt. That was the last thing he wanted. The original plan had been to grab Frankie and Ryan tomorrow night, get it done right away. But then Frankie and Ryan had stumbled upon them by the lake, and suddenly Crow had a problem that needed to be solved. It had required quick thinking. Grab the kids. Send Nikki to get Tom out of the way. That had left one major problem: how to stop Tom and the Butlers from calling the cops.

Leaving the notes, Crow thinks, was a stroke of genius. He's seen enough kidnap movies to know that if you leave a ransom note saying *Don't call the cops or your kids will die*, the parents always hesitate. Crow needs less than twenty-four hours. He's confident it will be enough. Even if Tom does call the police in the morning, Crow doesn't think they'll act immediately. Frankie and Ryan are teenagers. Everyone will assume they're holed up somewhere screwing or getting wasted.

'You should sleep,' he says to Nikki now.

She lifts her head. There's hatred in the way she looks at him. Hatred born of shame and defeat. 'How am I supposed to do that?'

'It will all be over soon,' he says. 'The resort will be closed. The Hollows will be peaceful again. We can all go back to how things were.'

She makes a scoffing sound. 'Until the next time.'

'What are you talking about?'

'Even if this works—'

'It will work.'

'Even if this works, even if you drive the tourists away, who's to say it won't happen again? Another campground, another resort. Maybe worse. A logging operation. A chemical factory. Everyone who believed in the sacredness of these woods is long gone.'

'I'm still here. Abigail's still here.'

Again she scoffs. 'People around here have to make a living somehow.'

'We'll all find other ways to live.'

'Yeah, that's right. Because all that matters is Abigail. You know—'

She stops herself.

'What were you going to say?' he demands. 'Were you going to tell me she's not real? That I'm crazy? Is that it?'

'Of course you're crazy,' she says. 'You took a job at the place you hate—'

'Only so I could get access.'

'What, access to the cabins? So you could sneak around and scare people, like we did last time? It didn't even work.'

'No!' He sees spittle spray from his mouth. Forces himself to swallow, take a breath. 'That wasn't me,' he tells her. 'That was Buddy and Darlene. They took the keys from the office. I didn't know they were doing it until I heard about them taking that woman's heart pills.'

They had stolen them because they thought they might be uppers or downers. Something they could take or sell. As soon as he'd found out about it, he'd told them to put them back.

He hadn't wanted the woman to die. He wasn't a bad person. Shit, he'd even left a flashlight for Frankie and Ryan, down under the cabin. He'd shuddered to think of how deep-dark black it would be under there. He didn't want them to suffer more than they needed to. One of his mom's boyfriends had worked in the big abattoir near the border, and he'd talked a lot about how important it was to ensure the animals weren't overly scared. 'We don't want 'em to panic before we put that bolt in their brains,' he'd said. Crow had never forgotten that.

'It was . . . unfortunate,' he says, mopping sweat from his brow. Was it his fault she had such a hair-trigger heart? Buddy could hardly breathe for laughing when he came back from returning the pills, grabbing his heart and popping his eyes and hissing 'Lucifer!' over and over. How was Crow to know this Donna woman was a religious nut, and that turning around to find Buddy standing there in his horned-up goat mask would send her over the edge?

Nikki stares at him. 'Unfortunate. That's one way of putting it.' Her eyes flash in the half-light. 'You were sweet once,' she says. 'But something snapped inside you, didn't it? When Abigail died.

I wish I'd seen that twenty years ago.' She's talking to him quietly now. Sadly. Almost like she cares about him. 'But I guess something snapped in all of us. Why else would we have gone along with your plan?'

He looks down at the crow mask in his lap and thinks back. He never snapped. He got wise.

And he wasn't crazy. He was smart.

ϖ

The first night he'd seen the teachers, he had been on his way to the cabin. He liked to commune with Abigail on his own, without Goat or Fox there to share her attention. He would light up a joint and sit out on the porch, starlight straining to penetrate the thick canopy of trees, and he would talk to her about his life and his worries and his hopes for the future. He told her how sorry and frustrated he was that the plan wasn't working. He raged about the stupidity of the campers. All those kids, crashing through the woods, dropping garbage and cigarettes and chewing gum. Trampling the hallowed ground. Polluting this pure realm.

And then, when he was halfway between Penance and the cabin, close to the clearing with the flat rock, he heard voices. Grown-up voices.

He scrambled behind the trees, fearful it might be someone he knew, and immediately recognised two of the teachers he'd seen around the campground. A man and a woman, though at that point he didn't know their names. He wouldn't find those out until the next day.

They murmured to each other in low voices; words he couldn't make out. They sat on the rock and the male teacher produced a bottle and swigged from it, passing it to the woman. They had brought a battery-powered lantern with them, which illuminated her face as she took a drink. She was skinny but kinda hot.

They passed the bottle back and forth a few times, and then they moved close together.

They started to kiss.

He must have made a noise because the woman broke free of the kiss and looked in his direction, though he was too well hidden in the trees, in the dark, for her to see.

The man said something, probably reassuring her, and then they were kissing again. They were deep kisses, like characters in movies, the grown-up movies he would sometimes watch when his mom wasn't around – VHS tapes one of her boyfriends had left behind. *9 1/2 Weeks. Basic Instinct.*

And then the teachers started to take their clothes off. The man first, pulling his T-shirt over his head, and then she did the same. The man kissed the hollow of her neck and she reached behind and unfastened her bra, letting it fall to the forest floor.

Crow couldn't believe his luck.

He watched the whole thing. It was over too quickly. But it was the greatest thing he'd seen in his life.

The teachers both stood, giving him a full view of their naked bodies. They embraced, and for one excited moment he thought they were going to do it again, but they parted and dressed hurriedly. They walked quickly across the clearing and vanished from sight.

The next day, he crept on to the campground, concealed in the trees, and watched them. It wasn't long before he overheard some kids say their names. Mr Daniels. Mrs Fredericks. It took most of the day to get their first names. Eric and Sally. He watched them huddled together, whispering, and wondered if they were making plans to return to the clearing that night. He saw their wedding rings. Different last names. He knew some people didn't change their surnames when they got married, but the way these two were acting, the sneaking around, the way they behaved during the day – the exchanged glances they didn't think anyone saw – he knew they were cheating.

When he got home, he looked them up online. Their school had a rudimentary website with a page that listed all the faculty members with brief bios.

And when he returned to the clearing that second night, he saw he'd been right about their whispering. They came back. Did again what they'd done the night before.

Suddenly, he knew what he could do.

He pushed the idea away at first. It was too awful, too risky. Wasn't it?

But he kept coming back to it. Thinking it through. He examined it, rejected it, then came back to it again. The idea excited and appalled him, but if he could pull it off, it would be perfect. The only really worthwhile thing he'd achieved in his short life. He barely considered the rights or wrongs of it. Certainly didn't care about the teachers. They were cheaters, just like most of the men his mom brought home, the ones who made her cry and curse their names. His dad had been one too, apparently. That's why she'd kicked him out when Crow was just a baby.

And these two – didn't they represent everything he hated? That damn campground. The invasion of this sacred space. Of Abigail's space. It was a cancer, just like the cancer that had spread through Abigail's body and that would continue to spread, to pollute, to ruin her eternal home. To kill her a second time.

Something had to be done.

And he was the only person who could make it happen.

Clever boy, Abigail whispered. *Always my most special boy. Do it*, she said.

ϖ

It's way past midnight now.

He ought to check on the kids in the basement, throw them down a couple of bottles of water. He'll do it in a minute. First, he wants to sit here for a moment before Abigail's altar, and give thanks.

Because today is a very special day. Tonight marks the new moon.

A new phase – not only in the lunar cycle, but in the history of the Hollows.

A beginning, and an end.

Chapter 39

Thursday

Somebody was knocking on my cabin door, calling my name. I jerked upright. There was saliva on my chin and my tongue felt like there was fur growing on it. Guilt slapped me. How could I have fallen asleep when Frankie was out there? I checked the time – nine fifteen!

I thought back to last night. After leaving Nikki's I had come back to the resort. I'd found David and Connie searching with help from Neal. There were still some stragglers from the barbecue around, drunk people half-asleep on the grass, a few revellers gathered around the embers of the bonfire. But there were no staff around. No sign of Greg, of course, or Vivian. Reception was still locked up. It felt like all the staff had gone home and abandoned us.

By three a.m. David and Connie had looked everywhere. Neal had gone around the whole resort knocking on cabin doors, waking people and asking if they'd seen a pair of teenagers, showing them a photo of Ryan on Connie's iPad. Nobody had seen them. Most people, Neal told us, seemed stunned to have been woken by the man they'd seen onstage a few hours before, as if they must be dreaming.

Yes, I wanted to say. *Surely they were starstruck. This is all about you, isn't it?*

But I didn't say anything, of course. Didn't say anything to any of the three of them. I wanted to take David and Connie aside and confide in them. How would the person who sent the note know I'd spoken to them? But I couldn't risk it.

I had eventually gone back to the cabin to attempt to think things through, make a plan. Sat down on the couch. That must have been around four thirty. I didn't remember anything after that. Exhaustion and stress had pulled me under.

And now somebody continued to bang on my front door and shout my name.

It was David.

He was holding a sheet of paper. A note. He'd had a note too.

He waved it at me. 'I was about to get in my car to find a police station, and this was under the wipers.'

I took it from him and read it as he came inside and paced around, his hands on his head, pulling at his hair. It was exactly the same as mine, except with Ryan's name instead of Frankie's.

I handed it back to him.

'It was on your car? Did you look at your car last night?'

'No. I didn't go near it.'

Had the note been put there at the same time mine had been left inside my cabin? I guessed so. I wasn't sure why the Butlers' note had been left on their car, but perhaps Greg or the twins hadn't been able to get into their cabin; they'd lost the key or been disturbed by a passer-by.

It didn't matter right now. But I wished David had found his note last night.

I fished out the note I'd received, screwed up and tattered after being in my pocket all night, and handed it to David.

He read it. 'When did you get this?' he demanded.

253

'Last night.'

'What, after you got back here?'

'No. Before.'

I thought his eyes were going to pop out. 'What the fuck? *Before?* You mean, while we were searching everywhere, you'd already seen this?'

'It says not to talk to anyone. An instruction you've already ignored by coming here.'

His mouth opened. He looked at the note he'd found on his car. He closed his mouth.

'Maybe it's okay,' I said, looking around. 'He's not going to know we've spoken to each other, unless—'

Something struck me. Greg was the manager of Hollow Falls. He could easily have bugged this place, couldn't he? He could be listening to everything we were saying right now.

I gestured for David to follow me outside. He didn't move until I hissed, 'Come on.'

I looked around for somewhere safe to talk. Greg couldn't have this whole place bugged. He couldn't have bugged the insides of our cars.

David seemed to catch up with my thinking. He unlocked his car, got into the driver's seat and I got in the other side. Maybe they were watching, but they wouldn't be able to hear. And maybe I was taking a huge gamble, perhaps we should both be sitting in our cabins doing nothing except waiting – but surely the important thing, from Greg's perspective, was for us not to go to the authorities. David and I talking to each other wasn't going to wreck his lunatic plan, whatever it was. He'd just been trying to buy himself time, cautioning us to remain isolated. Time for *what*, I had no idea.

A horrible thought struck me. Had he already hurt Frankie and Ryan, and wanted more time to get away before we called the police? Oh Jesus, is that what the notes were for? A stalling attempt so he could get on a plane or flee north?

I sucked in a breath and tried not to panic. What I needed to do was fill David in. We had to be operating with the same information.

'Okay,' I said. 'I need you to listen without too many interruptions or questions.'

I told him everything I knew, going back to Ryan's offending Instagram post, the threatening messages, my conviction that Buddy and Darlene, or maybe Greg himself, had taken Donna's beta blockers. I told him about Frankie seeing masked figures in the woods the night she and Ryan had argued. I described what Frankie and Ryan had seen yesterday, and how the twins had attacked them with rocks.

'Then, last night, we saw Buddy and Darlene with Greg. He's their dad. He must be the person in the crow mask. Then I talked with Nikki—'

'Hold up. Who's Nikki?'

'Someone I thought I could trust. I think she and Greg were involved in the murders of Eric Daniels and Sally Fredericks. It's—'

'Greg, the manager? You think *he* killed Eric and Sally, and now you think he has Ryan and Frankie? Why would you—'

'I know it sounds mad. But I'm telling you, he's insane. Nikki told me all about it. He believes that the Hollows are home to the spirit of this woman who befriended them when they were kids. That the Hollows have to be protected from outsiders. Nikki didn't finish telling me everything, but I think that's why they killed the teachers. They'd been trying to frighten people away by carrying out all these pranks around the campground but it wasn't working. So they decided they needed to do something more extreme. A ritual murder. Something that would ensure no one wanted to come and stay here again. No parent would want their kids coming to stay here.'

He stared at me, open-mouthed. He and Connie were supposed to be the experts on the murders. This was blowing his mind. 'Whoa . . . wait. So Everett Miller didn't do it?'

'I don't know. I think he was involved. Nikki said there were three of them. She was Fox, Greg was Crow, and I assume Everett was Goat.'

'And now these kids, Buddy and Darlene . . .'

'They were wearing the Fox and Goat masks. They're Nikki and Everett's replacements, it seems. But Nikki's helping him too, presumably because Greg has told her she needs to do it to protect herself from being found out for her role in the 1999 killings. Her job was to get me out of the way while they took Frankie and Ryan. And this whole thing – the notes and the abduction of our kids – is because I was getting close to the truth. I was going to expose Greg and ruin his plans before he could—'

'Murder someone else?' said David, finishing my sentence. 'Carry out another ritual? Holy shit – our kids! He thinks if he does the same thing again it will have the same outcome. Hollow Falls closing down.'

'Yeah.'

David faced the windscreen. The trees swayed in the morning breeze.

'But why would he wait?' he asked.

I was scared of the words I was about to speak, but forced them out. 'I think maybe the notes are a stalling tactic, giving him time to get away.'

'You think they're already dead?' He shouted it.

'I don't know.' Realising I was shouting too, I forced myself to lower my voice. 'Can you think of any other reason why he would wait? It's not, I don't know, the anniversary of the original murders today, is it?'

'No. That's not till next week.'

Of course. He and Connie had already told me that.

'Then what—'

But David wasn't listening. He started the car.

'What are you doing?' I asked.

'What the fuck do you think I'm doing? I'm going to find him.'

'But the instructions. The note says more will be coming today.'

'You said it yourself, they could already be dead and these notes are designed to make us sit here on our asses, doing nothing. Well, I'm not doing that when he could be killing Ryan and Frankie right now.'

The car was moving, accelerating through the resort. We were adjacent to the lake. A woman jogging along the path had to jump out of our way, her shock turning to fury in the rear-view mirror.

'Where are we going to go?' I asked as we sped out through the gates of the resort, leaving the *WELCOME TO HOLLOW FALLS* sign behind. In a way it felt good, a relief, to go along with someone else's plan.

'Do you know where he lives?' David asked.

'No.'

'It shouldn't be a problem. Everybody knows everybody around here, right? Tell me exactly what Frankie told you again, about when she went to find Buddy and Darlene. Did she describe where they went?'

I thought back, forcing myself to concentrate, to peer through the swirling chaos in my head. 'She said they paused to take photos of the junkyard, then walked to Main Street. They met Buddy and Darlene somewhere in between.'

I gave him directions and he turned left towards Penance. The sky was overcast, the morning sticky and unpleasant, like we needed a storm to clear the air. I checked the time. Almost ten.

The road cut through the trees. We passed a dead creature, its fur matted with blood. I wasn't sure what it was. A beaver? There was more roadkill up ahead. I tried not to see it as an omen, but it was all getting to me. These woods, the image of Frankie tied up in some dark room somewhere, terrified.

'This way,' I said.

We drove past Main Street and I considered asking David to stop briefly, so we could check if Nikki had gone back to the bookstore or her apartment. Get Greg's address out of her. But I decided it was unlikely. We would just be wasting time. I looked out for Wyatt too, but he wasn't at his usual spot beneath the statue.

We cruised along the road that ran parallel to the woods. The junkyard was ahead.

'This must be it,' I said, pointing to the right turn on to Paradise Loop.

David turned and we drove slowly, looking for someone to ask. Then I spotted them. Two small children, around six years old, playing out on their front lawn. They had to be the kids who had told Frankie and Ryan about the rabbit and the buried-alive cat.

'Stop the car,' I said.

I got out and went over to talk to the children. They were playing Jenga, concentrating hard as the boy tried to pull out a block from near the bottom of the tower. His sister clapped her hands with glee as it wobbled and almost fell.

'Hi,' I said. Two large pairs of eyes turned towards me. David stood on the edge of the lawn, watching.

'I'm looking for a friend of mine,' I went on, keeping my voice light and friendly. 'Buddy and Darlene's dad. Can you tell me which house is theirs?'

The girl pointed to the house next door. An unassuming, detached house surrounded by a white picket fence. The Stars and Stripes flew at the top of a flagpole out front, and there was a basketball hoop attached to the wall.

'Have you seen them today?' David asked.

'Uh-uh.' The girl shook her head.

'What about last night?'

'I don't think so,' said the boy, though he didn't seem too sure.

I glanced at the house. There was no sign of life. I assumed Greg hadn't turned up to work today. I imagined he must have called in sick, maybe blaming it on a bad burger from last night's barbecue.

'Okay, thanks,' I said to the children.

We approached the house, going through the front gate. It was well oiled, no squeak. The sky was looking increasingly overcast but the birds were singing, fluttering between the treetops. A normal summer's day in small-town America.

The birds weren't the only things fluttering. My stomach was like a butterfly house. Now we were here, I wasn't sure what to do.

'What are we going to do?' I asked. 'Knock?'

David looked as tense as I felt. There was a small car, a red Hyundai, parked outside, presumably Greg's.

'I'm going to go round the back and take a look first,' David said.

I followed him down the side of the house, through another well-oiled gate into a neat garden. I peered through a rear window into the kitchen. It looked totally normal, a few dishes piled in the sink, a loaf of bread on the counter. There was something else on the counter too. Leaning closer I realised it was candy, sweets in shiny wrappers, as if someone had torn open a bag and let it scatter.

'This doesn't feel right,' I said. 'I don't think they're here.'

But David ignored me. He tried the back door.

It opened.

'Wait,' I whispered, but he went inside and I followed.

It was silent inside the house. I could hear my own breathing.

David took a knife from the block on the counter, examined it, then took a sharper one. I noticed that the largest slot in the block was empty.

The kitchen door was open, and we went through it into a hallway that led to the living room. There was more candy scattered on the floor here. There were two PlayStation controllers on the couch and the case for *Resident Evil 7* lay on the carpet. Two open cans of Coke sat on the coffee table. Next to them was an item I knew. Frankie's Hydro Flask. I'd recognise its aquamarine colour anywhere.

I picked it up, turned it in my hand. It sent a chill through me. This was evidence that linked this family to my daughter, and it indicated to me that they were either stupid or indifferent about getting caught. Because they were already long gone? Our children already dead?

I had to hold on to the back of an armchair for a second while I gave myself a pep talk. This was not the time to give up. I followed David back into the hallway and stood at the foot of the stairs.

'There's no one home,' I said quietly.

But David was already going up the stairs. Again, I followed. We reached the upper floor.

'Look,' I whispered.

The closest door was pulled to, though not closed. The handle was smeared with something dark.

Blood.

David was pale, his jaw moving like he was chewing gum. I pushed the door open with my foot, expecting to see a horrific murder scene, a body.

It was an empty bathroom.

I exhaled with relief. But then I saw that the basin and the tap handles were smeared red, as if someone had had blood all over their hands and attempted half-heartedly to wash it off. There were spatters of it all over the floor, mixed with dried soap suds. In the bath was a white towel, stained with yet more blood.

David picked it up and turned to me, anguish on his face. He mouthed his son's name. Then he said it aloud. 'Ryan? *Ryan?* Are you here? Son, are you hurt?'

Silence.

We left the bathroom. There were three more doors. One of them had a small enamel sign that said *Darlene's Room*, with flowers around the edge. Presumably it had been there since she was a small child. On the door next to it, a sign that said *KEEP OUT*. Buddy's room, presumably.

The third door was closed. There were drops of blood on the carpet directly outside it and, looking closer, I saw a trail of specks leading to the bathroom.

I took a deep breath. I didn't want to do this. But what choice did I have? I couldn't call the police. Not yet. Not until I'd seen what was in this room.

I put my hand over my nose and mouth, pushed the handle down and let the door swing open.

Chapter 40

Frankie and Ryan huddled together in the corner, as far from the remains as they could get.

The human remains.

Frankie wasn't sure if she'd slept. There was no sense of time down here. Minutes felt like hours. Hours seemed like seconds. Her eyes were scratchy and there was a nasty, mossy taste in her mouth. Her bladder was burning too. Shortly after finding the body, she and Ryan had decided to turn off the flashlight, worried the batteries might run out, even though in the pitch-darkness it was easy to imagine the man on the other side of the room slithering towards them, dragging his bones across the floor. Reaching out a decayed hand, his fingers hovering an inch from her foot, preparing to touch her. Every so often, when she became convinced he was moving, she would have to flick on the light to check he was lying still.

Of course he was still. He was dead.

He'd been dead for a long time.

Last night, or whenever it had been, after they had realised they weren't alone down here, she and Ryan had crawled slowly, very slowly, across the concrete floor. Not wanting to see but *needing* to see.

There had still been a part of Frankie that believed she was mistaken. That it was a mannequin or a pile of clothes. Down here in the dark, it would be easy to see things; for the imagination to run riot. She wanted it to be a dummy. She wanted to be able to laugh about how stupid she had been. *It's just a pile of old clothes and some rocks! Aren't we silly?*

But then they'd got to within two feet of it and Frankie pointed the flashlight beam. It was unmistakable. It was a body. A skeleton, the flesh and organs long since rotted away. Frankie had tried not to think about rats and insects and all the other creatures that might have feasted on the corpse. Were there still rats down here? She wasn't particularly scared of rodents, but the thought of one running over her . . . She shuddered. Even worse, what if she and Ryan died down here and suffered the same fate as whoever this was?

She couldn't let that happen.

Frankie had found herself fixating on the skull. The eye sockets. She fought the fear that this, one day, could be her and Ryan.

And then Ryan had said, 'Oh my God.'

It seemed like a late reaction but then Frankie realised he was looking at the black garment that was draped across the pile of bones. That he'd noticed something.

'I know who this is,' Ryan said.

He inched closer and Frankie did the same. Now she could see what the garment was. A black leather jacket. A biker's jacket.

There was a design stencilled in white on the back. A large circle with an upside-down crescent on top.

'The horned god,' said Ryan.

Beneath the symbol was a single word: *Wolfspear*.

'This is Everett Miller.'

ϖ

Now, on the other side of the room, after Ryan – who had absorbed the whole story from his parents – had filled her in, Frankie speculated about what had happened. Everett Miller had come here to hide and, somehow, got trapped. Looking around with the flashlight, Frankie had found numerous pieces of rock scattered about. There were marks on the ceiling by the hatch. She could picture Everett down here, throwing rocks at the ceiling, trying to capture someone's attention. Except, of course, there was no one around. Nobody believed this place existed. She wondered if Everett had stumbled across it or if he'd always known; if it had once been common knowledge among the kids in Penance.

Everett had been hiding. He knew everyone suspected him of the murder. Frankie didn't know if he was guilty or not, but maybe that wasn't important, not any more. Everett hadn't run off to Canada. He'd come here. Most likely, he'd been walking through the house, looking for a place to hide in the dark, and the hatch had been open. He'd fallen through.

Even in her current predicament, Frankie could hardly imagine how scared he must have been. Hungry and cold and thirsty. Calling and calling with no answer. Praying for a miracle. Trying to figure out a way to escape before realising it was a puzzle with no solution. Had he sat here and thought about all the things he'd done wrong in his life – which might, or might not, have included murder? Did he pray the police would find him? Were there people – parents, friends – he wanted to apologise to? Did he picture his mother crying, believing he was a killer, wondering where she and his father had gone wrong?

And then she thought about her own dad, how frantic he must be right now, searching for her. She wondered if he'd called her mum to let her know what was going on, and if she was on her way to Maine. And what about the police? Were they combing these woods right now, searching for them?

There had to be other people in Penance, besides the ones who had put them here, who knew the location of this house. There *had* to be.

Except Everett Miller had probably thought the same thing.

Beside her, Ryan stirred and opened his eyes.

'Are we still here?' he said.

'I'm afraid so.'

He closed his eyes again. 'I need to go to the bathroom.'

She pointed to the corner of the basement. 'There it is.'

They both giggled, and Frankie wondered if they were losing their minds.

He shuffled off to the other side of the room and said, 'Don't listen.'

Frankie had already been, while he was asleep. A spider had run over her foot, and she had made a vow never to complain about any public restroom ever again, no matter how foul. When they got out of this. If they got out.

As Ryan came back, she heard footsteps above, followed by voices. A man's voice and a higher one. A woman? Or one of the twins? She was relieved they were still here, despite the hatred and fear she felt towards them. She wanted them to fall through the hatch and break their necks – but only after they'd let her and Ryan out.

Ryan sat back down on the mattress and they looked up at the ceiling.

'What do you think they want with us?' he asked.

'I'm trying not to think about it.'

'Sorry. It's just . . .'

'Just?'

'I keep remembering what those little kids said about Buddy and Darlene burying that cat alive. Maybe this is them doing that to us.'

'Jesus. Thanks, Ryan.'

They fell silent and Frankie tried to make out the words from above, but the voices were too muffled.

'A family of psychopaths,' Ryan said. 'Have you seen *The Texas Chainsaw Massacre*?'

'Ryan, please!'

'Sorry.'

'How old was Greg at the time of the murders?' Frankie asked, glancing in the direction of Everett's body.

'No idea. How old do you figure he is now? Thirty-something?'

'So he would have been around our age then.' She paused. 'Old enough to kill someone.'

Ryan appeared to let that sink in. 'Is this . . . is this all because I dissed Penance on Instagram?'

She reached out and found his hand. Squeezed it.

'The police will be looking for us. There'll be helicopters out searching. They'll find us.'

If only she could believe it.

'We're going to be—'

She stopped. There was a scraping sound, and then light flooded the basement. Somebody had opened the hatch.

Please let it be the police. Please let it be our parents.

'Stand clear,' came a voice, and something dropped through the hole and hit the floor. It rolled towards them. A bottle of water, followed by another one. Then something else landed. A paper bag.

Frankie craned her neck upwards. The man was looking down at her, still wearing his crow mask. He still wasn't letting them see his face. That was a good sign, right? Greg was under the impression they didn't know it was him.

'Some sandwiches for you there,' he said. 'A couple of bananas and apples.'

'Please,' Frankie said. 'Please. Let us out.'

266

'Please,' Ryan echoed.

'All in good time.'

He went to close the hatch.

'No! Can't you leave it open?' Frankie pleaded with him. 'It's so dark down here. There's no air.'

He appeared to be thinking about it.

'Please,' she said again. 'We'll tell people you looked after us. That we came with you voluntarily, that you didn't hurt us. Whatever you want.' She swallowed. 'We'll do whatever you want.'

'All right, Katniss,' he said. 'No need to beg.'

There was a long moment of silence as he realised what he'd done.

'Whoops,' he said. And now that he knew it didn't matter any more, he removed the mask.

Chapter 41

Greg lay on the floor of his bedroom, covered in his own blood.

The carpet beneath my feet was sticky with the stuff. It was spattered across the white paint of the door. Greg was a big man, and his body filled the space between the foot of the bed and the closet. He was wearing his red Hollow Falls polo shirt and I imagined him getting ready for work, another day in his new job. Although I didn't want to look too closely, I could see that some patches of blood were darker. It looked like he'd been stabbed in the belly. Twice at least. The room stank of something foul. Blood and sweat and excrement.

I stepped back, out of the room, not wanting to look at Greg's corpse for a moment longer, unable to bear the stench.

I flapped a hand at David, motioning for him to go downstairs. My legs were weak and I had to grip the handrail. It took all my self-control not to vomit. David was not so lucky. He bent double and threw up, splattering the carpeted hallway. He went into the kitchen and splashed his face with water, then opened the back door, gulping fresh air.

'The twins,' I said, standing behind him. The PlayStation controllers. The cans of Coke. The scattered candy. 'They did this. They killed their own dad.'

'That means . . .'

We were both trying to figure it out. Had Greg been innocent all along? Had I been wrong about Greg being Crow, having leapt to the wrong conclusion when I realised he was the twins' dad? One thing was for sure. Frankie and Ryan were not here. I doubted they'd ever been here.

'We've got to call the police now,' David said.

I pushed my hands through my hair. Out here in the back garden, I was able to breathe again. The air was thick with heat but at least it didn't stink. That cloying stench. The blood. I didn't think I'd ever forget it.

'Tom?' David urged. The sight of Greg's body had taken something out of him. He looked defeated. Almost resigned.

'Let me think,' I said. I had to believe that Frankie and Ryan were still alive. Buddy and Darlene and Crow, whoever that was – could it actually be Everett? – had taken them somewhere and were waiting, but for how long? If I knew what they were waiting for . . .

There was a calendar hanging on the wall in the kitchen. I went inside to study it. Something I had read in Jake Robineaux's book, his account of the murder scene, was niggling at me, just out of reach. And then I saw it, marked on the calendar. The symbol that gave me the answer.

'David, come here.'

He came into the kitchen, queasy and exhausted-looking.

I pointed to the calendar. 'What's special about today?'

He peered at it. 'Nothing.'

'Look again.'

He did as I asked. 'Wait. It's a new moon.'

'And the first murders happened on a new moon too,' I said. 'Is that right?'

'Yeah. Yeah, they did.'

'And the new moon symbolises . . . ?'

He stared at the moon symbol on the calendar. 'Connie covered this on the podcast. Fresh beginnings, sending your intentions into the world. Stuff like that.'

'Which fits with what we now know they were trying to do back in '99,' I said. 'Ridding this place of the campers. It would fit with their wanting to purify this place for the spirit of that woman. Abigail. It's a new moon tonight. That's what they're waiting for. Frankie and Ryan are still alive. I'm sure of it.'

I didn't believe in spirits or pagan gods or the dark power of rituals. But what *I* thought wasn't important. All that mattered was that *they* believed it. And besides, however it was dressed up, the original killings had achieved a concrete aim, hadn't they? The campground had shut down. Whether it was wrapped up in ancient beliefs or not, there was no reason to think it wouldn't work again.

'Tom, I think we need to call the police.'

He was right, wasn't he? We couldn't leave Greg's body here like this. And if the abductors needed to wait until the night of the new moon before conducting their ritual, surely that meant their threat to kill our kids if we called the authorities was intended purely to scare us. To stop us doing exactly that.

And I had fallen for it. I should have called the cops last night.

I took out my phone and dialled 911.

While it rang, David said, 'I'm going to drive back to the resort, let Connie know what's going on. She must be going out of her mind.'

'Okay.'

As I watched him run back to the car, 911 came on the line. I explained everything to the call-taker. It took a few minutes to answer her questions. I didn't mention new moons or rituals because I was pretty sure that would make them think I was a crank.

'How long will it take?' I pressed. 'Before somebody gets here?'

I could sense her tapping at a computer, and remembered what Wyatt had told me. The nearest police were ninety miles away. It would take them at least an hour to get here. The ambulance might be quicker, but they were already responding to a couple of emergencies in the area where the patient had some hope of survival.

An hour. I couldn't stand around waiting for that long.

ϖ

The children were still playing on the lawn next door, the picture of innocence. Sweet faces concentrating on their game. Had Buddy and Darlene been like this once? I remembered what Nikki had told me, about the twins' mother running off because she thought her kids were evil. It was hard for me to imagine looking at a two-year-old child and thinking that. Difficult, naughty, uncooperative. All two-year-olds are terrible; everyone knows that. What had she, their own mother, seen in them that made her run? Had she foreseen this? It made me shudder.

'The secret cabin,' I said as I crouched beside the children. I couldn't think where else my daughter and Ryan might be. 'Do you know where it is?'

In tandem, they pressed their lips together and shook their heads.

I got my wallet out of my pocket and pulled out all the money I had. Around fifty dollars. I showed it to them. 'If you can tell me, I'll give you all this.'

Their eyes widened but the girl said, 'We don't know.'

'Nobody knows,' said the boy.

I stood up straight and swore under my breath.

'Have you seen Buddy and Darlene today?' I asked.

Tight lips, shaking heads.

I went back into the house and upstairs, avoiding Greg's bedroom and the bloody bathroom. I headed straight into the room with the *KEEP OUT* sign on the door. I wasn't sure what I was hoping to find. Something that would give me a clue to the location of the hidden cabin. A diary. A map that had been passed down through the generations. I knew how unlikely it was, but I was desperate. Frankie was there. She would be terrified. They could be doing anything to her. Things I didn't want to think about.

Buddy's room looked like any other teenage bedroom. An unmade single bed. A computer on a desk. The funky smell that teenage boys exude. Nothing that screamed 'a psychopath lives here'. The posters on the walls looked like they'd been there since his childhood. WWF wrestlers. *Minecraft*.

I rifled through the drawers of his desk. I pulled out exercise books, pens and other stationery, ancient Pokémon cards and Lego mini-figures, tangled headphones and broken charger cables. Detritus, none of it useful. No diary. No map with a big arrow that said *Secret Cabin*.

I went into Darlene's room. It looked like it had been ransacked by burglars. Pens and scissors and glue sticks scattered across the desk. Dozens of perfume bottles, many of them almost full. I picked one up. Chanel No. 5. Where had these come from? I knew immediately. She had taken them from cabins at the resort. Using Greg's keys to go in and help herself.

There was a glass tank in the corner. Inside were several black and brown insects. I bent down to take a closer look. Madagascar hissing cockroaches. I'd seen them in a pet store once and wondered what would possess anyone to want to keep such creatures as pets. I took a step back, disgusted, and heard a noise outside the room. Something scraping. A breath?

Someone was here. Upstairs. And it was way too soon for it to be the police.

I looked around for a weapon, wishing I'd picked up a knife from the kitchen. Surely Darlene would have something lethal in her room? There was a glass paperweight on a shelf. It contained the body of a scorpion. I picked it up, hefted it in my hand. It was solid enough to knock someone out.

I peered out of the room. There was no sign of anyone in the hall. No shadows creeping up the stairs. All was silent and still.

Slowly, with the paperweight raised, I left Darlene's room. I kept my back to the wall and crept sideways along the hall, back towards the top of the stairs and Greg's bedroom.

I looked down the stairs. Was someone down there? Maybe I had imagined it. Maybe it was the wind, or the little kids outside. Perhaps David had come back. I stood still, barely breathing, feeling my heart thump inside me.

The noise came from behind me and I whirled round. It sounded like somebody trying to speak. A noise deep in someone's throat.

I rushed into Greg's room and saw his eyelids flicker.

He was still alive!

I crouched beside him. 'Greg?'

His eyes flickered again.

'There's an ambulance on its way,' I said, scrambling to get my phone out of my pocket. 'I'll tell them to hurry.'

'I tried,' he said.

'To call an ambulance?'

He gave his head only the tiniest shake, but I could see his frustration. His eyes were still closed but his lips were moving, just, like he was trying to say more. I spotted a glass of water beside the bed and leapt up to grab it. I brought it to his mouth and let a little trickle between his parted lips. It dribbled down his chin and he made a horrible gasping noise.

'I tried my best,' he said.

Was he talking about Buddy and Darlene? His eyelids moved again and he tried to open them, squinting like the light hurt him.

'Abigail?' he said.

'It's Tom,' I said. 'Tom Anderson. Greg, do you know where Frankie is? Where Buddy and Darlene might have taken her?'

His breathing was slow, ragged. Somehow he had survived so far. Perhaps his flesh had protected his organs to an extent, but he had lost so much blood it was a miracle he was still alive.

'This . . . my . . .'

I leaned closer.

'My punishment,' he said. 'What . . . we did.' He tried to focus on me again. 'Abigail?'

'Greg,' I said. 'Please. Can you hear me? Where is the cabin? The secret cabin?'

Blood bubbled from between his lips, swelling and popping.

'Greg?'

'My name . . . my name is Goat.'

'Greg. Please. The secret cabin. Where is it?'

He tried again to open his eyes, squinting at me.

'Carl?'

Carl? Did he think I was the archery teacher?

'You,' Greg said, attempting to lift his hand, like he wanted to point a finger at me. 'Your fault.'

I rocked back on my heels. Carl? Why had he . . . ?

It dawned on me.

'Is Carl Crow?' I asked, leaning closer. 'Greg? Where is the cabin? Please. I need to find Frankie.'

He blinked, apparently realising who I was.

'The cabin,' I urged. 'Where is it?'

But he didn't want to tell me. He wanted to confess. He beckoned for me to move closer, and whispered into my ear, gasping, every word causing him pain. And he told me what he'd done. What they'd done. Him and Nikki and Carl.

When he'd finished, he lay there, silent, his skin chalky and damp with sweat. But he seemed lighter, unburdened of the story he'd kept secret for twenty years. He was ready to die.

'Greg,' I said. 'Please. Tell me where to find the cabin.'

The corners of his mouth twitched into something resembling a smile. 'The wind,' he said, so quietly the words were only just audible. 'Follow . . .'

He fell silent.

'Greg?'

I grabbed his wrist, felt for a pulse.

He was gone.

Chapter 42

When Carl made his way home after coming up with his plan – after the second time he'd seen the teachers – he was given evidence that the Hollows were on his side. Something that showed him the dark power of this place; its desire to protect itself and to reward him. Because there, lying on the path at his feet, was a piece of cloth. One that Carl – or Crow, as he had thought of himself since Abigail had given him that name – recognised. Using a stick to touch it, he picked it up and examined it.

It was Everett Miller's bandana.

Carl had liked Everett Miller until recently. On the couple of occasions he'd encountered him, Everett had been nice. There was that time at Big Al's Records when Everett had recommended a couple of albums to him, expanding his horizons beyond Metallica and Korn. He'd told him to listen to Wolfspear, pointing out how he had their horned-god logo painted on the back of his leather jacket.

Carl had long been aware that other people in town looked at Everett with suspicion. His dyed black hair, his 'Satanic' T-shirts, his shyness. Carl overheard a guy at the store say that Everett was a shooting spree waiting to happen, like those Columbine guys. Carl thought that if they were worried about Everett taking revenge on the town that had ostracised him, then maybe they should be nicer to him and bring him into the fold. But he also understood that wasn't how people, in their infinite capacity for cruelty and stupidity, worked.

But then Carl had begun to despise Everett himself.

All because of Fox.

It hadn't taken long for Carl to discover who Nikki's secret new friend was. One afternoon, after she'd left the cabin early again, he'd followed her, tracking her through the woods as she walked back to Penance. She kept looking over her shoulder, but he was good at hiding now, at camouflaging himself.

She was, he soon realised, heading to the junkyard. What the hell was she up to?

That was when he remembered. This was where Everett Miller lived with his dad.

Carl almost vomited when he saw Everett come to the gate and let Nikki through. He felt sick to see the way she smiled at him, touching her hair and laughing at something Everett said. He was the town weirdo and this hot girl was into him.

It was the first time Carl truly understood how it felt to hate someone. The burn of bile in his throat. A pain in his stomach. Ice and fire competing in his veins.

He watched Everett and Nikki walk side by side across the junkyard to the house, disappearing from sight, and he tormented himself with visions of what they were going to do inside. Everett was seventeen, two years older than Nikki. Why did girls always seem to go out with older guys? It wasn't fair. Everett was a loser, a freak. Nikki was meant to be Carl's. Just because he hadn't gathered the courage to ask her out yet . . . He had been building up to it, waiting for the perfect moment, and Everett had swooped in and snatched her away.

Now, here, like a gift from the gods of the forest, was Everett's bandana. Carl stuffed it into his pocket.

He could close down the campground and get rid of Everett at the same time. After that, when Nikki saw how clever he was, and with Everett out of the way, she would surely fall in love with him. Especially if they had a shared secret. Something they could never tell anyone else.

Yes, that was the final piece of this puzzle. Something like this would bind them together forever.

He looked to Abigail for approval.

She shimmered before him, a smile on her face, and told him what he would need to make it work.

ω

Almost twenty-four hours later, Carl, Greg and Nikki stood together by the lake. Night had fallen and the sky was an inky black, only starlight illuminating the Hollows. It happened to be a new moon, which felt like another good omen. Everything Carl had done today to prepare for tonight had gone even better than he'd hoped, everything slotting into place. It was as if by dreaming up his idea, he had unleashed the power of these woods, this sacred, special place, setting in motion a chain of events that could not be stopped.

'Are you ready?' Carl asked.

Nikki looked so hot tonight. Pale and nervous, but he couldn't imagine any girl being more beautiful. He wished he had the courage to kiss her.

After tonight – with their shared, terrible secret – he was sure that *she* would kiss *him*.

They each held a cup in their hands. Greg sniffed at the liquid and wrinkled his nose.

'Are you sure about this?' he asked. 'It's not going to make us sick?'

'Of course I'm sure,' Carl replied. 'Abigail gave me the recipe herself.'

She had directed him to it, tucked inside the book *A Sacred Space*. They all knew that Abigail had often come into the woods alone, to meditate and commune with the spirits of the forest. They had stumbled across her once, when she was in the middle of one of these vision quests. She had been wild-eyed and spaced out. She had hugged all of them and Carl had noticed how her pupils covered almost her entire eyes. It had been kind of frightening to see her like that, sweat beading her brow, her mouth a little slack. The way she kept staring at things they couldn't see. Later, she told them she had taken a potion that she had cooked up herself, made from flowers and plants she had picked in the woods. Herbs and berries that were easy enough to find, though it had taken Carl all morning to gather them.

'What's in it?' Nikki asked.

'That doesn't matter. Just drink it.'

Nikki and Greg exchanged a glance. 'I'm not sure,' Greg said.

Carl wanted to force it down their throats. 'Listen,' he said. 'You want the campers gone, don't you? You want Abigail's spirit to be happy?'

'Of course we do,' said Nikki.

'Then drink. This is the first part of the ritual.'

Greg sniffed at his cup again. 'Can't we just, like, smoke some weed or something?'

'No! It has to be this if we want the ritual to work.'

He hadn't told them exactly what the ritual involved, just that Abigail would guide them. He hadn't told them about the teachers or any of the rest of it. He knew they would freak out, refuse to take part. They had to be led to it, so that when they got there they felt like they had no choice but to take part. That it was a joint idea.

The potion was part of that. Maybe he could have got them drunk or given them weed, but he didn't think either of those things would be intoxicating – *transporting* – enough.

279

This will be perfect, Abigail had said. And if anyone knew, she did.

'Drink,' he said again, and he raised his own cup to his lips. It was lukewarm and bitter, even though he had added sugar to make it go down easier.

'Gross,' Greg said, after he'd downed it.

'Come on, Nikki,' Carl urged. 'Please.'

She looked into the cup again. Then she sighed, shrugged and tipped the liquid down her throat.

'So gross,' she said, and that made her and Greg giggle.

'Do you think we'll see visions like Abigail did?' Greg asked. 'Spirits?' He seemed equally frightened and excited.

'Abigail said the spirits will guide us and show us what to do,' replied Carl. He checked his watch. It was time. 'Now, come on. Let's go. Don't forget your masks.'

They walked in silence, away from the lake and into the woods. It was even darker here beneath the canopy of trees, but Carl found he had no trouble following the path.

'This is freaky,' Nikki said. 'But it's like I can see in the dark. Like I actually am a fox.'

'Me too,' said Greg.

'It's the potion,' Carl said. It was actually working.

'Do you feel anything?' Nikki asked.

Greg replied that he wasn't sure and Carl wondered too. And then, like a rush, he felt it. A light-headedness. A strange taste in his mouth. At the same time, his vision sharpened further and then – *whoa*. The trees appeared to be glowing.

'Can you see that?' Nikki asked, reaching out to touch a tree.

'That's awesome,' breathed Greg.

Carl looked down at his feet, at the path, and saw the ground shifting, pine needles squirming like bugs, and he felt branches reaching towards him – not threatening, but like they were trying to touch him, to stroke him.

'I think I'm going to be sick,' said Nikki. She had stopped and was leaning against a tree. 'Everything's swimming. I don't like it.'

Carl stared at her, trying to think straight. She was smaller than him and a lot smaller than Greg. Maybe he should have given her a smaller dose. He hadn't thought about body mass and all that.

'I don't like it,' Nikki repeated. Her voice sounded like it was coming to him through a long, dark tunnel. Beside Nikki, Greg was motionless, as if he'd forgotten how to walk. Both he and Nikki turned their faces towards Carl and their pupils were like Abigail's had been. Vast. Black. It was like staring into the void, into a pit. Carl shivered and his heart plunged, his stomach cold, and he felt a terrible foreboding, like he had made a huge mistake, unleashed something he didn't understand and couldn't control.

It's okay, Abigail whispered in his ear. *It will be okay. Just wait.* She calmed him. Quelled the panic.

'I want to go home,' Nikki said. 'I don't . . . Oh Jesus, what's that?'

Carl followed her gaze. She was staring into the trees, a look of enrapt wonder on her face.

'Oh,' she said, her voice breathy. 'Oh.'

'What is it?' Greg asked. His voice had turned thick and deep, like he was a bear that had learned to talk, and Carl wasn't sure if it was an auditory hallucination or if Greg really did sound like that now.

Nikki didn't reply. She gazed between the trees like there was a unicorn standing there, something only she could see.

'Nikki?' Carl said. 'What are you looking at?'

Tears slid down her cheeks. They glistened and Carl saw that they were edged by rainbows, like oil in water. And then he saw it too. It was Abigail, shining in the dark, smiling at them.

'You can see her too?' he whispered, and Nikki nodded, unable to speak.

'Abigail?' said Greg, peering at the same spot the other two were looking at. 'Oh. Abigail.' His voice was full of wonder.

'She wants us to do this,' Carl said. The others nodded. Carl put a hand on Nikki's shoulder. He had no idea how much time had passed since they'd stopped – it could have been hours – but when he checked his watch he saw they were still on schedule.

In the intervening years, he would cook up Abigail's potion many more times, but it never worked like it did that night. Was never as intense, as magical. And he found he couldn't describe it, even to himself. Like a dream, it stayed out of reach. He recalled the glowing trees, the velvet blackness of the spaces between them, the way the sky above appeared to rush and flow like a river of stars. He remembered heat spreading from inside his belly, like there was a sun burning there, and how when he touched Nikki's shoulder she felt hot too. At one point he thought he heard wolves howling in the distance and saw a pair of deer rush across their path as if pursued, but the others had no memory of this. More than anything, he recalled feeling more alive than he had ever thought possible, his body vibrating with energy, and Abigail walking beside him, serene and beautiful, emanating love.

All the while, he felt absolute certainty that his plan would work. That it was happening now.

They arrived at the line of trees at the edge of the clearing, the spot from which he'd watched the teachers the previous two nights. Greg and Nikki stopped beside him. He could feel them breathing. He could feel, too, Everett's bandana in his pocket.

He looked at Nikki and Greg, at their black eyes and slack jaws, and spoke to them in a low voice.

'We're going to make an offering,' he said.

They nodded.

'To the forest, to the spirits. Do you understand?'

They stared at him.

'This is for Abigail. For the Hollows. Are you with me?'

'Yes,' they said together. 'Yes.'

'Put your masks on,' he whispered.

Nikki became Fox, Greg turned into Goat, and Carl slipped on his own mask, becoming Crow.

He parted two branches and stepped into the clearing, where the teachers lay wrapped up in each other. Entwined and pale in the darkness. So caught up in their passion that they didn't see or hear the three masked teenagers approach. Didn't see the boy in the crow mask with the rock raised above his head.

After Carl brought the rock down on the back of Eric Daniels' skull, Sally screamed once.

He silenced her as quickly as he could.

There was a moment when he hesitated. Almost stopped. It was the look in Sally's eyes, the unspoken plea for mercy. But Abigail whispered to him: *Do it.*

This is for me.

ϖ

Afterwards, when they were certain both teachers were dead, they arranged Eric and Sally's bodies on the flat stone. They were heavy, especially Eric, and it took all of Carl and Greg's strength to move them, with Nikki helping too. He produced Everett's bandana and Nikki didn't react at all. Perhaps she hadn't noticed. It was hard to tell what she was thinking. She was crouched on the forest floor, motionless, her hair hanging around her face, staring at nothing. He was so set on what he was doing, on carrying out the last steps of his plan, that he felt almost sober.

He dipped the bandana in Eric's blood and used it to daub the symbols on the flat stone, the symbols he'd seen in Abigail's book. The horned god, which was also on the back of Everett's jacket, and the triple goddess. He looked up at the sky, the moon invisible among the stars.

He gestured for Fox and Goat to follow him. When they weren't paying attention, he dropped the bloody bandana by the path.

ω

Now, just over twenty years later, he stands outside the cabin, looking up at the same spot in the sky. After the ritual in the clearing, they had gone back to the lake and he had waited for the potion to wear off. Abigail had been right. Both Nikki and Greg appeared to be dazed, unsure of exactly what they had taken part in. So he had told them; filled in the blanks.

He didn't sleep that night. In the morning, he tuned in to the local news channel, waiting for the bodies to be found, and discovered they already had been, by two kids from the camp. Carl had gasped at that, wondering how close he and the others had been to getting caught. He forced himself to relax and waited for news that Everett had been arrested.

But that was the only thing that didn't go the way Carl had hoped. It turned out that some idiot reporter, who must have spoken to an idiot cop, revealed live on air that the police were planning to talk to a local youth who was known to be 'interested in the occult'. It would have been obvious to any local watching that this youth was Everett, including Everett himself. By the time the cops turned up at the junkyard, Everett was gone.

It was only later that day, when Carl came out to the cabin to visit Abigail's altar, that he discovered Everett hadn't run to Canada as everyone suspected. He was here. Hiding out.

Carl found him cowering in the bedroom, convinced he was going to be sent to prison for life for a crime he would never have dreamed of committing.

'How did you know about this place?' Carl asked.

'Nikki showed me.'

Of course she had.

Carl was forced to think on his feet.

'They're in the woods with dogs, looking for you,' he said.

Everett made a sobbing noise. What the hell did Nikki see in this snivelling dick? 'I want to see Nikki,' he said, as though he'd read Carl's thoughts and found her there.

Carl made reassuring noises. 'I'll fetch her. But maybe you should hide in case the dogs track your scent.'

Everett had agreed that was a good idea and Carl had opened the hatch to the basement, inviting Everett to wait down there until the coast was clear. And as Everett had begun to descend the ladder, Carl had kicked him in the face, causing him to fall all the way to the hard ground. While Everett lay there, stunned, Carl pulled up the ladder and shut the hatch.

He never told Nikki that he'd seen Everett. And he discouraged her from visiting the cabin by pointing out that they should stay away from each other for a while, just in case.

He pretended, like everyone else, that he believed Everett had crossed the border. Disappeared.

And it was strange. In the aftermath of that night, he found he wasn't so interested in Nikki any more. His interest in her seemed trivial somehow. Juvenile. Of course, he would need to keep an eye on her, to ensure she didn't have an attack of conscience. Greg too. He worried they might find religion and decide they needed to confess. But that never happened, and over the years his interest in Nikki faded to a sepia memory. There was only one woman he cared about. Abigail.

She was all he needed.

All he would ever, ever need.

Chapter 43

The wind. Follow . . .

Greg's words. What had he been trying to communicate?

I left his now certainly dead body in his room, and went downstairs. How long had it been since I'd called the police? Fifteen minutes. They would still be a long way from here, presuming they'd even set out.

I went outside. While I'd been in the house, the sky had darkened further, black rain clouds converging over Penance.

My punishment, Greg had said as he lay dying. Did he mean being stabbed to death? Or was he talking about his children and how they had turned out? Did he believe he was paying the price for what he took part in back in 1999? Him and Nikki and . . . Carl? Greg had said Carl's name, had seemed to think I was him for a moment.

I had seen Carl last night, at the barbecue. I could hardly remember our conversation – the music had drowned most of it out – but I clearly remembered our previous encounter, when he had, it seemed clear now, pretended to help me look for Frankie's phone. He had teased me about Nikki, and I guessed it must have been obvious that I was attracted to her. What else had we talked about? His disdain for the dark tourists who flocked here. How it must have maddened him that his original crime had increased the popularity of this place. Rubberneckers drawn to gawp at the murder scene, trampling all over his precious woods. Had he been following me that day? Watched me bang on the door of the bookstore, worrying about my new friendship with Nikki? Thinking about how he could use it against me?

And as I replayed that encounter in my head, I heard what had been there in the background of our conversation.

The wind chimes.

The wind. Follow . . .

Greg had been telling me to follow the sound of the wind chimes.

The heavens opened. The rain – the first I'd seen since coming here – was sudden, heavy. No slow build-up. An instant downpour. The little kids quickly gathered up their toys and vanished inside.

I sprinted towards the woods.

Chapter 44

Carl hears a noise behind him and turns from the altar. Buddy and Darlene enter the cabin.

'Where have you been?' he asks.

They don't answer. They just stare at him in that maddeningly vacant way of theirs.

'What's going on out there? Have you been watching the parents like I asked? Any sign they've called the police?'

It's frustrating, having to rely on these two to be his eyes and ears. Anderson and Butler might have broken the rules already. The woods could be crawling with cops. But he really doesn't believe they would risk it.

'Well?' he asks.

They continue to stare. They're both wet, their hair a couple of shades darker than normal, clothes damp. He hadn't realised it was raining.

Carl notices that Darlene is holding a sharp knife down by her side.

'What are you doing with that?'

Buddy and Darlene smile in tandem.

'Whatever,' Carl says. 'Leave it here. I need you to deliver—'

'No,' says Buddy.

Carl can't quite believe his ears. 'What?'

'We're not going along with your stupid plan any more.'

'We've got our own plan,' says Darlene.

'Much better than yours.'

'What the hell are you talking about?' says Carl, looking from one of them to the other.

There's the slow, liquid drip of fear in his belly, and he has to remind himself they're just kids. He ought to punch the smirk off of Buddy's face right now, get control of this situation. But he sees the bulge of the gun in the boy's pocket, and Darlene is holding that big-ass knife, the one she presumably brought from her own house.

Now, looking at it more closely, he sees blood on the blade.

Darlene notices him noticing. 'It's Dad's,' she says with something like pride. Like if a cat could talk and tell you it's brought you a mouse.

'Greg's? What the hell are you talking about?'

'It seemed like the perfect time,' says Buddy.

Carl takes a step back. The bow and arrows are outside. He has no other weapon to hand.

'You want to spend the rest of your lives in prison?' Carl says, fighting to keep the tremor from his voice.

'We're not going to prison,' says Buddy.

'We're innocent,' adds Darlene.

'Innocent children.'

'Oh yeah? So who are you going to blame for killing Greg?'

'You,' says Darlene.

Carl attempts to force out a laugh but it gets stuck. Instead, a weak croak emerges and dies in the air between them.

There's a flash of contempt in Buddy's eyes before the bored expression returns. 'You came to our house, killed our dad, forced us to come here with you.'

'You and the woman from the bookstore.'

The icy drip of dread has grown to a trickle. Where is Nikki? He hasn't seen her for a couple of hours, since she came in from having a smoke outside earlier. Her cigarettes and lighter are still by the door. He thinks she's sleeping in the bedroom but can't be sure.

Buddy goes on in that bored tone. 'You'd gone crazy. You were ranting about how some woman called Abigail told you to do it. *Kill them all*, she said. *Kill Greg. Kill the twins. Kill the kids in the basement and burn this place down.*'

Darlene snickers.

'We begged you to let us go but it was obvious. You were insane. You told us you murdered those teachers too, and Everett Miller. You hid his body in the basement. All these years.'

'This is bullshit,' Carl says. He takes another small step back towards the table. Maybe if he can get outside he can use one of the arrows as a weapon. Get it against Darlene's throat.

'Don't even try it,' Buddy says, stepping in front of the door to block Carl's exit, and he takes the gun from his pocket, aims it at Carl's chest.

Carl blinks. There's sweat running into his eyes. He attempts a smile. Changes tack. 'Come on, kids. You're not seriously going to hurt me, right? After all I've done for you. All the fun we've had together. I gave you the run of the camp, let you take whatever you wanted.'

'Except the pills.'

'Well, taking those pills was dumb. It drew attention. But yeah, sure, maybe I was a little hard on you. It won't happen again, all right?'

'No, it won't,' says Darlene.

Buddy's eyes have fallen upon Abigail's altar. Carl follows his gaze.

'It's dumb,' Buddy says.

'Such crap,' adds Darlene.

'Ghosts,' Buddy scoffs. 'Spirits.'

Darlene giggles and puts on a high-pitched voice. '*Oh Abigail. I must protect your woods from all these scary tourists.*'

Buddy locks eyes with Carl. 'We're the scary ones.'

'And these woods are ours,' says Darlene.

Buddy marches over to the altar with its framed photograph of Abigail at its centre, and picks up the photo. He examines it with a sneer on his face.

'We're the big bad wolves,' he says, and he chuckles at the expression on Carl's face. 'What big eyes you have.'

Darlene grins. 'All the better to see you with, my dear.'

'What are you doing?' Carl asks. The icy trickle is a flood now, filling his insides. Buddy is concentrating on the altar and Darlene is behind Carl. They are both distracted. Of course they are. They have the attention spans of kittens. Carl calculates the distance between himself and the door. He could get to it within a second. Another second or two to get an arrow. Then what? He can't run because then everything will be ruined. He pictures what he needs to do: press the sharp tip of an arrow against Darlene's throat, tell Buddy to drop his gun, take back control. Or he could simply run. Get the fuck out of here.

He hesitates. All this planning. He can't abandon it now. Can't abandon Abigail.

'What big ears you have,' says Buddy, taking a step towards Carl, prodding the air with the barrel of the revolver.

From behind Carl, Darlene laughs again. 'All the better to hear you with, my dear.'

Carl is paralysed by indecision. The door. The gun. He waits for Abigail to tell him what to do, to advise him, but she is silent. With a shudder, he realises he can no longer feel her presence.

'What big teeth you have,' says Buddy.

The door. He's going to go for the door. He braces himself, inches closer. Behind him, Darlene is breathing heavily. She sounds excited. Panting like the wolf in the story.

'All the better to eat you with.'

They both laugh like this is hilarious.

He's going to do it. On the count of three. He's going to run. But . . . the plan. The ritual. He can't let Abigail down.

Except he must. Survival comes first.

One.

'What big claws you have,' says Buddy, his back fully to Carl now, facing the altar.

I'm sorry, Abigail, Carl says in his head. *Another time. We'll do it another time.*

Two.

Wait. Claws? That's not . . .

'All the better,' says Darlene, and her voice is right in Carl's ear, her breath on his neck. When did she get so close?

She slides the knife into his back.

'All the better to kill you with.'

ϖ

Carl lies on the dirty wooden floor of the cabin, gazing up at them. He can't move. He's vaguely aware of his blood seeping out of him, pooling around him. He turns his head and sees Abigail's picture, the glass of the frame smashed to pieces, lying in the path of his blood. Two faces look down at him. A fox and a goat. Nikki and Greg. His friends. His family. He smiles, not feeling the blood on his lips. They're all so young. They have their whole lives ahead of them.

Then he remembers. This isn't Greg and Nikki. It's Buddy and Darlene. Behind them, in the doorway, he sees another face. A

292

woman's face. Abigail? Has she come for him? Come to take him away? Oh, such relief. She hasn't abandoned him, hasn't fled this place. She's been waiting, waiting to welcome him to the next life, to take his hand and lead him into the woods, her woods, the place he protected for her, and they will roam and dance and laugh and be together forever.

He takes one last look at Abigail's broken portrait and closes his eyes. He hears Buddy say something about burning this place down, but that doesn't matter now.

He waits.

Waits for Abigail to stretch out her hand.

He's still waiting when the last breath leaves his lungs.

Chapter 45

Frankie's throat was sore, her voice hoarse, from pleading with Carl to let them out. Ryan's too, despite the bottled water Carl had dropped into the basement.

Finally, realising it was futile, that they should save their energy, Frankie stopped yelling. She touched Ryan's arm and he fell quiet too.

All was silent above them.

Frankie tried to picture what it was like up there. They had been led into the house, through the room with the altar in the corner and into another room. That's where the hatch was. If Carl was in the first room with the door shut, he probably couldn't hear them, or they were muffled enough to make ignoring them easy.

Ryan sat back on the ground, his arms wrapped around his knees.

'We're gonna die down here,' he said. He turned his face towards the remains of Everett Miller. 'Like him.'

Frankie, who had sat down too, scooted over to him. 'Don't say that. We're going to get out of here. We're going to live long, wonderful lives. We'll be grateful to be alive. We won't take it for granted. And that will give us an edge over all our friends and peers. Because we'll have been given a second chance.'

'Huh.'

'Hey, that was my best motivational speech.'

'It was a good one.'

'But wasted on you, huh?'

He smiled. In the dim light of the torch his face was like a skull; bone-white, eyes sunken. The sight of him made Frankie shiver, as if it were a premonition. She wondered if, in their final moments, they would cling to each other. Which of them would die first? Would the other be left here for hours or days with the corpse of their friend?

She reached out and gave Ryan a hug.

The hatch opened.

Frankie jumped to her feet, forcing herself not to start yelling and begging. She didn't want to anger Carl and make him leave them alone again. She would be reasonable with him. Try to persuade him that she would never tell anyone. She would take his secret to the grave in many, many years' time.

Except it wasn't Carl.

It was Nikki. And she was pushing something down through the hole.

'Stand back,' she said. She was whisper-shouting it.

Something came sliding down into the basement, hitting the ground with a loud thump, which made Nikki swear and turn her face away from the hatch as if she knew the sound must have drawn attention. But Frankie didn't care. It was a ladder. They had a ladder! They were getting out of here. She grabbed Ryan's hand, pulled him to his feet and told him to start climbing.

'No, you first,' he said.

Nikki stuck her head through the open hatch and whispered, 'Hurry.'

Frankie stepped on to the first rung and started to climb.

There was a noise from above. A voice. A male, teenage voice, saying something to Nikki. It must be Buddy. Above Frankie, Nikki vanished from sight and began to talk in a pleading tone, her words low and indecipherable.

Frankie froze in her position halfway up the ladder. She looked down at Ryan beneath her, his face turned upwards. And then, looking back to the hatch, she could see Nikki again. The backs of her legs. She was standing right by the edge of the open hatch, still pleading with Buddy.

And then he must have pushed her.

Nikki's falling body filled the open hatch. There was a thump as her spine banged against the far side of the opening and she tried to twist, scrambling to hold on to the edge. Her legs kicked at the air beneath her, a few feet above Frankie's face.

Frankie froze. Nikki was going to make it. She was going to hold on, haul herself back up.

And then Buddy must have stamped on her hands or kicked her in the face.

Frankie saw Nikki plummeting towards her, legs first, but there was nothing she could do about it. It took less than a second. The falling woman crashed into her and Frankie tried to cling to the rung she was holding, but the force was too great. Pain exploded in her shoulder and she was thrown to the side, hitting the ground face down, knees and hips and belly smashing into the hard floor.

Nikki hit the ground beside her with a crack.

Ryan rushed over to Frankie. 'Are you okay? Frankie? Speak to me!'

Frankie lay still for a moment, all the breath gone from her body. Pain pulsated through her but began to fade as her breath returned. She was aware of Ryan crouching beside her, saying something that was drowned out by a high-pitched drone in her ears. She managed to turn on to her side and look upwards.

The ladder was moving. Buddy was pulling it upwards.

'Ryan,' she gasped. 'The ladder.'

He turned, got to his feet, but it was too late. The bottom of the ladder was out of reach. Buddy hauled the remaining rungs through the gap then peeked through, a grin on his face.

He slammed the hatch shut.

Chapter 46

The weather was getting worse, the wind picking up and shaking the branches of the trees opposite Paradise Loop. Rain lashed against my face and ran into my eyes, half blinding me. I stood by the tree line, trying to figure out where the clearing was, the one where Frankie had seen the masked figures, where I'd looked for her phone with Carl. I thought I knew how to reach it following the path back to the resort, but that was a long way round. There had to be a shortcut, another way through.

'What ya doing?'

I whirled round. It was Wyatt, coming across the road towards me. Rain had flattened his long, matted hair to his bony skull, and the water bounced off his cheeks and nose. It had removed some of the dirt from his face, though it was still hard to tell his age. Fifties? Sixties? What did it matter? Maybe he could help.

'The wind chimes,' I said. 'I need to . . . find them.'

He squinted at me like I wasn't making sense.

'My daughter's missing. I think she's wherever those wind chimes are. There's a clearing. Do you know—?'

He held up a hand. 'All right, there's no need to shout. I know it. What's going on?'

'I don't have time to explain. Please. I have to find my daughter. But if you can't help . . .'

'I can help.'

Wyatt suddenly pushed his way between two trees and vanished into the woods. It was like a disappearing trick. One second he was there, the next – gone. Like it was a portal into another timeline.

I followed and found myself pushing through the tightly packed pines, their needles dragging against my cheeks and stroking my hair. Creepers clutched at my ankles. The path was so overgrown it was hardly a path at all. But Wyatt pushed through it ahead of me using his shoulders, one then the other, with the occasional grunt. As we walked, I told him what had happened, having to yell to make myself heard. Finding Greg and hearing his dying words. Wyatt had his back to me so I couldn't see his reaction.

'Guess their mother was right,' he said after a long pause. The trees had been packed tight from the start, but . . . I knew it was my imagination, but it felt like they were squeezing even closer together as we pushed our way through. As if they were trying to block our way.

'You knew her?' I asked, as he muttered and cursed at the branches.

'Yup. Knew her folks. They ran the gas station on the road outta town. God-fearing type, she was. They all were. Baptists. Go in there and you'd be likely to get a Bible reading along with your gas. After Lainey took her own life—'

'Lainey? That was Greg's wife?'

'Yup.'

'She killed herself? I thought she left town.'

He grunted into his beard. 'Killing yourself is one way of leaving town, ain't it? Anyways, after that happened, her parents shut down the gas station and moved somewhere far away.'

We emerged into a clearing. We were surrounded by pines that stretched to the mottled grey sky, as dark as twilight.

'Are we nearly there?' I asked, as Wyatt lurched off to the east. The rain hadn't eased up and I still couldn't hear the wind chimes.

'Not much further.'

'Were you around when the first murders happened?' I asked. 'In 1999?'

'Yup.'

'Did you know Abigail?'

'Sure I did. Everyone knows everyone around here.' The Penance town motto.

We had entered another thick patch. The rainwater that clung to the needles of the trees continued to drench our clothes as we thrashed our way through them.

'What was she like?' I asked.

He appeared to be thinking about it. 'She was the kind of woman who would have been burnt at the stake if she'd been around during the witch trials.'

'Because she was a hippie?'

He grunted. 'She was more than that. She didn't fit in, not round here. People were always after Logan, that was her husband, to rein her in. Folk didn't like it, the way she went around collecting plants and herbs. There was a lot of talk about potions and spells. When she got the cancer, a lot of folk muttered about how the Devil was finally taking her home.'

'Did people know about her and the teens she hung out with?'

'There were rumours. As I remember, there was talk of doing something about it, and then the cancer came and it wasn't a problem any more.'

'And what did you think of her?'

300

He hissed with laughter. 'I liked her. She was always happy to share her weed.'

We emerged into another clearing, exposing us again to the lashing rain – and, finally, I knew where we were. This was where Frankie had lost her phone.

And I could hear them. The wind chimes.

They were ringing out from behind the trees on the far side of the clearing. Wyatt shambled towards them. Then he stopped, sniffing the air like a dog that had caught a scent.

'You smell that?' he asked.

I sniffed. At first, all I could smell was the heavy aroma of wet pine needles. Damp earth and petrichor. And then I caught the scent too.

Smoke.

Chapter 47

Frankie managed to get into a sitting position. She quickly checked herself over. Her head was fine. Nothing was broken.

The same couldn't be said for Nikki.

Frankie crawled over to where the woman lay on her back, not far from Everett's corpse. Nikki's eyes were wide open, a grimace of agony on her face.

'I can't move my legs,' she said.

Frankie couldn't deal with that right now. 'What were you doing here? Does anyone else know we're here?'

Nikki closed her eyes for a moment and whispered, 'I'm sorry.'

'Why are you apologising?'

'Frankie,' Ryan said, but she ignored him. She repeated the question to Nikki, but she didn't answer right away. When she did, tears had begun rolling down towards her ears.

'I couldn't go to jail,' she said. She began to sob for herself and Frankie stood, appalled and angry. This woman was involved in them being here. Frankie didn't know exactly what she'd done, or why Buddy had pushed her through the hatch. Maybe it didn't matter. The ladder was gone. The hatch was shut.

And Ryan was still trying to get her attention.

'Frankie.' He was on his feet, looking up at the closed hatch.

'What is it?'

'Can't you smell it?'

Frankie stood too, shaking her head. 'I can't smell any—' And then she caught it.

Smoke.

'They're burning the cabin,' Ryan said.

Frankie threw herself on to her knees beside Nikki. 'Do you have a phone?'

'It's upstairs. It doesn't work out here anyway.'

Ryan was pacing the floor, swearing over and over again.

'And there's no other way out of here?'

Nikki looked at her like she'd asked if she could do magic tricks.

Frankie got back on her feet. She looked around. The smell of smoke was getting stronger now. There was a tiny gap around the perimeter of the hatch, just enough to let smoke through. In the dim light, Frankie could see it swirling around the ceiling. The fire might not get into this room, not unless the floor collapsed – was that possible? – but Frankie knew from countless fire-safety videos at school that most house-fire victims died from smoke inhalation.

'Carl!' Frankie screamed. 'Let us out!'

'Carl's dead,' Nikki said from the floor. 'It's just Buddy and Darlene up there now.'

Buddy and Darlene. Frankie thought back to the messages they'd sent her. The threats. The dead rabbit. The buried-alive cat. This was what the twins had wanted all along, from the moment Ryan had insulted Penance.

Frankie picked up the flashlight and pointed it at the ceiling, illuminating the swirling smoke as it thickened and moved lower, thin tendrils reaching down towards them, making Frankie cough and giving them a little taste of what was to come. Soon the smoke would fill this whole space.

Nikki had closed her eyes and fallen silent, presumably passed out from the pain.

Frankie sat on the ground and lay flat, as far from the smoke as possible, though what good would that do? Buy her another second or two? She pushed herself up into a sitting position and beckoned to Ryan, putting her arms around him.

She waited to die.

Chapter 48

I overtook Wyatt and reached the tree line first, then realised I had no idea what I was looking for. I had scanned this area before, searching for a path with no luck. Was I supposed to just push my way between the trees? Follow the sound of the wind chimes and the smell of smoke? At least it was raining. That would surely slow the fire. But even as I thought that, I realised the rain had eased off to a drizzle.

I ran along the line of trees, searching for an opening. A path. There was no way through. I squeezed between two thick trunks but found my path blocked by another huge pine. I could try to thread my way through, but it was impossible to tell if I was going in the right direction or if I would get stuck. Trapped.

I retreated into the clearing. Wyatt had vanished. Where the hell was he? It seemed that he had done as I'd asked, led me to the clearing, then left me to it.

It was up to me.

Again, I scanned the tree line. There had to be an opening. I heard Greg's final words in my head, rearranged and expanded to make sense. *Follow the wind chimes.* But I couldn't find my way through to wherever they hung.

Maybe Greg had simply meant *Follow the wind.*

I stood back, a couple of feet from the pines, and closed my eyes. Felt the wind around me, blowing at my back, trying to believe in the power of this place, that it was alive, that it would direct me.

Nothing happened.

What was I doing? Relying on some ancient, supernatural force to show me the way to my daughter? Even if I believed in that stuff, why would the Hollows care about me or Frankie? Why would the spirits guide me? That was the kind of thing Carl believed in. The beliefs that had led us here.

My eyes snapped open.

I watched the wind stir the branches of the trees directly ahead of me, forcing them to sway back and forth.

It is showing you the way, said a voice in my head. *It actually is.*

But the rational side of me shut that voice out. The wind was shaking the branches, that was all.

And as they shook, I caught a glimpse of a space between. A line of light, stretching between the pines. Just a glimpse, but it was enough.

I barrelled forward into the trees, branches raking my cheeks and scraping my scalp. The path was narrow but clear, like one of those magic-eye paintings that suddenly reveals itself. I thrust forward. And there it was before me.

The old cabin.

Thick smoke poured through the broken windows. The wind chimes hung from the porch, swinging wildly. The front door stood open and I could see flames dancing within. There was no sign of anyone. No Carl, no Buddy or Darlene.

'Frankie? Ryan?' I called their names and waited. Nothing.

I ran up to the door and peered into the front room, squinting through the thick smoke. The heat hit me hard but the fire wasn't yet out of control. There was an open door to the left which revealed another room that burned orange, smoke pouring through into the front room. It seemed that whoever had set the fire had started it in the room to the left, then fled before it reached this room. Perhaps they had intended to set fire to all the rooms but had been scared off by the flames, which looked like they would come roaring into the front room at any moment.

I looked down at my clothes. I was soaked through. My skin was drenched too. Surely that would provide some protection. I wasn't certain, but I had no choice. My daughter could be in here.

I went inside.

I could barely see. My foot bumped against something, and I looked down and saw a dark shape on the floor. A body.

It was Carl, lying on his side, the back of his shirt thick with blood. Dead.

'Frankie?' I called again.

I couldn't hear anything above the crackle of flames to my left and the roar of the wind outside. The manic cacophony of the chimes.

'*Frankie?*'

There was an open doorway on the far side of the room, straight ahead of me. I went inside. There were no open or broken windows in this room and the smoke was thicker, filling the air, making it almost impossible to see anything. I retreated back into the front room.

'Frankie!' I called again, as loud as I could.

And I heard it. A faint voice, coming from a long way away. 'Here.'

'Frankie? Frankie, where are you?'

'Dad!'

'Where are you?'

'Down here! Beneath the hatch.'

I covered my mouth and nose with my sleeve and followed the sound of Frankie's voice. There was so much smoke I couldn't see anything. A hatch? Where was it? I dropped to my hands and knees and crawled forward, patting the floor in front of me. I heard a roar in the room I'd just left. Fire bursting through and taking hold. Soon, it would be in this room. I ought to get out. But this was my daughter. I would do anything. Risk third-degree burns; sacrifice my life.

I bumped into something. A heavy, old-fashioned armchair. I shoved it aside and my hand found something metal. A large ring.

I hesitated. I assumed the basement would be full of oxygen. If I opened the hatch, would the extra oxygen feed the flames and cause them to rush into this room? I glanced over my shoulder and watched orange consume the room I'd just left.

I had no choice. I had to risk it.

'Get on the floor!' I yelled. 'Cover your face.'

Bracing myself, I opened the hatch. The flames stayed put. But it was getting hotter. I had seconds. I stuck my head through the gap. Again, there was so much smoke I could hardly see.

'There's a ladder!' Frankie cried. 'We need the ladder.'

Her words were followed by a volley of coughs. Two people coughing, presumably her and Ryan.

I groped around on my hands and knees. The ladder. Where was it?

'Dad, please, hurry!'

My hand fell upon something solid and wooden. It was a ladder, lying on the floor. I pulled it towards me with one hand, feeling for the opening to the hatch with the other. Blindly, barely able to breathe, I manoeuvred the end of it into the gap and stood, gripping its sides, almost dropping it as I lifted it above my head and it made contact with the ceiling.

'Stand back,' I yelled.

I dropped the ladder through the gap, letting it slide across my palms, scraping the skin. I heard a thud far beneath me as the ladder struck the floor of the basement.

'Come on!' I screamed.

Ryan climbed the ladder first, coughing and spluttering. I helped drag him out. The front room was burning but there was no other option. I thumped Ryan on the back. 'That way. Run.'

He didn't hesitate. And a moment later my daughter, my beautiful daughter, appeared in the hatch. 'Dad,' she said, smoke swirling around her head. I wanted to embrace her, kiss her, tell her I was sorry, but that would have to wait. I pulled her up through the gap and she collapsed against me. I put my arm around her.

'We're going to run,' I said. 'Straight to the front door. You ready?'

'Wait—' she said.

But I didn't let her speak. I took hold of her arm and pulled her, into the burning front room, through the heat, the flames, the walls buckling around us. There was a terrible roaring, rushing noise, and I shoved Frankie, sending her flying through the open door. I leapt after her, convinced the hair on the back of my neck was about to catch fire, the heat like nothing I'd ever felt. If I hadn't been soaked through, I'm certain I would have gone up in flames too.

I landed on my knees on the porch. Carl's bow was there, along with a quiver of arrows. Frankie, who had already got to her feet, pulled me down the wooden steps into the soaking grass. I lay on my back and looked up at the sky, ashes dancing above me. Two pairs of arms took hold of me – Frankie's and Ryan's – and pulled me towards the trees.

I sat up. Coughed uncontrollably. Struggled for breath. I opened my mouth and tried to catch the rain, which was falling more heavily again. Frankie was crouched beside me, her hand on my back.

'Nikki's in there,' she said.

The roar of the fire. The wind. The rain. I wasn't sure if I'd heard her correctly.

'She was in the basement with us. I think she's broken her back.'

I looked at the burning cabin. There was nothing I could do. They were all dead now, the original three. Crow, Goat and Fox.

'Everett's body was down there too,' Frankie said.

I couldn't take any of it in. 'We need to . . . get out . . . Back to the resort.' My body was racked with coughs again. The smoke was in my lungs. My insides felt charred and black.

I tried to get to my feet but fell back. Everything swam. The heat from the burning cabin was making me want to vomit, and smoke swirled all around us, black embers and orange sparks flying above our heads. It was like being in Hell. But Frankie was alive. She was fine. Ryan too. I had got them out, and if I died now it would be fine.

I wanted to lie down on the grass, the exhaustion and shock and relief taking over, but Frankie stopped me.

'We need to get away from the fire and the smoke.'

She was right. I let her help me to my feet. With the smoke billowing around us it was hard to find the path, but Ryan said, 'This way', and we followed him. As we pushed through, the smoke grew thinner and soon I was gulping down clean air as we entered the clearing.

I collapsed on to my knees. I needed to rest again. Needed oxygen. I lay down on my side and concentrated on breathing. Surely the fire would attract people from the town and the resort. Let them come to us. I was spent.

'Dad, what are you—?'

She stopped talking.

Two figures appeared before us, out of nowhere.

Buddy and Darlene.

They were wearing their masks. Goat and Fox. I watched them lift their faces towards the blaze beyond the trees, then swivel their attention back to us. Frankie was behind me, near the entrance to the hidden path, and Ryan was beside her. Somehow, I found some strength and pushed myself into a sitting position.

Buddy held a gun and Darlene had a knife.

I watched as Buddy lifted the gun.

'Go back,' I said. 'Now!'

Frankie and Ryan understood immediately. They darted back into the trees. I followed, realising that once you had seen the entrance to the path it was impossible to unsee it. I still have no idea how I managed it, where that final burst of strength came from, but I guess it's like one of those fabled mothers who is able to lift a car to free her child. I wasn't only trying to protect myself. Frankie still needed me.

Or so I believed.

I could hear the twins crashing through the trees behind us, and somewhere in the distance, above the rain and the wind, I heard the drone of an engine. A plane or helicopter sent to check out the fire? I didn't have time to think about that right now. The three of us – Frankie, Ryan, me – emerged into the clearing around the cabin. I stopped running. The cabin was burning hard, flames erupting from the roof, black smoke pouring into the sky. Fortunately, the wet weather and clear ground between the cabin and the surrounding trees had stopped the fire from spreading and setting off a wildfire. An image of Nikki trapped in the basement, unable to move, flashed before my eyes, and I pushed it away, knowing it would return later to fill my nightmares.

311

I looked around for somewhere to hide, was about to head for the space between two thick pines, but Frankie was still running towards the cabin.

'What are you doing?' I yelled.

She vanished into a cloud of smoke.

Buddy and Darlene emerged from the path, and Ryan and I turned to face them.

Buddy took off his mask and let it fall by his feet. He looked in awe at the burning cabin, then pointed the gun, a revolver, at me using both hands.

'Killing us won't help you,' I called over the noise of the fire. 'They'll know you did this. Know you killed your dad.'

'I don't care,' he replied.

Beside him, Darlene had also removed her mask, though she still held it. She had the knife gripped in her other fist. The same knife, I guessed, that had killed Greg and Carl.

'I knew you were assholes the first time we met you,' Ryan said.

Buddy pointed the gun at Ryan and said, 'You're the asshole.'

'You're a pair of freaks,' said Ryan.

Buddy took a step closer, still gripping the revolver with both hands.

'They're not going to close down Hollow Falls,' I said.

'We don't care about that either,' said Darlene.

'Then what's the point of all this?' I asked.

Darlene shrugged. 'We were tired of being told what to do.'

'We were bored,' said Buddy.

Flames danced in his eyes, and his sister's.

'Where's Frankie?' Darlene said.

And Frankie replied, from behind me, 'I'm here.'

I turned to look.

Frankie was standing in front of the cabin, a silhouette against the blaze. She had her legs apart, back straight. She held the bow that had been on the porch, where the flames hadn't yet reached, the string pulled back with her right hand, an arrow pointed straight at Buddy.

I saw what I had to do.

I threw myself to the ground, yelling Buddy's name as I fell. Instinctively, he followed my voice, kept the gun trained on me. Too late, he realised what was about to happen. He tried to shift his aim towards Frankie, but the revolver was too heavy and he was too slow.

Frankie let the arrow fly.

If she had missed, he would have shot her. For a long time afterwards, I replayed this scene in dreams, in nightmares where the arrow sailed over Buddy's head. In these dreams, Buddy would grin, aim at her and squeeze the trigger. My daughter would fall, and then he would turn the gun on me.

But Frankie didn't miss.

The arrow struck Buddy in the chest. He went down like a dropped brick. The gun fell with him. I snatched it up.

Darlene froze for a second, then ran. Before Frankie or I could take aim at her, she vanished into the trees.

I collapsed back on to the earth, all my strength gone. Before I blacked out I heard two things. The *whup-whup* of helicopter blades overhead, and Ryan saying of Buddy, 'He's dead.'

Chapter 49

Saturday

David and Connie came to see me when I was packing up the car.

'How are the lungs?' David asked.

'Getting better,' I replied. 'The doctors said there shouldn't be any lasting damage, but I shouldn't try running a marathon any time soon.'

He grinned and slapped me on the back. Ever since I'd left the hospital – where they'd checked me over and kept me in overnight – and returned to Hollow Falls, the Butlers had acted like I was some kind of hero. I didn't feel like a hero. If I hadn't trusted Nikki, Frankie and Ryan probably wouldn't have ended up in that basement. My daughter wouldn't have had to kill someone. Nikki might still be alive too.

I was going to have a lot of shit to deal with over the coming months.

'Have you seen Frankie?' I asked, as I lifted the suitcase into the back of the rental.

'She and Ryan are saying goodbye,' Connie replied.

'They've already arranged for Frankie to come stay with us next summer,' David said. 'And you're welcome too. Any time, Tom. Our home is your home.'

'We don't live near any woods,' Connie added.

I closed the boot of the car. 'I guess you're going to get a great podcast episode out of this.'

They both shifted uncomfortably. 'We don't want anyone to think we're exploiting what happened to our son,' said Connie.

'But we think our listeners deserve to know the truth.'

'The *world* needs to know the truth. Everett Miller was innocent. I think we owe it to him to spread the word.'

I wasn't going to argue.

'What about you?' David asked. 'You still planning on writing that article?'

'I don't know.'

I hadn't decided. I was going to have to do something for money. Something to resuscitate my career. But for now, I didn't want to think about Hollow Falls or murders or burning cabins.

'I need a vacation,' I said.

We all laughed.

'Well, if you do write about this, we'd love to have you on our podcast as a guest,' Connie said.

At that moment, Neal Fredericks came over from where he had been packing up his car, lifting a hand in greeting. When I had returned to the resort after my hospital visit, I was surprised to find he was still there. I thought he would have gone back to Portland. But he had lots of questions. For the past twenty years, he had believed Everett Miller had murdered his wife. I imagined all of this must have opened up old wounds. He'd wanted to know everything I'd found out. What Carl, Greg and Nikki had said to me and Frankie.

Now, he clapped me on the shoulder. 'Heading home too?'

I nodded. I was cutting our trip short by a couple of days. I just wanted to get out of here. 'Got to take Frankie back to Albany, then I'm going to hang around there for a few days.' The police

315

had asked me not to leave the US quite yet, in case they had any more questions.

He nodded in return. 'I just want to thank you again. For finding out the truth.'

I was uncomfortable with all of these thanks, so I shrugged.

'It never sat right with me,' Neal said. 'About Everett Miller, I mean. It always seemed too easy, you know? Too convenient.' He turned his face towards the woods, in the direction of the clearing where Sally and Eric's bodies had been found. 'But I still didn't get justice. The three of them oughta be rotting in a jail cell.'

He looked around, a curl of distaste on his lip.

'I hate this fucking place,' he said.

He walked back to his car, and then Frankie and Ryan appeared. They stood close together. Ryan said something in Frankie's ear and she smiled, then caught my eye.

I was proud of her. And when I thought about going back to the UK and not seeing her for another year, I had to fight back tears.

But at least I would see her again.

ϖ

'Dad.'

The night before, after I'd got back to the cabin and started packing up our stuff, Frankie had come up to me and given me a long hug. Then she'd stood back, arms wrapped around herself.

'I feel different,' she said.

'That's . . . not surprising.'

'I had to do it, didn't I?'

I put my hands on her shoulders. 'Of course you did. You saved me and Ryan. You were amazing.'

She pulled away and crossed to the window. 'Do you think they'll ever find Darlene?'

The police had been searching the woods for her for over twenty-four hours now. The helicopter had failed to find her. Sniffer dogs hadn't been able to pick up her scent in the wet grass. Just like Everett twenty years before, she had vanished, except we knew she couldn't be hiding in a hunting cabin, trapped forever in its basement.

'She'll turn up,' I said. 'One day.'

'Maybe she's gone to Canada,' Frankie suggested.

'Poor Canada,' I said.

ϖ

I did a final sweep of the cabin to make sure we hadn't left anything behind, then shook David's hand, then Ryan's. Connie gave me a quick hug, and Frankie gave Ryan a long hug.

Then we were in the car.

On the way out, I stopped at reception to drop off the keys. Vivian, who had been made temporary manager, was on duty.

'Hey,' she said. I could tell she was pleased we were leaving. She wanted everything to get back to normal. Maybe that was possible now the ghosts of the Hollows' past had finally been exorcised.

'Hi.'

I handed her the keys and spotted a cat carrier on the side. She noticed me looking at it.

'I've volunteered to take in Nikki's cat,' she said.

'Cujo? That's great.'

'He's a cutie,' she said.

I turned to leave.

'Hey, Mr Anderson,' she called. I looked back. 'Don't forget to leave us a review on TripAdvisor.'

317

I was still chuckling when I got back to the car. Neal Fredericks drove past us, also on his way home, and I raised a hand to say farewell. Then something else occurred to me that made me laugh more. I stopped and took a final look back at Hollow Falls. It was beautiful. There was no denying it. And we were never coming back here again.

'What were you laughing at?' Frankie asked as I slid into the driver's seat.

'Oh,' I said, 'I was just trying to figure out what we're going to tell your mum.'

Epilogue

There are places in the woods that only she and Buddy knew. Dark spaces. Hollow tree trunks. The abandoned den of some long-dead animal in which, for hours, she has lain still, concentrating on slowing her heartbeat to a crawl, something she has always found easy. Once, a doctor told her she had both an unusually slow resting pulse and a surprisingly low body temperature. She has always been proud of that. Buddy was the opposite. It was as if they balanced each other out.

Now that balance has gone.

Thanks to the girl.

Katniss, Crow called her, which made Darlene sick. *The Hunger Games* was one of her favourite movies. She'd watched it over and over. Had taken part a thousand times in her own mind, picturing kills, weapons, plotting out exactly how she would survive – and win. The English girl was no Katniss. She'd gotten lucky with that arrow, that was all, though Darlene guessed that was a lesson. Even the weakest competitor can win sometimes, through a fluke of fate, or a moment of weakness on the part of a natural-born winner.

Her brother paid the price for that. He had thought himself invincible.

Darlene would not make the same mistake.

All yesterday, they searched the woods for her. Men with dogs. A helicopter that swept overhead. But the men hadn't been looking too hard. At one point, a pair of them came within feet of her and she heard one say he was certain she would have gotten the hell out of here by now.

'Waste of time,' the other grumbled.

She had been tempted to surprise them. Slash one's throat, then the other's, just that quickly. They wouldn't have seen her coming. A pair of stealth kills. But in the end she let them go, deciding not to take the risk.

The important thing was that she remained free. That she lived to fight another day.

ω

Morning comes. The second sunrise since the fire and Buddy's death and her escape into the woods. All night, the scene replayed in her head. The arrow, thwacking into Buddy's chest. The way he fell.

This she could not bear, so she ran it in reverse: the arrow, sucked from the fresh wound, leaping back to the string of the English girl's bow.

But then the bitch would just unleash it again. That awful sound. Buddy falling.

Back and forth, up and down, all night.

The last time, Darlene leaps forward, knocks the arrow aside with a forearm and drives the knife into the girl's skinny throat.

In reality, she crawls from the abandoned den into sunlight.

She is filthy. Black with smoke and slick with mud. She can smell herself, stinking like a real fox, not one who wears a mask. She licks her lips, tastes dirt. Her stomach growls and she remembers how thirsty she is. She sucks rainwater from leaves, wonders about

320

trapping a rabbit or a bird. How long will she survive out here in the forest?

She thinks of the refrigerator at home, always stocked with Coke and Dew. The full cupboards. The eggs Dad used to fix them for breakfast. Sunny side up. Doused in ketchup. The way she liked them.

She thinks of how Dad squealed when she cut him and feels a wave of self-pity. He'll never cook her breakfast again.

But her house is so close to here. The refrigerator and the cupboards will still be full. And upstairs, her babies will be missing their mommy. Her cockroaches. She misses them. The feel of their little legs on her skin. The sound they make.

Hisssssssss.

Like music.

Thirst and hunger and thoughts of her babies send her in the direction of Penance. She reaches the edge of the woods and crosses the road, climbs a fence and sneaks across a pair of gardens. Through a back window she thinks she glimpses those annoying little kids from next door. She is worried they might see her, but they are absorbed in some dumb game.

She climbs up and peeks over the fence of her own house.

There's a cop standing by the front door. Another by the back.

Shit.

She imagines herself dropping over the fence, commando-crawling across the lawn, one stealth kill, then another. Grab them from behind and slide the blade across their throats. Easy. Not a sound.

Her stomach growls again. She drops from the fence, turns.

The little bitch from next door is there.

'Hey,' the girl says.

'Hi,' says Darlene. Her eyes flick towards the house. 'Where's your mom?'

'Still asleep,' replies the girl. Then she frowns, eyeing the knife in Darlene's hand. 'Are you going to bury me? Like that cat?'

Darlene smiles. 'Not if you do as I say.'

Five minutes later she's running back into the woods with a bottle of Dew, a bag of chips and a couple of Twinkies. She stops and stuffs the food into her mouth, barely pausing to chew. She washes it down with the soda. Thinks.

She doesn't know how to hunt or fish. And she can't live like a scavenger, like some homeless bum. She can't hide here forever.

She knows what she has to do.

ω

It takes a couple of hours to get across the woods to the road that leads to the highway. It's a hot morning, and by the time she gets there she's thirsty again, wishing she'd told the girl to fetch her a bottle of water. She's going to have to get better at this stuff. Learn to think ahead; something she's never been good at.

She crouches by the side of the road. The sun is bright and hurts her eyes but she is concealed by the low branches of the trees and they provide some shelter. She sits down and feels herself slipping towards sleep. She jabs at her leg with the tip of the knife to wake herself up. Pictures herself jabbing it into the English girl's soft throat, imagines the sound of her gargling blood. The dad too, he needs to die. Poke out one eye, then the other. Cut out his tongue. These sweet visions keep her going as she waits.

When she hears a car coming along the road, she jumps up and runs in front of it.

The car swerves and screeches to a halt.

It's a brown car, a station wagon. Kind of old and shitty but she's not fussy. The door opens and an old man gets out. He's bald with a pink scalp. She recognises him. He's the guy who gave that big speech at the resort a few nights back. The one who was boo-hooing about his dead wife.

'What the hell?' he says. He stands there blinking at her in the hot sun.

'Mister,' she says, stepping towards him. 'I'm lost and—'

'You're that girl,' he says. 'The one they're looking for.'

He puts his hand in his pocket, presumably to take out his phone, but she's on him before he can get his hand out of his pocket. She stabs him in the belly. He makes this weird gasping noise, mouth open in shock, and she stabs him again, in the chest. He falls and, just to make sure, she drops to her knees and slashes his throat, jumping back to avoid the blood spraying her.

When she's sure he's dead she takes him under his arms to drag him the few feet into the trees. At first, she can't budge him. It's like he's this enormous bag of flesh filled with sand. But there's a trick to it. There's a trick to everything. Hauling on one leg and rolling him halfway over, then hauling on one arm and finishing the roll. Repeat. By the time she's done and he's out of sight of the road, she's panting and sweating and thirstier than ever.

But there's a bottle of water in the car! She gets behind the wheel and forces herself not to drink all of it at once. The keys are still in the ignition. There's a GPS and, hallelujah, a bunch of snacks on the back seat. She's already taken his wallet, which contains a bank card and almost a hundred dollars.

She pauses for a moment to remember the driving lessons Dad gave her. She'll be okay, as long as she sticks to quiet roads. She'll get the hang of it quickly. She's a winner. She can do whatever she sets her mind to.

She starts the engine and drives a little way along the road. After a couple of minutes she hears another car behind her and, worried it might be the police or someone from the resort who would recognise her, she turns on to the little side road ahead, and pulls to a halt.

The car goes by, not too fast, the occupants not seeing her.

But she recognises them.

It's the English girl and her dad.

Instinctively, Darlene reaches for the knife, then grips the wheel with both hands and looks for Reverse. She'll back out of the little road, put her foot down, chase them, run them off the road.

She stops herself.

Think.

It's more important to get away, find somewhere safe. Somewhere she can get food and something to drink. Maybe find some sucker who'll take her in, look after her. She bets there are plenty of guys out there who'd do that.

Because what's the rush? She's been through that girl's phone. She knows where she lives, where she goes to school. She knows who her friends are. She's seen photos of her house and her back garden. The hutch where she keeps her pet rabbit. She knows everything.

Darlene looks over to the passenger seat and finds Buddy there, smiling. Proud of her for not acting on impulse, for thinking about the future.

Then she starts the engine and drives away from the Hollows, towards the rest of her life.

Acknowledgments

I very much hope you enjoyed *The Hollows*. If you want to get in touch and let me know what you thought, my email address is mark@markedwardsauthor.com. Or you can contact me via Facebook (@markedwardsauthor), Instagram (also @markedwardsauthor) or Twitter (@mredwards). A review on Amazon or Goodreads is always very welcome.

You can also download a collection of four short stories by going to www.markedwardsauthor.com/free and joining my Readers Club.

This book was written during the pandemic of 2020. Fortunately, for me, I had already decided to set it during the summer of 2019, so I didn't have to worry about my characters social-distancing or being obsessed with hand sanitiser, although I wonder whether the important role played by masks in this book was some kind of subconscious reaction to what was going on beyond my study. I'm writing this letter at the start of December 2020, seven months before publication, and I am keeping everything crossed that the world will be in a better place by the time you read these words. I know that reading has been a solace for many people, including myself, and wonder how much of an appetite there will be for reading novels set during the pandemic. That's a question I will have to face when it comes to writing my next book . . .

I have a few people to thank:

David Downing, Jack Butler, Gemma Wain, Madeleine Milburn and everyone at the agency. Sarah Lotz, for pointing me in the direction of dark tourism. Lisa Harrison, whose hard work and organisational skills allow me to concentrate on writing. My crime-writer friends for all the title brainstorming and for helping to keep me sane this year. I miss you all. Lucie Whitehouse, who came up with the town name, Penance. Matthew Farrell, for baseball advice. And, of course, my family: Sara, Poppy, Ellie, Archie and Harry – and Peggy the Maine Coon, who is always there when I'm working, keeping me company, though it's not helpful when she lies on the keyboard or steals my chair . . .

Glen Troiano won the 'honour' of having a character named after him in this book. Hope you enjoyed seeing your name in print, Glen!

This book contains several Easter eggs, with references to *The Magpies*, *The Lucky Ones*, *The Retreat* and *The House Guest*. Did you spot them all? If not, send me an email and I'll tell you where to look.

Thanks for reading.

Mark Edwards

About the Author

Mark Edwards writes psychological thrillers in which scary things happen to ordinary people.

He has sold 3 million books since his first novel, *The Magpies*, was published in 2013, and has topped the bestseller lists several times. His other novels include *Follow You Home*, *The Retreat*, *In Her Shadow*, *Because She Loves Me*, *The House Guest* and *Here to Stay*. He has also co-authored six books with Louise Voss.

Originally from Hastings in East Sussex, Mark now lives in Wolverhampton with his wife, their children, three cats and a golden retriever.

Mark loves hearing from readers and can be contacted through his website, www.markedwardsauthor.com, or you can find him on Facebook (@markedwardsauthor), Twitter (@mredwards) and Instagram (@markedwardsauthor).

Did you enjoy this book and would like to get informed when Mark Edwards publishes his next work? Just follow the author on Amazon!

1) Search for the book you were just reading on Amazon or in the Amazon App.

2) Go to the Author Page by clicking on the author's name.

3) Click the 'Follow' button.

If you enjoyed this book on a Kindle eReader or in the Kindle App, you will be automatically offered to follow the author when arriving at the last page.

THOMAS & MERCER